THE FRENZY WOLVES

THE FRENZY WOLVES

The Frenzy Wolves Cycle

Author of the Bram Stoker
Award–Nominated
Johnny Gruesome

GREGORY LAMBERSON

MEDALLION
P R E S S

Medallion Press, Inc.

Printed in USA

Dedicated to Terry Wright,
a great writer and one hell of an inspiration

Published 2014 by Medallion Press, Inc.
The MEDALLION PRESS LOGO
is a registered trademark of Medallion Press, Inc.

Typeset in Adobe Garamond Pro
Printed in the United States of America

ISBN 978-1-60542-716-4
10 9 8 7 6 5 4 3 2 1

First Edition

Acknowledgments

Special thanks to everyone at Medallion Press, from my editor, Lorie Jones, to freelance artists Tommy Castillo and Patrick Reilly for their wonderful covers, and, once again, to Chris "the cop" Aiello for his police expertise in all three of my Frenzy novels.

"Two wolves fight inside me," an old man said to his grandson. "One is Evil—he is anger, envy, sorrow, regret, greed, arrogance, self-pity, guilt, resentment, inferiority, lies, false pride, superiority, and ego. The other is Good—he is joy, peace, love, hope, serenity, humility, kindness, benevolence, empathy, generosity, truth, compassion, and faith."

The grandson said, "Which wolf wins?"

The old man said, "The one you feed."

—Cherokee legend

Angus Domini watched his wife, Dawn, lying upon their bed with her knees raised, pushing with all her strength, her face contorted and beading with sweat, her swollen belly rising and falling in time with her tortured gasps. Blood glistened on the mat beneath her, and Dr. Edward Kurtz tended to her needs while the midwife, Jessica Collins, watched.

Dawn had gone into labor four hours earlier, and Angus had summoned the caregivers to the house. Members of the Greater Pack of New York City did not go to hospitals to give birth; the risk of a newborn babe emerging from the womb in Wolf Form was too great. All Dawn's checkups had been with Edward, who maintained a state-of-the-art facility in Queens.

"Push, Dawn," Edward said. "You can do it."

Dawn's lips quivered, and the muscles in her throat

bulged. Angus half expected her to Change.

"Here comes one," Edward said.

A form wiggled free of Dawn's bloody opening, covered with afterbirth. Edward held the child, and Jessica cleared wet discharge from the newborn's eyes, nostrils, and mouth, permitting the babe to cry. Edward raised the infant for Angus and Dawn to see. "You have a son."

Dawn wept, and Angus's chest swelled with pride. He had attended dozens of births, but this was his first child, his heir apparent.

Gabriel, he thought. Dawn had chosen the name.

The midwife produced a surgical scissor, and Angus cut the umbilical cord. Edward placed the baby—so tiny and delicate—in Angus's hands. Angus moved closer to the bed and showed Gabriel to Dawn, who laughed through her tears. Jessica collected the baby and set him in a crib with a raised bottom.

"You're not done yet," Edward said to Dawn.

Angus took his wife's hand. Six minutes later, a second infant wailed.

"You have another son," Edward said.

Raphael, Angus thought as he cradled the baby.

"They're both beautiful," Jessica said. "And *healthy*."

In the old days, when Wolves ran through the country in their true form, litters of four to six pups were common. But after the Europeans invaded the territory and the Wolves adopted human form to survive, litters of three became the norm. In the last hundred years, most females gave birth to a single pup, although some gave birth to twins. Angus had been a lone pup, and so had Dawn. When Edward informed them that Dawn carried triplets, they had been overjoyed and concerned at the same time: in many cases, twins and triplets were stillborn. Gabriel's and Raphael's survival was a triumph for the species. The odds of all three pups living were slim.

Seven minutes later, a third newborn cried to the world.

"Your daughter has arrived," Edward said.

Angus grinned. *Angela.* She was smaller than her brothers but no less vocal.

Dawn sank into the bed, exhausted, and Angus held their daughter. He knew the pack would regard the pups as special, but his thoughts were not of starting a feral dynasty but keeping his offspring safe.

Gabriel ran through the woods below the domed Adirondacks, followed by Raphael and Angela. He and Raphael had been Changing for a year now and Angela for nine months. Their parents had brought the three of them to the mountain retreat to experience running in the wild, and after a week, Gabriel felt as if he had undergone an even more radical change than transforming from a human into a Wolf: he felt he *belonged* in the wild. Fire consumed his senses; trees towered overhead; the aroma of pinecones filled his nostrils; his ears pinpointed birds hopping on tree branches and rabbits scampering along trails.

At thirteen, the siblings were recognized as young

adults by the elders in their pack, and now they sprinted on all fours between trees in the thick woods, chasing squirrels and nipping at each other's hindquarters. Gabriel didn't know how he could return to New York City; *this* was the life he desired. Running in Wolf Form, he forgot about everything that had mattered to him back home: video games, television, and music. The feeling of his heart beating in sync with nature soothed and exhilarated him. Another sensation tingled in the back of his mind: a desire to hunt, to kill, to taste raw meat. He knew if he stayed here, the urge to prey upon a fellow animal would become impossible to resist, and if he returned to the family's Manhattan domicile, the veneer of civilization would prevent him from ever being true to himself.

Gabriel led the way into the sunlight and along the muddy embankment of a stream, then back into the shadowy woods. Beams of sunlight shot through the tree branches overhead, and leaves struck his snout as his paws kicked up dirt. Raphael, ever competitive, pulled beside him. Gabriel increased his speed, but Raphael passed him. Gabriel allowed his brother to have his moment of glory. They leapt over a fallen tree and ran down a gulley. Gabriel slowed in the gulley, but Raphael charged on at full speed, lengthening his lead. Angela panted behind Gabriel.

Gabriel ran faster, keeping his brother in sight. Caution rose within him: they had reached the border of the property owned by the pack, and their father had warned them never to venture beyond their own territory in Wolf Shape. Angela yelped a warning, and he stopped, but Raphael continued running, shrinking from view. Angela caught up to Gabriel, and the two Wolves looked at each other. Gabriel knew his sister feared danger. They chased their brother.

Raphael crossed the border, ignoring a No Trespassing notice posted on the thick trunk of a tree. When Gabriel reached the tree he stopped, tilted his head toward the sky, and issued a short howl, calling Raphael back, even though it would alert predators. Hunting season was six weeks away.

Ignoring Gabriel's plea, Raphael sprinted into a clearing and glanced back at his brother and sister, daring them to follow.

Resisting the urge to do so, Gabriel dropped his hindquarters to the earth and waited. Angela stood beside him, panting.

Raphael stared at Gabriel.

Come on, Gabriel thought.

A gunshot split the air, blowing a chunk of bark from a tree near Raphael's head. Gabriel recoiled from the sound, which echoed through the woods. Raphael turned rigid, then took off in the opposite direction. Before Gabriel could stop her, Angela bolted past him and ran after Raphael.

Now Gabriel had to worry about both of them. A second shot rang out, tearing through bushes behind where Raphael had hesitated. Raphael disappeared from his view, and Angela followed the same path. Gabriel expected the unseen shooter to fire another shot, but he didn't. Turning his head left, Gabriel headed in the direction the shots had come from, using bushes for cover. Thirty seconds later, he glimpsed their enemy: a burly Caucasian male wearing a baseball cap and a down vest over a red plaid shirt. The man held a scoped rifle and trotted after the Wolves.

The man was a poacher, and he was on our property. What good did it do to obey Father's orders if their enemies broke the law? Gabriel circled behind him and followed at a distance. The poacher entered the clearing and moved through the same bushes Raphael and Angela had. Gabriel kept trees between them, peeking around them to see the man intent on killing his brother and now his sister. He wondered if the land they had crossed onto belonged to the man or if he had trespassed like them.

The poacher stopped at dense brush, set one boot on a boulder, and raised the stock of the rifle to his shoulder.

Gabriel hesitated as the man lined up a shot. Wolves obeyed a rule never to kill humans. To disobey meant exposing the pack and their species to danger. But if he failed to act, the poacher might kill Raphael or Angela, and if that happened, a carcass would reveal the Wolves' existence, and Gabriel would have no choice but to kill the man anyway.

Seeing no alternative, Gabriel broke into a run. When he had cut the distance between himself and the poacher in half, the man spun in his direction. Gabriel skidded to a stop and froze, paralyzed with fear, looking at the barrel of the man's rifle. One second that felt like thirty passed, and Gabriel braced for the impact of a bullet.

A dark shape burst through the brush on the man's right side. Angela clamped her fangs around the man's shin just as he fired, and a round tore into the earth behind Gabriel. Another shape sprang from the bushes to the man's left, slamming into his shoulder and toppling him over Angela. The man's rifle flew from his hands. Raphael landed on the ground beside the man and bared his canines at him, a menacing growl rising from his throat.

The blood drained from the man's panic-stricken features, and he flopped onto his belly and groped for his rifle. Raphael bounded over him, landing between him and his weapon with a snarl that caused the man to go still. Seeing the bloodlust in Raphael's eyes, Gabriel barked at his brother. Angela passed between the man and Raphael, separating them, then fastened her teeth on the rifle's stock and dragged it away.

Gabriel and Raphael locked eyes. Gabriel bared his own fangs and issued a deep warning. Raphael stayed his ground, then backed away from the poacher. Angela rejoined him and nudged him forward. The two Wolves padded away from the scene. Gabriel stared at the man, whose eyes revealed astonishment, and ran after them.

Back in human form and dressed in jeans and T-shirts, the three teenagers stood on the back deck of the cabin, facing their father, who sat in a wooden chair. Angela cursed herself for allowing her brothers to get her into trouble once more.

"Human rules are made to be broken," their father said. "We live by pack rules. We live *because* of pack rules. Do you understand?"

Gabriel nodded on Angela's right, Raphael on her left.

She nodded as well.

"When you break our rules you endanger yourself, the other Wolves in our pack, and our entire species." He stared at Gabriel. "Explain this violation."

Gabriel looked at Raphael.

"I didn't tell Raphael to speak; I told you to speak. You're the oldest. One day you'll lead the pack in my place. Tell me the truth."

Gabriel met his father's gaze. "Raphael crossed the border. I called him back, but he ignored me. When the hunter shot his rifle he ran away, and Angela ran after him."

"I only wanted to protect him," Angela said.

Her father silenced her with a look.

"I followed them for the same reason. When the man turned his gun on me, Raphael and Angela jumped him. They saved my life."

He regarded Angela, then Raphael. "You each broke my rule and made the decision to cross that boundary."

"It's my fault," Raphael said.

"No, all of you are to blame." He turned to Gabriel. "But I hold you responsible."

Gabriel's voice grew shrill. "But Raphael—"

"It's time for you to take responsibility for the actions of your brother and sister. How can you lead the pack if you can't lead your younger siblings?"

Angela loved her father, but she felt herself burning with anger. Gabriel was older than her by minutes, not years. She had her own mind and knew how to make her own decisions. She considered herself responsible.

Gabriel said nothing.

Their father turned to Raphael. "If anything ever happens to Gabriel, you're next in line to lead when I'm gone. You're old enough now to put childish behavior behind you. Follow his example."

Raphael bowed his head. "Yes, sir."

Their father rose. "I brought you up here to learn about yourselves, to discover how we once were. I think you've all learned an important lesson today. Go inside and do your homework. We're going back to the city tomorrow."

Gabriel entered the cabin, followed by Raphael.

Their father looked at Angela. "Yes, dear?"

"Don't I have to be responsible in case I have to lead the pack?"

He got down on one knee and stroked her hair. "We all have to be responsible for each other; that's what it means to belong to a pack. But your mother and I have other plans for you."

"To have pups," Angela said with disappointment in her voice.

"How else can we survive as a species?"

"Can't I have pups and lead the pack?"

He smiled. "I'm not a king. I'm the alpha male. If I pass my mantle to a strong son, the others in the pack will respect that. But if I choose my daughter as my successor, other Wolves would doubt my judgment. Someone stronger than you would challenge you, and you would lose. Is leadership worth dying for?"

"It isn't fair."

"Nature dictates our roles, not human sentiment. If I could bear children I would, but that's not how things work. Go inside now."

Angela went inside, but she still felt cheated.

PART ONE
THE FRENZY WOLVES

one

Jonas Tudoro inhaled. Through the black fabric covering his head he discerned a lightbulb glowing in the ceiling. His hands had been zip tied behind his back, his ankles secured to the metal legs of the chair he sat upon. He did not know how long he had been sitting in the room, perhaps forty minutes, after spending hours in the sky. The hood had covered his head the entire trip.

When the plane landed, his captors had moved him into what he decided was a troop transport truck because of the smell of wet canvas. As the truck growled across the tarmac, his mind told him they had landed on a military base. In what country, he did not know. The plane could have flown to Europe, or it could have remained in the air to confuse him and landed on a base in the States. It did not matter. The only thing that mattered was that he, Father

Jonas Tudoro of the Catholic church, had been taken into custody by federal agents at JFK International Airport in Queens, New York, while attempting to escape the country. Now he sat like a common criminal—worse, like a terrorist. Or a caged animal.

A key rattled in the metal door, which swung open with a loud squeak like a frightened rat. Tudoro heard footsteps. A shadow passed over the hood. A ring of keys landing on a metal table produced a sharp sound that made him wince. Fingertips grazed the crown of his head, and Velcro separated. The hood came loose, and Tudoro blinked in the dingy light. A man came into focus before him: Caucasian, muscular, short brown hair, dressed in a polo shirt and jeans.

CIA, Tudoro thought. He had expected regular army.

The man, who had a square jaw and all-American good looks, stepped behind Tudoro and pushed the priest and his chair over to the metal table. He circled the table, his waist narrow and his back wide, and Tudor saw the empty holster clipped to his belt. He must have turned his gun in as a precaution.

The man pulled out the chair on the other side of the table and sat. "Good evening, Father."

"Is it? Evening, I mean."

"It is in the US. You slept on the plane."

"Were you on board too?"

"No, I get airsick. I try to fly as little as possible. But I heard you slept well."

"Where are we?" The room was stuffy. Underground, maybe.

The man offered a sympathetic smile. "Does it matter?"

"I'd like to know."

"Our location's classified."

"Doesn't a prisoner have the right to know his prison and captors?"

"Call me Jim."

"That isn't your name."

"No."

"What am I being charged with?" Tudoro said.

"You're not being charged with any crime. You're classified as an enemy combatant of the United States of America."

"I've committed no act against your country."

Jim smiled again. "You've withheld information vital to the safety of the United States, and the members of your cell went on quite a rampage in New York City."

"What do you mean by 'cell'?"

"Father, I don't want to hurt you, but I won't lose sleep over it if I have to remove a few of your teeth and break all your fingers. When you were taken into custody at JFK, you were told we have the laptop used by the Brotherhood of Torquemada. We've identified all the members who were killed in Newark, and we can trace your movements around the globe in relation to theirs and to transactions made into their bank accounts. You were one of the ringleaders of this cell. Now they're all dead, and your superior, Cardinal Delecarte, died in Rome last week. As far as we can tell, you're the last man standing, and we have a lot of questions."

Tudoro sat straight. "I'm a priest with the Catholic

church. I demand to call the Vatican."

"Does it look like we're treating you with kid gloves? That we're going to give you a quarter to make a phone call? Forget it. That ain't happening. But just to put your mind at ease, we've already contacted the Vatican on your behalf. They deny any knowledge of your activities and suggested that you and Delecarte embezzled funds for this rogue operation. They want nothing to do with you. We got the feeling they'd prefer it if you sat in this cell until your dying day or if something worse happened to you. The last thing they want is a scandal."

This did not surprise Tudoro. The Brotherhood was a clandestine organization only partly rooted in the church, and when Delecarte had passed, its other backers had withdrawn their support. Delecarte had played everything so close to the vest that Tudoro didn't even know who else in the church knew about the Brotherhood's mission, and Tudoro had been Delecarte's chief assistant. "That's it, then? I'm to be left to rot here?"

"That depends on how willing you are to cooperate. Tell me. What did you envision for your retirement?"

"I once wished to return to a simple life in Tuscany."

Jim made a face. "That's a little close to home. How about the Dominican Republic? You once served there."

Jim missed the point; Tudoro wanted to retire where he knew no one, and no one knew him—a difficult task given his globe-trotting history. "Now I'd prefer to see the sunrise from someplace warm and unfamiliar."

"How about Costa Rica?"

Tudoro considered the suggestion. "The idea has appeal for me, but I'm concerned about my safety."

"From the church?"

"And our enemies."

"Well, we never considered setting you free anyway. You'd have to be watched and protected in a compound somewhere. But at least you'll see the sun, which is more than you'll do here."

"An expensive proposition."

"Not in Costa Rica."

"You'd do that for me?"

"Sure, why not? You're sixty-eight. How long could you have left?"

Tudoro grunted. His parents and maternal grandparents had lived into their late eighties. "So I can stay here and be tortured or cooperate and be treated like some deposed dictator."

"That's not a bad analogy."

Drawing a breath, Tudoro stared at the dirty mirror behind Jim. "Are we being recorded?"

"Of course."

"If I agree to your terms, how long will it be until you relocate me to my new quarters?"

"That depends on how fast you talk."

"Please untie my hands and feet. I'd like to be comfortable."

Jim stared at Tudoro's eyes. Then he rose and walked over to the door, which he banged on. As Jim walked back to Tudoro a second man entered the cell and closed the door. The second man held a machine gun.

"Is that to protect me or you?" Tudoro said. "I assure you I know no martial arts and possess no superpowers."

"Your assassins knew a lot of tricks," Jim said. He set one boot on the table and rolled up his jeans, revealing a hunting knife that he unsheathed.

Tudoro's gaze did not leave the blade until Jim moved behind him with it. The interrogator cut the ties binding the priest's ankles, then the zip tie around his wrists. It felt good to be somewhat free.

Jim returned to his seat.

"I'm hungry," Tudoro said.

"You'll be fed."

"I'd like some red wine too."

"We planned ahead."

"Where shall we begin?"

"Start with the werewolves."

TWO

Seated in the second pew of the worship hall at the Church of Saint Paul the Apostle on the corner of Columbus Avenue and West Sixtieth Street, Captain Anthony Mace felt his stomach tighten as Father Shepherd called his name. His wife, Cheryl, had remained at home with Patty, their two-year-old. She had stayed there all week since Mace had rescued her and Rhonda Wilson, an eighteen-year-old Wolf, from the New Jersey lair of the Brotherhood of Torquemada.

Karol Williams, a detective serving on his task force, squeezed his hand. He looked at her brown eyes, shiny with suppressed tears, and gave her a grim smile. Then he rose and made his way toward the flag-draped coffin on the dais. A statue of Jesus Christ, crucified and in agony, overlooked the closed casket. Mace avoided the statue's tortured eyes, instead focusing on those of Willy in a framed eight-by-ten photo atop the coffin.

Stepping up to the pulpit, Mace nodded to the priest and faced the mourners. Willy's parents and other family members sat in the front pew on Mace's right-hand side. Willy's mother wore black and sobbed into a handkerchief. His father resembled Willy, only with silver hair and a mustache. Civilians filled the pews behind them, an invisible blue wall separating them from the police who occupied the other half of the church, all of them in dress blues, like Mace. Ken Landry and Candice Smalls, the other two surviving detectives from Mace's task force, sat on Karol's other side. Special Agent Kathy Norton, the surviving FBI member of their task force, had flown to Washington, D.C., to attend the burial of her partner, Special Agent Shelly, also killed in the raid.

In the front pew on Mace's left sat the big brass, including Mayor Branson and his wife, Deputy Chief of Operations Jim Mint, Commissioner of Public Information Craig Lindberg, and Police Commissioner Robert Benson. The power of the police department stared at him. They knew about the existence of Class Ls, the government's classification for lycanthropes—Wolves. Jim had pressed Mace to head the task force because Mace had tangled with Wolves even before the Brotherhood of Torquemada showed up, and Mace had dragged Willy into the operation. Guilt gnawed at his insides.

Mace gave Willy's parents a sympathetic look and then spoke into the pulpit's microphone. "Willy Diega served under me for five years, first in Manhattan Homicide South . . ."

Mace recalled Willy working cases with Patty Lane, who had been murdered two years earlier by Janus Farel, a rogue Wolf. Mace and Cheryl named their daughter after the fallen detective. He wondered how many other good cops might die under his command.

". . . and then on a special task force assigned to apprehend the Brotherhood of Torquemada. I can't discuss that case because the investigation is ongoing, but Willy served his community with honor and died in the line of duty. His bravery helped bring down a terrorist organization we didn't even know existed until they arrived on our shores. He died a hero, and today he'll be recognized as one. My thoughts and the prayers of the department go out to his family, friends, and colleagues. His loss is a blow to our community, and we must make it our personal missions to carry on as he would have wanted us to, living up to his ideals. He was a good man, and I'm better for having known him."

Mace lost focus as he descended from the pulpit. He ran his right hand along the polished surface of the casket, then took his seat beside Karol.

Karol's breathing was shallow. He knew she would not allow herself to cry, even though she and Willy had been lovers. The relationship between his subordinates had come as a surprise to Mace but not as big a surprise as the secret Karol carried with her every day: she was a Wolf and belonged to Gabriel Domini's pack. Karol had served the task force while reporting its activities to Gabriel. Mace should have felt betrayed, but he and Gabriel had formed an uneasy alliance to rescue Cheryl and Rhonda Wilson.

Mace's desire to protect Gabriel—as he had protected Gabriel's sister, Angela Domini, before him—conflicted with his loyalty to the department, and that conflict intensified now that the skirmish with the Brotherhood had become public news. Everyone who had survived the battle in Newark had left the presence of the Wolves out of their accounts. As far as the brass and the public knew, only police detectives and FBI agents had battled the Torquemadans.

Bagpipes played outside the church as mourners exited. Another hundred police officers stood on the sidewalk, and civilians stood across the street. Snowflakes drifted through the air, almost invisible.

Waiting for the uniformed pallbearers to emerge with the casket, Mace scanned the crowd and spotted Colleen Wanglund. Cheryl worked for Colleen at Manhattan Minute News. The two women had been together when Rodrigo Gomez, the notorious Full Moon Killer, had given Cheryl a stunning interview from Sing Sing prison, where he had proclaimed himself a werewolf. Colleen had driven Cheryl home from the interview, but the Brotherhood intercepted them. They drugged Colleen and took Cheryl prisoner, which provoked Mace into leading the charge on their Newark, New Jersey, base—the offense that had gotten Willy and Shelly killed.

Mace's gaze drifted away from Colleen, and he took in the faces of the members of the press corps. Cameramen trained their lenses on him, the price of being branded a hero cop in the tabloids. A familiar figure stood in the crowd: a flabby man with blond hair, wearing a red scarf. Carl Rice. Mace's body stiffened.

Rice had authored two true crime books that featured Mace in a central role, *Rodrigo Gomez: Tracking the Full Moon Killer* and *The Wolf Is Loose: The True Story of the Manhattan Werewolf.* The first book was a sensationalized account of how Mace had apprehended Gomez. It had been made into a cable TV movie, much to Mace's consternation. The second book tried to make sense of a series of brutal murders committed by Janus Farel, the rogue Wolf Mace had killed in secret. The book was largely conjecture. How could it be anything else? Farel had been a shapeshifting Wolf, and no rational mind could accept such a being's existence with ease.

Mace disliked Rice on principle: he was a shoddy journalist and an opportunist. Rice had also made Mace something of a celebrity and had spoken to Cheryl hours before her abduction, implying Mace had killed the Manhattan Werewolf. Rice's theory was correct, and since freeing Cheryl from the Brotherhood's makeshift prison, Mace had told her everything. Now Rice watched him. Mace knew the reporter was on the scent of a story.

The gang's all here, he thought.

But that wasn't true. Gabriel Domini had gone underground; he was wanted for questioning because both the funeral home and the occult bookstore he and his brother, Raphael, owned had been destroyed in explosions set by the Torquemadans. And Rhonda Wilson was nowhere to be seen.

Six police officers exited the church with Willy's casket supported between them. They descended the front steps, and the bagpipes swelled. The pallbearers carried the casket to the waiting hearse and loaded it into the black vehicle.

Mace, Karol, Landry, and Candice got into Mace's department SUV and joined the procession en route to the Police Arlington Burial Grounds at Cypress Hills in Brooklyn for Willy's twenty-one gun salute. Neither Landry nor Candice knew Karol was a Wolf.

"Nice job, Tony," Landry said.

Keeping his eyes on the motorcade ahead of him, Mace did not answer.

"Any idea when we're going to get some help in the squad room?"

"I've requested five more detectives," Mace said.

"How long is this operation going to continue?" Candice said. "I know we have to cooperate with Justice as far as wrapping up what just went down—whatever that was—but new detectives mean new business. We did our duty; the Brotherhood's finished. So let's go home."

"Mint wants us to keep surveillance on the Class Ls."

Karol looked out the passenger side window.

"That isn't what we signed up for," Candice said.

"I realize that," Mace said. "Objectives change."

"I didn't become a police to spy on werewolves. I wish I didn't even know they existed."

"I'm sorry for getting Willy and Shelly killed and dragging you all into this. But we're part of something bigger now, whether we want to be or not. We know the truth.

The department's not going to let any of us off the task force. They're going to keep us in that shabby squad room for as long as they can to keep an eye on us if nothing else. If they want us to watch Class Ls, then that's what we're going to do."

It doesn't mean we have to hurt them, he thought.

"How are we supposed to identify them?" Landry said.

"Good question." But he already knew the answer.

THREE

Sitting in the passenger seat of a silver minivan, Gabriel Domini exhibited no reaction as the Hauppauge Industrial Park, one of the largest industrial parks in the country, came into view. Modern-looking buildings and decrepit factories rose to the sky like great mesas. The park occupied fourteen hundred acres and employed fifty-five thousand employees. Gabriel thought it was a city unto itself.

George Allen, his driver, lowered the volume on the radio. "Civilization."

Gabriel smiled. George had served as advisor to Gabriel's father, Angus, the leader of the pack until Angus appointed Gabriel to fill that role in preparation for the day when Gabriel would succeed him. When Angus passed away just over two years ago, Gabriel became the alpha, and his brother, Raphael, served as his advisor. Now that

Raphael and his subordinates had separated from the pack, Gabriel had turned to his father's former advisor for help. "You don't have skyscrapers on the Upper East Side?"

"Of course we do. That doesn't mean we have to like it."

"Today I'm glad this park is here."

George snorted. "*Park*."

They drove through the industrial park, passing stout buildings and lawns that had lost their green sheen in the December cold. Christmas lights blinked in a single window in one building.

"Thank you for your help," Gabriel said.

"Thank you for asking me. My retirement has been a disappointment, especially since Katherine died. I've felt useless."

"I should have consulted you earlier." Gabriel hoped his sincerity showed.

The older man waved him off. "Forget it. I'm old; I get it. Young people think old people are out of touch just because it takes us longer to learn new technology and we have little patience for modern music."

"I'm hardly young. I have a wife and two children."

Thinking about Melissa, Damien, and Gareth pained his heart. He had sent them to Canada to stay with his sister, Angela, when the Brotherhood of Torquemada came to New York City to exterminate the Wolves in his pack.

They reached the far end of the park. A factory that looked ancient in comparison to the other buildings loomed ahead. A man stood outside a steel door set in dirty brick.

"There he is, as promised," George said.

Gabriel recognized the Wolf in human form: Bennett

Jones, a grocer from Staten Island. Gabriel had been reluctant to enlist Bennett, who had challenged him at several pack councils, but George had insisted. Seeing the burly man now, Gabriel was glad George had been so stubborn.

George parked near a rusted old truck, and he and Gabriel got out. Across the lumpy pavement, Bennett spoke into a cell phone. George opened the hatch, and each man withdrew an old guitar case. Metal clanged inside the heavy cases. George closed the hatch, and they met Bennett halfway to the steel door.

"Warren's on his way down," Bennett said. "I came an hour early. The morning shift went inside. No sign of Raphael or his men."

"That doesn't mean they aren't watching us right now," George said.

"They're not here," Bennett said in a flat voice.

"It doesn't matter if they are," Gabriel said. "Raphael's got no reason to stop us from doing what we came here to do."

"That isn't what I'm worried about," George said.

Gabriel knew George feared Raphael intended to assassinate him and take over the pack. Gabriel did not share that fear. Raphael posed a threat, but he had been raised with the same code as Gabriel. If the younger brother intended to seize power, he would do so in accordance with the pack's law by challenging Gabriel at council.

Bennett took out a cheap-looking cell phone. "I just bought this, and I'll chuck it as soon as we're done here. Give me a number so I can warn you if anyone with an unfriendly disposition shows."

George removed a scrap of paper from his coat pocket and read a phone number aloud, and Bennett entered the number into his disposable phone.

So many precautions, Gabriel thought.

"Got it," Bennett said. Pocketing his phone, he withdrew a key card and turned to the door. He waved the key card before a sensor, and the door clicked.

George opened the door, and as he and Gabriel moved to enter the factory, Bennett held the card out.

"Give this back to Warren," Bennett said.

Gabriel followed George inside, and the door clanged shut behind him.

Warren Schneider led Gabriel and George across the shop floor of Schneider Metal Works. Each man wore a safety helmet, protective goggles, and earplugs. Dozens of workers pushed carts, welded iron, and poured fiery molten metal. The heat made Gabriel dizzy, and he unbuttoned his coat. They passed through plastic strips over a threshold wide enough to accommodate a forklift, and the temperature dropped. Inside this new space, chargers for the forklifts' batteries lined one wall.

A forklift came around the far corner, beeping a warning. Its driver wore a protective yellow vest in addition to the gear Warren and his guests used.

Warren stopped at a door in the side wall, near an eyewash station, and waved a key card at a sensor. He opened the door and led Gabriel and George into a large room filled with silent machinery. Closing the door behind them, he removed his earplugs. Gabriel and George did the same. Warren walked over to what looked like a giant oven. It reminded Gabriel of the oven he and Raphael had used to cremate people at their funeral home.

Warren patted the side of the metal construction. "Here she is. I'm glad I kept her around. Let's see what you've got."

Gabriel and George set the guitar cases on a motionless conveyer belt and flipped their latches. They opened the cases at the same time, revealing the silver gleaming inside: six swords divided between the cases.

Warren moved closer to the cases, a mixture of dread and awe on his features. "The symbols of our persecution. I know they have no real power, but I'm afraid to touch them. How many of our kind have they killed over the centuries?"

Gabriel clasped the handle of one sword and raised the heavy blade. "That's why they have to be destroyed. Their symbolism is their power."

The six Blades of Salvation had been forged during the Spanish Inquisition and had been wielded by the Brotherhood of Torquemada. Hundreds of Wolves in human form and hundreds of humans accused of being Wolves had been executed with them.

Funded in part by the Catholic church, the secret, modern Brotherhood had wiped out the Wolves in Europe, then set its sights on the US. A group of six men and women had entered New Jersey with the swords in their possession. They murdered Jason Lourdes, his parents, and the parents of Rhonda Wilson, Jason's girlfriend, and they kidnapped Rhonda. NYPD assigned Tony Mace to head a joint task force with the FBI to stop the Brotherhood and prevent the public from discovering the Wolves' existence. The swords had come into Gabriel's possession after the battle in Newark.

Warren gazed at the silver blade in Gabriel's hands. "If the Brotherhood's really finished . . ."

"The Brotherhood's assassins are dead, and the church has publicly denied any association with it," George said. "But a society that's functioned in secret for centuries has supporters and believers. These must be destroyed now."

Warren nodded. "Let's get on with it, then." He slid open the heavy front door on the oven.

Gabriel tossed the sword into the oven, and George and Warren carried the rest of the Blades and threw them clattering inside the metal box. After Gabriel gave the weapons a last look, Warren pulled the door down. He threw a series of switches, and the oven rumbled to life.

"Silver melts at 1,763 degrees," Warren said. "I've set this oven's temperature at 2,000."

The room grew hot.

"What should I do with the melted silver?" Warren said.

"Bury it," George said.

"No, sell it," Gabriel said. "We're going to need all the money we can get our hands on."

FOUR

fter Willy's burial, Mace strode into One Police Plaza as if he worked there, flashing his shield at the police guards, and made his way to the elevators. It wasn't long ago that he had been treated like a pariah in these halls of power, banished to Floyd Bennett Field to administrate the K-9 Unit.

Mace rode the elevator to the seventh floor and walked along the corridor, the squeaks of his rubber-soled shoes echoing on the tile floor. He opened a door and entered a wide anteroom where a civilian female with red hair worked at a computer.

"Can I help you?" the woman said in a thick Long Island accent.

"Tony Mace to see Jim Mint."

"Do you have an appointment?"

"He'll see me."

The woman picked up her phone and pressed a button. "Mr. Mace is here to see you."

"Captain Mace," Mace said. He wore his dress blues, for Christ's sake.

"Yes, sir." She hung up. "You can go right in. Do you know the way?"

"I do." Mace crossed the room to another hallway and opened an office door.

Jim Mint rose behind his desk. "Tony, what are you doing here?"

Mace entered and closed the door. "It's all over the news that I led the raid in Newark. The task force isn't a secret anymore."

Jim sat. "That's only fair, isn't it? You were the golden boy until the Manhattan Werewolf came along. Now you've redeemed yourself. You and your people did well."

Mace eased himself into a chair facing the desk. "I didn't take the assignment to reignite my career. I was pretty happy living a simpler life. I took it because my experience with Janus Farel made me the best man for the job."

"Well, it paid off. In a sense, you're vindicated."

"Why, because my superiors now know I told the truth? You guys didn't make me the face of this investigation to throw me a bone. You did it because there was no way to cover up what went down this time. When sword-wielding maniacs blow up New York City buildings, the public demands answers. My team provided a convenient solution."

Jim spread his hands apart. "There's nothing wrong with that. You had a job to do, and you did it."

"And Diega and Shelly got killed in the process."

Jim's expression turned serious. "That's the chance we take every day. It comes with the job."

Mace looked around the office. The bosses didn't risk their lives. "My wife's involvement only sweetened the pot."

"It's a sensational story; I'll give you that. How is she?"

"Resting."

Mint's voice softened. "That was some send-off, wasn't it? I always get the chills during the salute."

"Since the whole world knows my team took down the Brotherhood, there's no reason to continue this cloak-and-dagger routine any longer, is there? If my banishment's been lifted, I should be free to walk in and out of here as I please."

"Not so fast. You're still on assignment, and that assignment remains classified."

"Spying on Class Ls."

"Identifying them and tracking their activities."

"What if we can't find any?"

"If they're out there, you'll find them. I have faith in you. Jason Lourdes was in mid-Transformation when he was killed. His parents were in Class L form when we found their corpses. Begin with the parents' friends and coworkers, any organizations they belonged to. Build a list, then start bringing people in for genetic testing."

"You promised me more men."

"That's what this is about?"

"Norton's in D.C. I've only got three people, and Williams needs a partner for any fieldwork."

"Assigning more people to your task force means

bringing them into the fold. We're trying to minimize the number of people who know these things exist. Norton will be back."

"I need more people."

Jim sighed. "I'll see what I can do, but it isn't as easy as you think. This is a joint task force. I'm not calling the shots. FBI has a say in this too. I'm sure they'll assign a new partner to Norton, and then you can pair Williams with Smalls."

"We'd also like to know if there's an end date for this assignment."

"What do you think? If you're to be believed—and the feds sure seem to—there's a secret species of shape-shifters walking around under our noses, and we're standing on the front line. If you'd never voiced your theory about Janus Farel, you wouldn't be sitting here now."

It always came back to Farel. The monster's killing spree had attracted the Brotherhood in the first place.

"Any word on the Domini brothers?" Jim said.

"No."

"They've disappeared just like their sister. Convenient, isn't it? Find any of them, and you'll find more Class Ls."

Mace remained silent.

"How's the Wilson girl doing?"

Mace knew Mint had an ulterior reason for asking. "She's still in hiding from the press. I'm told she's staying with friends."

"You heard this from Detective Williams?"

"That's right. I assigned Karol to be her liaison."

"I don't like it. We should know where she is at all times."

Mace didn't like it, either, but for different reasons.

"The Brotherhood came here to kill Class Ls, and they took that girl prisoner."

"Rhonda's DNA test shows she's 100 percent human. What remained of her parents' corpses after the Brotherhood blew up their house was human."

"Then why take her?"

"She witnessed Jason Lourdes's execution. Maybe they didn't want to kill a human. They kidnapped Cheryl too. Do you think she's a Class L?"

"Of course not."

"Williams took the genetic test. Every member of my team did. We passed with flying colors." Karol had explained to Mace that if a Wolf provided materials for genetic testing while in human form, the DNA would appear human. He kept that to himself.

"Find the Dominis."

Mace parked his Jeep Cherokee in the lot of the Fifth Precinct headquarters on Elizabeth Street and walked through the crowded streets of Chinatown to a four-story brick building on Mott Street. He unlocked the door, then punched in a code on the alarm keypad and boarded the elevator.

On the fourth floor, he used a key card to open a gray metal door. He had grown to hate this place as much as Candice did. Passing the empty reception station, he entered the bull pen. Karol looked up from her cubicle, and

Candice and Landry looked up from the desks in the office they shared. Shelly's cubicle and Willy's desk served as grim reminders of their losses. Space heaters hummed.

"You look lonely out here by yourself," Mace said to Karol. He needed to speak to her alone.

"I'm getting used to it," Karol said.

Landry came out of his office. "Any word on reinforcements?"

"I'm working on it. Mint wants us to compile a list of all the Lourdes's known friends, coworkers, and associations."

Landry held his gaze as if waiting for additional information. "We'll get right on that."

Mace walked into his glass-faced office, hung his coat, and sat at his desk, where he opened his e-mail and called Cheryl. "What's happening on the home front?"

"I just put Patty down for her nap."

"I'm sorry I couldn't call earlier."

"How could you? I saw you on TV."

"They carried the funeral live?"

"Manhattan Minute and every local station. I think the networks may have too; they carried Shelly's. It's the story of the day."

Mace's stomach tightened again. The increased press coverage, especially in the national media, made his covert operation harder to run.

I'm going to get an ulcer.

For as long as he could remember, he had suffered pains in his body when he grew tense or excited, but no doctor had ever been able to diagnose them.

"Are you sorry you weren't in on the action?" he said.

"I couldn't have gotten any closer to the real action." Cheryl kept her tone light, but Mace knew her experience with the Wolves and Torquemadans had left deep emotional scars on her psyche. "I told Colleen I won't be going back."

"How did she take the news?"

"She told me to take a six-month leave. I told her I'd made up my mind."

Before her abduction, Cheryl had wanted Mace to resign from NYPD. Now that wouldn't be possible. She wouldn't even be eligible for unemployment benefits.

In the bull pen, Candice crossed the squad room and disappeared into the reception area.

"You were working too hard anyway," he said.

"I haven't told Anna yet."

Anna Sanchez, the twenty-year-old daughter of their downstairs tenants, worked as their nanny.

"Why don't you hold off on that for a while? You need some rest, and I'm sure you could use help around the house."

"If I'm not working . . ."

Mace stiffened as Candice led Carl Rice into the squad room. "Cut her down to part-time, then. She can leave after you put Patty down every day. Our savings account can handle it while she looks for other work."

Karol rose from her desk, and Landry exited his office. Karol moved to Carl, who said something to her and gestured to Mace. Karol and Landry turned to Mace, who raised his hand palm out.

"I've got to run. Something just came up," Mace said.

"Something serious?"

"No."

"I love you."

"I love you too." Mace hung up and walked into the bull pen.

Carl stood with his hands stuffed into the pockets of his coat, smiling. "So, this is where you do whatever it is that you do." He looked around the squad room. "It's very humble."

"You followed me from the funeral, didn't you?"

"Nice to see you're allowed back in One PP again. Did you meet with the big man himself?"

"No comment."

"Probably not. He needs plausible deniability, so you probably deal with a trusted middleman. How does that line go in *The Godfather*? You needed a buffer. Is Seely your buffer? Or does he need plausible deniability too?"

Mark Seely was the chief of operations. Jim was the deputy chief.

"No comment," Mace said. "Except you're thinking of *The Godfather II*. How did you get into the building?"

"You're not the only tenant. Your neighbors have limited English, or at least they pretended to when I asked about a police operation in the building, so your secret is safe. For the moment." Carl nodded at Mace's subordinates. "Is this your whole team? You're kind of shorthanded."

Mace said nothing.

"I thought this was a joint NYPD and FBI task force?"

"The task force is closed. This is a mop-up operation. All we're doing is working with federal agencies to make sure they know everything they need to know about the Brotherhood of Torquemada. Any information related to what we're doing here is classified. Contact Craig Lindberg if you have any burning questions."

"I tried several times. The esteemed commissioner of public information isn't very keen on sharing information with the press."

Mace shrugged, which caused pain to flare in his left shoulder, where Valeria Rapero, a member of the Brotherhood of Torquemada, had stabbed him with her sword in Newark.

"I guess I can understand why no one wants to go on the record about werewolves," Carl said.

Damn it. Mace showed no reaction.

"Would you like to invite me into your office?"

"I have nothing to say to you."

"Then I'll do all the talking."

Keeping his eyes on Carl, Mace motioned to his office. As Carl proceeded in that direction, Mace looked at Candice, gestured at her dress blues.

"What could I do?" she said. "We need a civilian receptionist to keep inquiring minds away."

Mace followed Carl into his office and closed the door. The reporter didn't wait for an invitation to sit.

"Jesus Christ," Carl said, unbuttoning his coat. "It's freezing out there and boiling in here."

"You have five minutes," Mace said.

Carl smiled. "It hurts me that you haven't been returning my calls."

"Why should I start now?"

"Touché. I'm sure your wife told you about the conversation she and I had the day of her big interview with Rodrigo Gomez, right before her abduction."

"You mean when you stalked her?"

"We just share an affinity for overpriced coffee. How is she, anyway?"

"She's fine."

"That interview was pretty hairy, if you know what I mean. She must have told you that I know you met with Gomez two years earlier during the height of the Manhattan Werewolf scare."

Mace feigned a bored expression.

"What a coincidence that in your wife's big televised interview, the Full Moon Killer announced he was a werewolf."

Mace checked his watch.

"But he wasn't the *Manhattan* Werewolf. How could he have been? He was already in Sing Sing, where you put him. But isn't it funny how those killings just stopped?"

"I understand you theorize I had something to do with that."

"You were hot on the case and at the top of your game. The next thing the world knew, you were sent to the K-9 Unit on Floyd Bennett Field. Why would a rising star like you suddenly get benched? And why would the killings stop at the same time?"

"Don't forget the National Guards came to town."

"Just like they did last week. And now they're gone again. The difference is, this time we know that the people they wanted were stopped—by you."

"I had more than a little help."

"If you say so. The thing I wonder is, why were you put in charge of this operation? What did you do to earn a reprieve? Why did the powers that be pull you out of mothballs?"

Mace stared without answering.

"I have other questions, of course. We've been led to believe the Brotherhood of Torquemada was a terrorist organization, but no one's revealed their objective beyond decapitating a teenage boy and kidnapping his sweetheart."

"They blew up and torched two buildings, two houses, and an SUV and decapitated several people, not just the boy. I'd say their objective was clear: to cause a panic."

"May I quote you on that?"

"How can you quote me when I made no comment?"

"The buildings they blew up were co-owned by Gabriel and Raphael Domini, the brothers of Angela Domini, who's wanted for questioning in connection with the murder of John Stalk two years ago. The Manhattan Werewolf case again."

Mace sat silent.

"Coincidentally, several witness claimed to have seen a wolflike creature disembowel and decapitate Stalk on the fire escape of a building across the street from the Dominis' bookstore. You were at the scene of the crime, though I've been unable to find any statement from you on the record."

"I have no comment."

"Did a werewolf kill John Stalk? Or any kind of wolf, for that matter?"

"No comment."

"Did you kill the Manhattan Werewolf?"

No answer.

"Why were you put in charge of this secret task force to stop the Brotherhood of Torquemada?"

"I thought you were going to do all the talking." Carl rose. "Fine, let me take a crack at it. Fourteen men and women were killed by the Manhattan Werewolf. They were ripped to pieces as if by a real werewolf. Stalk was a policeman on an Indian reservation upstate, and he just happened to show up in the middle of this. On the night Patty Lane—one of your detectives—was murdered while undercover trying to nab this mad dog killer, you arrested Stalk in the Astor Place subway station. Then the National Guard rolled into town, the killings stopped, and you wound up on doggy duty."

"It sounds like a story that would make a great book. Too bad nobody wrote one."

"Did you read it?"

"No."

"My publisher rushed me to write it, so they could put it out before anyone else did one. As a result, it's more incomplete than I would have liked. The missing pieces didn't really fit together until these last few weeks." Carl counted on his fingers. "A boy is decapitated by a sword and a girl kidnapped in the Dominis' bookstore, then the boys' parents are killed and their house is torched. You get called back into the field to lead a joint NYPD and FBI task force. Why the hell would you be put in charge of anything after you were punished for some unpardonable crime? And why would the FBI answer to you? *Because you had valuable experience and information related to the case.*

"But nobody had heard of the Brotherhood of Torquemada before . . . except for a guy named Terrence Glenzer, an eccentric NYU professor. He wrote several books on the occult, and in one he self-published, he wrote about this Brotherhood. The book went out of print, but guess who laid his hands on a copy?" He tapped his chest. *"This guy.* According to Glenzer, the Brotherhood was made up of *werewolf hunters* during the Spanish Inquisition. Glenzer was the Manhattan Werewolf's first victim. One of the pieces of evidence you found in his apartment was half of a broken sword that belonged to the Brotherhood. The Vatican claimed the sword, and now they're denying any knowledge of the Brotherhood. The two cases are linked tighter than virgins on their honeymoon."

Mace stood. "You've had more than five minutes."

"One hour after Rodrigo Gomez told your wife he's a werewolf, she was kidnapped by the Brotherhood. Then you and the gang here rode to the rescue, and all the Brotherhood and two of your own people got dead. The Brotherhood is related to the Manhattan Werewolf, and the Manhattan Werewolf is related to Rodrigo Gomez."

"Are you hoping to write another book?"

"I need another installment to make it a trilogy."

"If I were you, I wouldn't tell anyone your theory until you have conclusive evidence."

"Is that a threat?"

"Hell, no, it's friendly advice. You may not like where your bosses send you if you overstep the boundaries of common sense."

Carl chuckled. "I'm between bosses. I write these books because no legitimate news organization will have me. I burned my bridges and my rep years ago, but if I can crack this story—real news—I'll get another shot."

For a moment, Mace felt sorry for him. "I can't help you."

"I can go live with what I have now."

Mace opened his door. "You could, but who would believe you?"

FIVE

As soon as Carl left, Mace turned to his detectives. "Ken, make sure Rice leaves the building. Candice, man the fort. Karol, I'd like to speak to you outside for a moment."

Candice returned her attention to her monitor, and Ken, Mace, and Karol filed into the hallway and waited for the elevator. When the door opened, Landry boarded the car and held the door.

"Go on without us," Mace said.

Landry released the door, and the elevator descended.

"Let's go onto the roof," Mace said.

He and Karol entered the emergency stairwell and climbed the stairs, their footsteps echoing. Mace opened the door and stepped outside, and Karol followed. He set a splintered block of wood between the door and its frame, so it wouldn't latch. Wind blew Karol's hair as they scanned the skyline around them.

"How are you doing?" Mace said.

"I can't really articulate how I feel right now. Like my heart's been ripped out of my chest and won't stop beating is just the start."

"You should have taken more time off."

"What good would that do? I'd still feel the same way, and the FBI, CIA, and Homeland Security would all still be hounding me for statements about what went down."

"What you really mean is, Gabriel wants you to keep an eye on everything here, right?"

Karol exhaled. "I can't exactly say my loyalties are torn. I am what I am before I'm who I am."

"This puts me in a difficult position."

"Are you going to turn me in?"

"Of course not, but if anyone finds out, I don't know anything about it. Do you understand?"

She nodded.

"How's Rhonda?"

Karol seemed to consider her words before speaking. "Worse than me, I think. She's angry, but that's to be expected. The Brotherhood killed Jason and spent days torturing her. We're both licking our wounds."

Mace had taken Rhonda's full account before Kathy Norton had taped an official version for the FBI. Both accounts neglected to mention torture, because Rhonda's wounds had healed and her severed arm had even regenerated. It also skipped the part of her transforming into a Wolf and ripping off the head of one of her captors.

"Mint brought her name up when I went to see him. You'd better find her a sublet to solidify her cover."

Karol digested this news.

"I'm going to have to partner you with Candice starting tomorrow. Legwork to determine the associates of the Lourdeses. It might be a good time for some sloppy police work."

"Is that it?"

"No. I want you to contact Gabriel. Tell him not to underestimate what's coming. I think he should come in ASAP to give a hair sample and deflect attention from himself. It will buy him some time. Don't use a phone. Get word to him in person. Do it on the clock if you have to, but get back here before anyone asks questions."

Karol stared at him as if weighing his words, then turned and walked to the door. In a moment she was gone.

Mace walked to the edge of the roof and looked at the mass of people below. Failing to see Carl Rice, he shivered in the cold.

"Warden Strand speaking."

"Hello, Jeff." Carl spoke into his smartphone while attempting to light a cigarette outside on the sidewalk. A man walking ahead of him carried a dead pig over one shoulder, and Carl found himself staring into the carcass's empty eye sockets.

"Why do you keep calling, Mr. Rice?"

"Because I want to speak to Rodrigo Gomez."

"I keep telling you that isn't possible. He's in solitary confinement."

"He didn't kill anyone. Lately, I mean."

"Mr. Gomez misbehaved. He isn't speaking to anyone. When he becomes available, I'll be sure to notify you. Now please stop calling."

"Is it possible you're keeping him under lockdown because he really *is* a werewolf?"

"Don't be ridiculous."

"So you think he was just making that up?"

"Of course I do."

"Isn't it true that since his incarceration at your fine institution, Gomez is suspected of killing three other inmates and maiming six others?"

"We have many violent offenders here. None of them are werewolves. Good-bye, Mr. Rice."

"Just one more question—"

Click.

Carl contemplated how to place Warden Strand's words into a new context.

Karol drove her department issue SUV to Booth Street in Rego Park, Queens. Parking at the curb, she walked to the front doors of a pre–World War II building, entered the vestibule, and pushed the buzzer for the superintendent.

"Yes?" a man said over the speaker.

"Karol Williams."

A moment passed. The door buzzed, and Karol entered the deep lobby. She followed the green tile floor to the elevator, which she rode to the basement. When the door opened, a tall Hispanic man waited for her.

"I'm here to see the man," Karol said.

The man looked her up and down, then turned on one heel and led her through a long corridor. They turned right and entered a spacious office with an old desk. The super knocked on another door, which he unlocked. Karol entered a smaller office with a newer desk and a cot. Gabriel rose from a seat at the desk. Karol didn't know the man who sat beside him.

"Karol, what brings you out here?" Gabriel said.

The super closed the door.

"I have a message from Mace."

Gabriel gestured to his companion. "I don't believe you've met George Allen."

"I know the name. It's an honor."

George smiled. "Charmed."

"Have a seat," Gabriel said.

Karol sat in his chair, and Gabriel sat on the cot. She looked around the office.

"I'm moving from safe house to safe house. Some are fancier than others."

"You don't have any bodyguards."

"I don't need them. The Brotherhood is finished."

"But Raphael—"

"Raphael and his men aren't going to sneak attack me. Right now, I want to keep as low a profile as I can. What does Mace want?"

Karol glanced at George.

"Speak freely in front of George. We have no secrets."

"Tony told me to tell you not to underestimate what's coming. He wants you to stop in right away to give a hair sample. He thinks that will take the heat off you."

"Anything else?"

"We have to find a sublet for Rhonda, something that can be verified. Mace says our boss is starting to ask questions."

Gabriel looked at George.

"I'll take care of it," George said. "Anyplace in particular?"

"Not the Bronx, that's too close to home," Karol said.

"It will be easy for me to find a place in Staten Island," George said. "You can get the address from your Bronx rep tomorrow."

"Carl Rice discovered the task force's location."

"Mace will have to deal with him."

"I wouldn't count on that. He's down with the cause, but his hands are tied. Once Rice blabs about the task force, it will be even harder for Tony to do anything without scrutiny."

"Better him than us." Gabriel turned to George. "Give her a burner. Make it two."

George opened a desk drawer and took out two disposable phones, which he handed to Karol. "For emergencies. Use them once and throw them out." He handed her a slip of paper with several phone numbers on it. "A different number for each day of the week."

Karol slid the phones and numbers into one coat pocket.

"Thanks for coming," Gabriel said. "I won't keep you from your duties."

Karol stood.

"How's Rhonda?"

Karol hesitated. "Troubled. She's desperate to leave the apartment, but the minute she shows her face in public the press will be all over her."

"Give her my best. Tell her we're thinking about her."

"I will."

"And how are you?"

She shrugged.

"I'll respect your privacy, but I'm thinking about you too."

"Thanks." Karol bowed and exited the office, and the door closed behind her.

When Carl arrived at the two-family home on Eighty-fourth Street in Bay Ridge, Brooklyn, he registered the black bars over the door and the first-floor windows. It surprised him more to see bars over the second-floor windows as well, an unusual security measure. Carl wondered if the bars had been in place prior to Cheryl Mace's abduction. He mounted the concrete steps and rang the doorbell. When no one answered, he rang it again. He knew better than to leave.

After several minutes, the door opened, and a young woman with Mexican features and glasses stood before him.

"Is Cheryl home?" Carl said.

"Mrs. Mace isn't seeing anyone."

"Can you tell her it's Carl Rice? I'm an old friend."

"She isn't seeing anyone."

"I'll wait."

"I've told you politely that she isn't seeing anyone. If you really are her friend, then you know she's married to a police captain. If you don't leave now, I'll call the local precinct and tell them you're harassing her, and then I'll call Captain Mace."

"There's no need for that."

"I think there is." The young woman closed the door, and Carl heard locks turning louder than necessary.

Goddamn college students, he thought. *She's probably a journalism major.*

Descending the steps, he stopped at the sidewalk and turned. In a second-floor window a woman looked down at him through the bars. Carl raised one hand to wave, but Cheryl dropped the curtain.

I had to try, he thought.

Mace's office phone rang, and he picked it up.

"It's Norton."

He felt relieved to hear her voice. "How goes it in Washington?"

"My funeral was dark and depressing. How was yours?"

"The same."

"I'll be back tomorrow."

He didn't press her for information. His phone could be tapped or hers. "We can use the help. Do you need someone to pick you up?"

"That won't be necessary. Expect me before lunch."

"I'll see you then." Mace hung up.

Now that the FBI believed Class Ls existed, the bureau would want a much more active role in running the task force. He would be happy to turn the entire operation over to them, but then he would be in no position to protect Gabriel, Karol, Rhonda, and the other Class Ls.

He glanced at the bull pen: Karol, Landry, and Candice continued to key in reports requested by different government agencies, even though they had already given statements following the warehouse raid. He knew Karol held an even more difficult position than he did, with more to lose. He looked at the clock—4:40 PM. Disappointment that Gabriel had failed to present himself weighed heavy on his shoulders. Tomorrow the feds would be back, and covering for Gabriel would be more difficult.

He walked into the bull pen. "Let's wrap it up and get out of here in an hour. I miss my family."

"I hear that," Candice said.

Mace entered the lavatory and relieved himself at the urinal, then washed his hands and gazed at his reflection in the mirror. His short dark hair was turning salt-and-pepper. Sighing, he rotated each shoulder and winced. The right one had been bitten by Janus Farel. The Wolf bite had healed, but the sword wound in his other arm flared with pain.

This damn war, he thought, splashing cold water on his face. He exited the bathroom and found Landry standing in the bull pen with a visitor.

"Hello, Captain," Gabriel Domini said.

SIX

"Mr. Domini," Mace said, "thank you for coming in."

Gabriel nodded. "Certainly."

Landry and Candice stared at Gabriel, and Karol mimicked them. Mace had told all of them the Dominis were Wolves, and Karol had told Gabriel that. Both Mace and Gabriel depended on their sworn secrecy.

"Please come into the conference room. Ken, set up the camera. Can I get you some coffee, Mr. Domini? It's not as bad as fictional depictions of police departments would have you believe."

"No, thank you. I'd like to get this over as quickly as possible."

"I understand. This way, please." Mace led Gabriel into the conference room, where Landry mounted an HD camera to a tripod. Mace lowered the blinds, then sat on the far side of the table. Gabriel sat opposite him.

Landry switched on the camera, which beeped, and set the focus. "Mr. Domini, would you mind saying something?"

"First they came for the communists, and I did not speak out because I was not a communist," Gabriel said. "Then they came for the trade unionists, and I did not speak out because I was not a trade unionist. Then they came for the Jews, and I did not speak out because I was not a Jew. Finally, they came for me, and there was no one left to speak out."

"Uh, great. We just need you to fill out that paperwork in front of you."

Gabriel picked up the printed document, skimmed it, and signed it with a pen. He slid the paper over to Mace, who eased it aside.

"Thank you, Ken," Mace said.

"Just let me know if you need anything." Landry exited and closed the door behind him.

Mace and Gabriel stared at each other.

This is a farce, Mace thought. *A stage play.* He and Gabriel had confided in each other and had fought side by side. Cheryl never would have made it out of the Brotherhood's lair if it hadn't been for the Wolf. Now both men had to play a game for the camera. *It has to be done.*

"Please identify yourself for the camera," Mace said.

"My name is Gabriel Domini."

"Middle name?"

"None."

"Do you have family?"

"A brother, Raphael, and a sister, Angela. Also, a wife, Melissa, and two boys, Damien and Gareth."

"How old are the boys?"

"Six."

"Twins?"

"Yes, and my brother and sister and I are triplets."

"How old are you?"

"Thirty-four."

"And what's your occupation?"

"I currently have none. Until recently, I co-owned the Domini Funeral Home and a bookstore called Synful Reading with my brother. Both businesses were destroyed."

"By whom?"

Gabriel smiled. "According to the police and news media, they were destroyed by a terrorist organization called the Brotherhood of Torquemada."

"Did you ever hear of the Brotherhood of Torquemada before?"

"Never."

"Have you seen the photographs of its members?"

"They would be hard to avoid. Our country loves to celebrate people who crave attention."

"Did you ever see any of those men or women before?"

"No."

"Did you ever have any contact with them or anyone connected to the Brotherhood of Torquemada?"

"No."

"Why do you think they targeted your businesses?"

"I have no idea."

"Surely you've wondered."

"Every waking moment. I'm an honest businessman. I've had no illicit dealings, and my businesses served the community. I'd like to know why my life has been turned upside down, why my family faces an uncertain future. But with those people dead, I have no reason to believe I'll ever get the answers I want."

"Was Jason Lourdes an employee of yours?"

"Yes, he worked at Synful Reading."

"Can you tell me what happened to him?"

"I wasn't there, but he was murdered in the store. Decapitated by a sword, I'm told. Raphael and I visited the crime scene and spoke with two of your detectives."

"Do you remember the detectives' names?"

"I remember Detective Diega's name, because his murder was recounted in the newspapers. A tragedy. I don't remember his partner's name, but the young woman is sitting at a desk outside this room."

Mace sat back in his seat. "Let the record show that Mr. Domini is referring to Detective Karol Williams, part of this task force. Do you know Rhonda Wilson?"

"She also worked at Synful Reading. I understand she and Jason were romantically linked, though I didn't learn that until after Jason's murder."

"You're aware that Jason's and Rhonda's parents were also killed by the Brotherhood?"

"Yes."

"Did you know any of them?"

"I knew all of them but only casually. That's why

Raphael hired their children in the first place."

"It's taken a while for you to come in for questioning. What took you so long?"

"My businesses were destroyed, and my livelihood's been taken away. I've had a great deal of work to attend to with regards to insurance claims. I've also had several funerals to attend, an ironic development for a former funeral director."

"We've been unable to reach your brother. Do you know where he is?"

"No, I don't. I'm afraid we've had a bit of a falling-out as a result of all this chaos."

"Two years ago, your sister, Angela, was wanted for questioning and disappeared. Can you tell us her whereabouts?"

"My sister is traveling across Europe. She never stays in one country for more than a few months, and I have no addresses for you."

"Have you been in touch with her?"

"She writes me on occasion. I'm unable to reciprocate. To my knowledge, she has no idea any of this has occurred."

"Did you save these letters?"

"I did. Unfortunately, I kept them at the funeral home."

Nice touch, Mace thought. "Where were you the night your businesses were destroyed?"

"Hiding."

"Excuse me?"

"I had just left the funeral home when it blew up. If I'd left work one minute later, I'd be dead now. I raced home to make sure my family was safe and learned on the news that the bookstore had been destroyed as well. Fearing the worst, we stayed with friends."

"Why didn't you call the police?"

Gabriel smiled. "If you were able to help, my businesses wouldn't have been destroyed in the first place. We resurfaced when we learned you'd actually killed those terrorists. What other questions can I answer for you, Captain? I'm afraid I can't be very helpful to your investigation, because I don't know anything."

"Do you believe in the supernatural?"

Gabriel's expression turned to one of surprise. "Excuse me?"

"Synful Reading was an occult bookstore."

"My father, Angus, owned the store before us. He saw an opportunity for a niche business and turned it into a world famous mail-order company. In later years, he became too old to shoulder the responsibilities and made my sister his manager. When he died, we inherited the business. None of us took it seriously. It was a lark, almost an embarrassment. But it continued to turn a modest profit."

"The Brotherhood of Torquemada was reportedly formed during the Spanish Inquisition to exterminate werewolves throughout Europe."

"Really?"

"That information hasn't been made public. Professor Terrence Glenzer wrote about it in a book you sold at Synful Reading."

"I only worked at the store part-time when I was a boy, breaking down boxes and taking out the garbage. I wouldn't know about the inventory, especially during the later years."

"I need to speak to your brother and your sister. When

you hear from them, tell them to get in touch with me."

"I will. Are we finished?"

"Not yet. I need you to give me a hair sample for genetic testing."

Gabriel frowned. "What in God's name for?"

"I can't tell you that."

"Then I'll have to refuse your request."

Mace stared at Gabriel. *Is he kidding?* "Aspects of this investigation are classified. The Brotherhood of Torquemada was an international terrorist organization."

"Why do you need *my* hair? I'm an American."

"I'm sorry I can't tell you more, but I really need that hair sample."

"Am I suspected of something?"

"Not exactly but this sample could eliminate you from the possibility of future suspicion."

Gabriel pointed at Mace. "I came here on good faith, without counsel. Do I have to—?"

"There's no need to be upset. If you want us to go through your lawyer, we will. Just give me his name. If you want us to get a subpoena, we can do that too. Or you can allow us to do what we need to do, and that way you won't have to come here again, and with any luck you'll never have to see me again. If you have nothing to hide, what's the problem?"

Gabriel hesitated, then crossed his arms. "Get it over with."

Mace walked over to the door and opened it. "Candice, would you mind doing the honors?"

A moment later Candice entered the conference room

with a small plastic kit in one hand and a paper envelope in the other.

"Mr. Domini's consented to assist us with our investigation."

"That's nice." Candice set down the plastic kit and removed a pair of scissors, which she raised toward Gabriel's head. Her hand shook, and she glanced at Mace, who stared at her. She pressed the blades against Gabriel's hair and snipped two locks, which she deposited into the envelope. "Thanks," she said in a forced cheerful tone and then hurried out of the room.

"Now we're done," Mace said.

"I'll show you out," Mace said in the bull pen.

Gabriel faced Landry, Karol, and Candice. "I'm sorry about what happened to your colleagues."

Mace led Gabriel to the elevator and boarded it with him. "Don't let that empty squad room fool you," he said. "It will be swarming in another day or two or someplace else will be."

"I have no doubt," Gabriel said.

"Don't go home."

"I haven't been there in over a week."

"You need to go underground."

Gabriel smiled. "That isn't possible. I have responsibilities, just as you do. But your responsibilities are work related. Mine pertain to the survival of my species."

"Something tells me your species will survive better if you and Raphael take a page from Angela's book and disappear."

"Thank you for the warning. I appreciate it. But you saw my brother and his Wolves at the warehouse. They complicate matters."

"What did you do with the swords?"

"We destroyed them. They'll cause neither one of us any more trouble."

The elevator lurched to a stop.

"If you need me, reach me through Karol," Mace said. "I don't trust my phones."

Gabriel gave Mace a concerned look. "You be careful."

The elevator door opened, and he was gone.

SEVEN

With cigarette smoke curling up from the ashtray next to his Mac, Carl pecked at his keyboard, then stopped and reviewed what he had written. Nodding, he smiled. Then he pressed Autodial on his phone and waited.

"Hello?" John Beaudoin, an editor at the *Post*, sounded tired.

"Long day?" Carl opened an e-mail and attached the article.

"Who's this?" Now he sound irritated.

"Carl Rice." He pressed Send.

"Oh, Christ, what do you want?"

"Congratulations on your coverage of the Brotherhood of Torquemada. Very sensational, far better than that dry stuff they're running at the *Daily News*. I've just sent you an article on the same topic."

"You're persona non grata here. You know that."

"Morty's retired."

"Saul doesn't like you, either."

"He may not like me, but he doesn't hate me."

"That's debatable. Okay, let me see this. What am I reading? The sword . . ."

"The Blade of Salvation."

"And the Vatican . . . Is this for real?"

"You bet your sagging ass it is."

"Glenzer . . . the Manhattan Werewolf . . . Are you shitting me?"

"The connection is real. These cases are linked."

"I don't know. It's awfully speculative . . . Wait a minute, *werewolves?*"

"I didn't say there *are* werewolves. I just said that killing werewolves is what the Brotherhood was all about."

"Sounds like malarkey to me, but you've got some fresh angles here. Give me the night to think about it."

"Not a chance. I'm breaking this story before anyone else does. *We're* breaking it."

"This isn't a story; it's a sidebar."

"You're crazy. This story provides a motive for the Brotherhood."

"What, werewolves? You got us confused with a supermarket rag. This is background, nothing more."

"What about the link to the Vatican?"

"Just because they claimed the broken sword doesn't mean squat, if it's even true. It could be sitting in a museum somewhere."

"It isn't. I checked. Guess what mysteriously disappeared?"

"You'll have to do better than that."

"I expect to see the first paragraph on the front page tomorrow. If I don't, I'll see it on the front page of the competition."

"They'll never touch this."

"We'll see."

John exhaled on the other end. "All right."

"Really?"

"Yes, really. I should have my head examined for giving you another chance. Rewrite the opening paragraph so it's a little less desperate, and it will make tomorrow morning's edition."

Carl pumped his fist in the air. "Thanks. You won't regret this."

"Too late." John hung up.

Carl leapt to his feet and shouted at the ceiling, "Yes! Front page, baby!"

Karol shivered as she followed the concrete walkway to her apartment building on Pelham Parkway in the Bronx. A trio of Albanian boys standing out front fell into silence as she approached the door. They had made the mistake of catcalling her once before, and she'd given them a lesson on manners they wouldn't soon forget. As she passed them now their sudden silence turned palpable. Their muted voices rose only when the inside glass door had closed behind her. Little did they know that her keen ears heard every syllable they whispered.

"We should get that bitch alone and rape her ass," one of them said.

Try it, honey, she thought. She had never killed a human being, had never even tasted a freshly killed wild animal, until battling the Brotherhood of Torquemada in the warehouse raid. The taste of hot human blood had awakened her senses in an intoxicating manner that contradicted her mourning for Willy. In the week that had followed, her temples throbbed, she wiggled her fingers and toes, and she chewed on the inside of her mouth. Every cell in her body told her she would feel so much better if she tore someone to pieces. She fought the urges, restraining her wild side. She had never expected to feel such bloodlust.

Karol opened her mailbox, searched through bills, and boarded the elevator. Loneliness massaged her tired muscles. Wolves were monogamous, and Willy had worked his way into her heart, only to be torn from her, slain before her eyes. The sight of him lying on the floor of that warehouse lingered in her mind. She squeezed her eyes shut, but the mental picture wouldn't go away. Willy's funeral had been agony. She had spoken to his parents at the cemetery, but they only knew her as Willy's partner, not as his mate.

The elevator door opened, and she crossed the carpeted floor to her apartment door. Bowing her head, she took a deep breath and got her emotions under control. Dealing with Rhonda required patience. She unlocked the door and went inside.

The apartment was dark, so she turned on the lights. Rhonda stood near the window by the radiator, gazing at falling snow. She did not react to Karol's arrival.

"Hi," Karol said.

"Hi." Rhonda spoke in a flat, emotionless voice.

"I don't suppose you cooked dinner?" Karol said.

Rhonda shook her head.

"Did you eat anything?"

Another shake.

"Then I guess I'd better get started." Karol hung her coat in the closet and went into the kitchen, where she removed steak from the refrigerator. "Do you like salad?"

No answer.

She went back into the living room. "Hey, I'm not a mind reader. Help me out here."

"Salad's fine."

"How do you want your steak?"

"Rare."

Of course. "I missed you at the funeral."

"I couldn't go. Those reporters would have been all over me."

"I told you we would have kept them at bay. I'd have sent a squad car for you and everything."

"They would have followed me back here."

Maybe she was right. "We could have made arrangements."

Rhonda snapped her head in Karol's direction. "I didn't want to go, okay?"

Karol debated whether to press the girl and decided Willy deserved a certain level of respect. "Two men died rescuing you. I cared about one of them a lot."

Rhonda screwed up her face. "That makes me sick to

my stomach, if you have to know. It's disgusting."

Karol blinked as if struck. "Don't you care—?"

"I hate them *all*, every last one." She raised her regenerated hand, which had been chopped off while she had been in captivity. "I shouldn't have to explain myself."

"We all suffered. Mace was stabbed, Willy and Shelly killed. You might show a little gratitude."

Moving forward, Rhonda snorted. "Gratitude. I was *tortured* for days. Jason and my mom and dad were killed." Tears filled her eyes. "They cut Jason's head off in front of me."

"And they all but cut Willy's off in front of me. Do you think I'm feeling any less pain than you are?"

"I loved him. Do you understand? And I loved my parents."

"I do understand. I loved Willy. We mated. That means it's over for me—no love, no pups. At least you still have a chance. Your wounds will heal."

Rhonda raised her voice. "What do you know?"

"I know that Mace, Willy, and those two FBI agents risked their lives to get you out of that warehouse, and only two of them walked out alive."

"They didn't come for me. They came for Mace's wife."

Karol felt her rage coursing through her veins. "That isn't true. We busted our asses looking for you."

"Funny how you didn't find me until Cheryl Mace got kidnapped too. She wasn't there long enough to lose any limbs. I guess that was my good luck, wasn't it? The cavalry came for her, and I got to tag along on the ride home."

Karol moved forward too. "If you want to sit here and

stew in your own hatred, go ahead. But show a little consideration. You're a guest in my house. Don't disrespect the people in my life who matter to me, especially after the sacrifices they made for you."

The irises of Rhonda's eyes expanded, blotting out the whites.

Reining herself in, Karol spoke in a tight voice. "You don't want to do that, girl. Don't make me teach you how to behave."

Rhonda pulled her lips back into a snarl.

Karol stood her ground. "I mean it."

Rhonda's irises shrank to their normal size, her breaths coming fast and hard.

"Go to your room."

Rhonda leaned closer to her, showing Karol she felt no fear. "Don't act like you're my mother." She sniffed the air around Karol. "You might as well be one of them."

Karol slapped her. The impact turned Rhonda's head, and when Rhonda looked back at her one side of her face was red. Her lips quivered, and then she stormed down the hall. A moment later a door slammed.

Taking a deep breath, Karol wondered what she had gotten herself into and whether she and Rhonda would both be better off if Rhonda really did move into a sublet.

Darkness had fallen when Mace and his crew left their headquarters and made their way to the Fifth Precinct lot where they parked their vehicles each day. They exchanged good-byes like any office colleagues and went their separate ways.

Mace listened to Dean Martin on the drive to Brooklyn. He parked in the driveway, mounted the steps, and unlocked the gate over the door and then the door itself. The aroma of sizzling pork from his tenants' first-floor apartment greeted his nostrils. Anita Sanchez must have spent hours each day on her meals. The wooden stairs creaked as he climbed them. Hanging his coat on the hall rack, he stepped out of his shoes and wiggled his toes. Then he unlocked the door to the upstairs residence and basked in steam heat.

"Dada!" Patty ran into his arms.

He picked her up despite the pain in his left shoulder. A groan escaped from his lips, but he spun it into a laugh as he raised her in the air. "How's my girl?" He held her high and buried his face in her belly and blew on it, eliciting a storm of giggles.

Cheryl and Anna came into the dining room.

"Your dinner's almost ready, Anna," he said.

Clutching an armful of textbooks, Anna gave him a quizzical look.

"So is ours," Cheryl said. She wore slacks and a sweater.

Anna kissed Patty. "I'll see you tomorrow, kiddo."

"Bye-bye," Patty said.

"Good night," Anna said to Mace and Cheryl.

"Good night," Mace said.

Anna exited, and Cheryl locked the door.

"How was your day?" Cheryl said.

"Rough," Mace said.

She leaned her head on his shoulder. "I'm sorry. I wish I could have been there."

"That's okay."

She took Patty from his arms. "We had a visitor today."

"Oh?"

"A certain pseudo journalist."

Mace frowned. "When was this?"

"Around three o'clock."

After he came to the squad room. "Why didn't you call me?"

"Because it wasn't necessary. I had Anna send Carl away. I suppose he's working on another book."

"It wouldn't surprise me."

"At least this one will have an ending, even if it can't possibly include the most important details."

"I guess we'll have to wait and see." Mace had become so accustomed to keeping information from Cheryl when she was a reporter that he had no trouble doing so now that she wasn't. "What's for dinner?"

"Chicken Marsala."

"Fantastic. No offense to Anna, but I prefer your cooking. I'm going to take a shower." He moved down the hall, hoping she didn't realize he was being evasive.

EIGHT

Lying on the bare mattress of his cot in solitary confinement, Rodrigo Gomez inhaled when the lightbulb in the ceiling turned dark. For a normal human prisoner, lights-out meant darkness. Gomez wasn't normal; he wasn't even human. He was a Wolf, which he had discovered only upon his imprisonment.

On the outside, no one had taught him about his true nature, and the beast raging within him had driven him to the brink of insanity. Many people—like Tony Mace and the journalist Carl Rice and the state prosecutor—believed he had crossed that line, but he knew better. A Wolf who devoured his human victims was not a cannibal but a predator acting on instinct. His years in prison had given him ample time to get in touch with his inner being, and he had made his televised interview with Cheryl Mace his coming-out party.

I am werewolf. Hear me howl.

Cheryl had sat before him, so smug and self-confident, but she didn't know shit. Neither did Mace or Rice. They claimed to want the truth, but their minds couldn't accept it. Mace had come to see him here at Sing Sing when the Manhattan Werewolf was loose in the streets of New York City. The cop had sought insight from Gomez, who had been dubbed the Full Moon Killer because he killed when the lunar cycle drove him to do so. Gomez had only begun to suspect his true nature after Mace's visit. The Manhattan Werewolf—whoever he was—had inspired him to look inward. When other inmates threatened him, he unleashed his fury in drips and drabs: a throat slashing here, a broken neck there. He had found the urge to kill difficult to rein in and wanted nothing more than to gnaw on the innards of his enemies, but he knew discretion was required to enjoy some sort of freedom within the prison's walls.

Following his interview, Warden Jeff Strand had relocated him to solitary confinement, and three days later had him moved into this old building. Gomez's cell had a shower and a toilet, and for one hour each day his captors allowed him onto a caged balcony.

Exhaling, Gomez rose in the darkness. He saw every detail in the cell, minus color. He stepped out of his clothes and left them on the floor, then proceeded to stretch his muscles. It was time to bring his time in Sing Sing to a close. He wanted out. Lying on his back on the cold floor, he tipped his head and unleashed a human scream as loud and melancholy as any Wolf's howl.

Jose Alvarez marched back and forth across the hard floor of the isolated wing of Sing Sing, counting his footsteps to pass the time. The shuttered building had stood empty for years and had just been reactivated to accommodate Rodrigo Gomez because the powers that be decided the inmate needed to be isolated even from those condemned to solitary confinement.

Jose didn't understand why some nut hollering he was a werewolf posed a threat or why he warranted the Rudolf Hess Spandau Prison treatment, requiring his own detail of corrections officers, but he didn't mind the assignment. He found it a pleasure to be away from the felons he usually watched. Since the new arrangement had gone into effect, Gomez had proven to be a model prisoner: no babbling, no screaming, no howling.

This was a babysitting job compared to his regular duty, but Jose wasn't complaining. He made decent overtime and had a great pension plan, and he was halfway to easy street. The only thing that bothered him was the daily commute from the Bronx, but he preferred driving along the Hudson River to riding the subway into Manhattan. He'd take tree-lined scenery over standing shoulder to shoulder with sweaty straphangers any day, even with the cost of gasoline.

Reaching the far end of the corridor, he turned on one heel. A spasm of pain shot through his right knee, and he felt old. His kids, Desi and Ramona, were both in middle school and would be in high school soon, and he had promised his wife, Jackie, that they would move out of the Bronx, maybe someplace close to his job. She wanted to move now, but houses out here were expensive, and if they rented one he knew they would never save enough to own one.

So close . . .

A loud wail came from the only occupied cell in the building.

Oh no, here it comes.

He moved toward the cell. The wailing continued.

At least he isn't howling.

Jose slid open the hatch in the steel door. "Let me have light in the tank," he said into the radio clipped to his collar.

Five seconds later the overhead light in Gomez's cell came on. Jose pulled his black baton free of his belt and leaned close to the hatch.

Gomez's cot was empty, but the wailing continued.

Squeezing the handle of his baton, Jose leaned even closer to the hatch. Gomez lay nude on his back on the stained concrete floor, his feet aimed at the door and his head at the far wall. He supported himself on one elbow, his face contorted with agony and his body speckled with sweat.

"What's going on, Gomez?"

"My heart . . ."

Jose's eyes widened at the sight of Gomez's chest. Its center expanded as if a fist inside his trunk was trying to punch its way out.

"Hurry . . ."

Jose holstered his baton and spoke into his radio. "Get a medical team in here right away. I think Gomez is having a heart attack."

"Copy that," CO Alex McBryde said inside the control room.

"Let me in there."

"You know that's against protocol."

"I see his heart pounding in his chest. There's no way he's faking it. Let me in!"

A moment later a clanging sound echoed in the block, and Jose opened the door.

Gomez had been practicing Transformation for two years, ever since the Manhattan Werewolf had inspired him to find the answers to the questions he had been asking: *Why am I different from everyone else? Why do I feel like an animal masquerading as a human being?*

He had lain awake each night, transforming a different body part: a hand, a foot, a leg, an arm. One night his head, another night his back. All on the cot in his cell, beneath the covers and away from the prying eyes of the guards. When he awoke each morning his muscles burned with pain, which gave him deep satisfaction. He never pumped iron in the yard, but his physique became more pronounced than those who did.

Now he concentrated on his heart and the muscles around it, causing his chest to expand to an alarming degree.

Jose ran over to him. "Get your feet on the cot."

Gomez groaned. "It hurts so bad."

Jose set Rodrigo's ankles on the cot one at a time, elevating his legs. Then he crouched beside the inmate. "Help is on the way."

Now.

In the span of seconds, Rodrigo willed his right hand to expand into a claw that he drove into Jose's face. His elongated index finger pierced the man's eyeballs while the thumb penetrated the flesh beneath his jaw, then his tongue, and then the roof of his mouth, preventing the man from screaming. A high-pitched whistle came from the corrections officer's nostrils, followed by blood.

Setting his left hand on the floor for support, Gomez sprang upright and slammed the corrections officer down in his place. Jose dug his fingers into Gomez's bare arm and kicked at the wall. Gomez raised the corrections officer's head like a bowling ball and smashed it on the floor with all his strength, splitting the man's skull. Jose's hands fell at his sides, and he stopped kicking.

"We have a medical emergency in the old building two," Alex McBryde said into his radio in the control room. He sat at a console with a live monitor feed of the cell block. "Inmate Gomez appears to be suffering a heart attack. Send a medical team."

"Copy that," the dispatcher said.

"No need to hurry," McBryde said. *Screw this scumbag.*

The monitor showed a uniformed figure running out of Gomez's cell.

"What now?"

Jose raced to the steel door below the camera and pounded on it. Blood streaked his face.

"Oh, shit." Pulling a manual lever, McBryde unlocked the door.

Jose staggered inside, head bowed.

McBryde ran around the console to help him. "What the hell happened?"

Jose turned away from him to close the steel door.

"Are you all right?"

When the CO turned back, McBryde saw the man wasn't Jose. For a sickening instant, he thought Gomez stood before him. Then the man's irises expanded, obscuring the whites of his eyes, and as he lunged forward his jaws opened wider than McBryde thought possible. Ferocious canine teeth sank into his face, and McBryde felt hot wet breath on him, followed by blinding pain. The teeth bit through his flesh and muscle, sinking into his cheekbones.

McBryde screamed, and his assailant knocked him to the floor. Claws shredded his torso, splashing his blood. Pain blazed through McBryde's body, and he tried to wrestle free of the grasp of his attacker. As the raging figure on top of him growled, McBryde felt coarse fur rubbing against his bloody flesh. He pounded at the monster, but it seized his wrists in powerful claws and forced his arms to the floor. McBryde heard a tearing sound, and it wasn't until the creature sat up and gobbled a large piece of flesh that he realized he no longer had a face.

Gomez swallowed human blood, and it tasted good. Fully transformed, he tore the remains of Jose's uniform from his powerful frame and opened and closed his fur-covered claws, admiring their awesome beauty. At that moment he wanted nothing more than to give in to his primal urges and wallow in the gore beneath him, but he knew he had only moments to execute the rest of his plan.

With lightning speed, he strode on his hind legs across the control room and opened the door, revealing a long corridor with cinder-block walls. Dropping to all fours, he raced down the corridor, his limbs assuming a more canine configuration. He turned the corner and entered another corridor, his claws scrabbling on the floor. A steel barred door loomed ahead. Gomez hurled himself at one of the bars, and the door flew open. He struck the floor of the old visitors' entrance, rolled, and galloped for the front doors.

Another leap and he felt cold air on his snout. He landed on a craggy surface outside and ran along the cement between the two old buildings, each four stories high and almost five hundred feet long. Moonlight reflected off the marble surface, and he felt as if he had entered deserted Roman ruins.

He slowed as he reached the end of the buildings. Work lights illuminated the dead grass separating him from the twenty-foot-high prison wall with an octagonal guard tower built into it. The windows in the tower glowed, but it was the full moon that held his attention. He broke into a run, tearing up dirt and grass, and headed straight for the tower.

A corrections officer emerged from the enclosed control room and stood gaping at the railing, then rushed back inside.

By the time the man returned with a Remington 870P shotgun, Gomez had circled around to the left of the tower's base and leapt halfway up it. He climbed to the top of the wall with ease.

The CO moved along the railing, looking at the yard below, until he stood next to Gomez. When he turned his head in Gomez's direction, his eyes went wild, and he raised the shotgun to his shoulder. Rodrigo seized the barrel and aimed it at the sky, then dug the claws of his other hand into the man's throat. The man gurgled blood and fired a blast at the moon, and Gomez sent him screaming to the ground below.

As the searchlight from another tower illuminated the other side of the control room, Gomez tilted his head back and let loose a shuddering howl, then leapt over the wall and plummeted twenty feet to the ground. Landing on the sloped embankment upon which the prison had been built, he sprinted across a paved road onto grass and bolted for the tree line. Shouts rose behind him and a searchlight swept over him, but no shots were fired and he vanished into the brush.

NINE

A cell phone rang in the darkness. Tony Mace stirred in his sleep, but it was Cheryl, lying wide awake, who heard the call. She had suffered insomnia all week, and now she nudged him before the ringing awakened Patty. Cheryl had moved the toddler into bed with them following her abduction.

"Mm?" Tony reached for the cell phone and answered it. With his back to her, Tony stiffened. "What? How? . . . Right, right. Call the Six-Eight and have them send a car to watch my house. I want two men."

Cheryl sat up.

"No, I want them parked outside my front door where my wife can see them. Give me an hour." He hung up and turned on the light.

"What is it?" Cheryl said.

Tony rose and switched on the bedside table lamp. He had taken to wearing T-shirts to bed to cover his wounds. His expression was grim. "Gomez escaped from prison half an hour ago. He killed three guards."

Cheryl's heart beat faster, but her voice stayed steady. "And where are you going?"

"To Ossining."

Her journalist's instincts kicked in. "He's one of them, isn't he? Just like he said. You wouldn't be running off like this if he wasn't."

"Yes."

"Who called?"

"Mint."

"And he wants you on the scene."

"I'm the head of the task force. It's my job."

"The task force was supposed to stop the Brotherhood of Torquemada. You did that. I thought it was just going to be paperwork now."

"That was the idea."

"Maybe I don't want you to go. If Gomez comes to the city, he could come after me."

"I'm not leaving until you have protection." Tony gestured to the bars on the windows. "You're safe in here, and I taught you to use my .38."

She got out of bed. Patty stirred but didn't awaken. "If Gomez is a Wolf, then no two police officers will stop him."

He moved closer to her. "The bars over the doors and windows will keep him out."

"He could set the house on fire, burn us out."

Tony set his hands on her shoulders. His hands felt strong and reassuring. "You're giving this too much thought. There's a manhunt for him. He probably won't make it to the city, and if he does his face will be posted everywhere. We'll catch him."

"Then what? How will you stop him?"

"They're not indestructible, babe. You saw that. They can be killed. Angela Domini told me Gomez doesn't even know he's a Wolf."

"In my interview, he said otherwise." She felt guilty for allowing Gomez to use her.

Tony put his arms around her, and she held on to him. Then he went into the bathroom and ran the shower.

Cheryl opened the door, stepped inside the closet, and took down the metal gun case. She set it on the bureau and opened it. Snug in its foam compartment, the .38 gleamed. She picked it up. It felt heavier than it had when Tony had taught her how to handle it. She popped open the cylinder and loaded six bullets into it, then snapped the cylinder shut.

Now what? Was she supposed to carry it in a holster around the house? Patty would love that. She placed the loaded revolver in its compartment, closed the case, and set it on top of Tony's armoire, where her daughter couldn't reach it. Then she went into the kitchen and brewed coffee.

Dressed in a black suit, Mace put on his long coat and kissed Cheryl. Sniper circled them wagging his tail.

"Don't worry," Mace said. "Everything will be okay."

"Are you coming back here before you go into the office?"

"I'll try." He opened the door and stepped into the hall-way. The door closed behind him, and Cheryl turned the locks. He descended the stairs and opened the glass-paneled inside door.

Before he could step into the vestibule, the apartment door behind him opened. Eduardo Sanchez stood there in flannel pajamas. "Is something wrong? I saw the police car outside."

Mace hesitated. He didn't want to worry Eduardo or his family, but he felt they had a right to know. "A felon's escaped from prison. I have to go to the scene. This crimi-nal isn't very happy with me or my wife. You should know there's a slim chance he'll come here. We all have to take security precautions."

Eduardo furrowed his brow. "Who is this man?"

"I can't say." *It will be all over the news soon enough.*

Eduardo raised his gaze to the ceiling. "Does Mrs. Mace know?"

"Yes."

"I'll send Anna upstairs to keep her company."

"Thank you, but that isn't necessary. I'm sure Cheryl will be happy to see her in the morning, though. She's likely to be focused on the TV all day."

Eduardo nodded. "I'll keep an eye on things while you're gone."

Mace smiled at the man. "I appreciate that, but those officers outside aren't going anywhere. They'll keep an eye out for everyone in the house."

Eduardo shrugged. "Still."

"Good night," Mace said.

"Good night, Captain."

Mace closed the inner door behind him and opened the front door, then the security gate over the door. A police cruiser idled double-parked out front. Shivering, he walked down the front steps to the cruiser. The officer behind the wheel lowered his window.

Mace leaned forward. "Hi, what are your orders?"

"Fugitive watch, right? Rodrigo Gomez."

Mace took out his card and handed it to the PO. "You're watching for Gomez or anything else out of the ordinary. If you see anything at all, radio it in and then call me. If either one of you needs to use the bathroom, call me and I'll work it out. Don't ring that bell unless you call me first."

"Sure."

"This may be a babysitting assignment, but don't treat it like one. I don't expect Gomez to get anywhere near here, but if he does, he's wily. That's how he escaped. I doubt your CO will call you away, but if he does, call me. At the end of your shift, don't leave until relief has arrived. Am I clear?"

"We get it."

"We have tenants downstairs, a Mexican family. No one receives visitors, not them and not my wife. No press. Keep your eyes peeled for a chubby guy with blond hair named Carl Rice. He's a persistent devil."

"Copy that."

Mace glanced at the upstairs window, where Cheryl stood watching him. He gave her a wave and she returned

it, and then he walked to the driveway and got into his department issue Jeep Cherokee.

On the road, Mace called Karol, who answered on the
fourth ring.

"Rodrigo Gomez escaped from Sing Sing," he said.

"Shit," Karol said.

"I'm on my way there now. Why don't you meet me?"
Keeping Karol in the loop was the easiest way he knew to
keep Gabriel in the loop as well.

"Okay, what about Landry and Candice?"

"Notify Landry. Tell him there's no need to go in now,
but I want him at the squad room early. Let Candice get
a good night's sleep." Mace hung up and autodialed Jim
Mint, who answered on the first ring.

"I'm en route to the scene," Mace said.

"So am I," Jim said.

"Welcome to my world. Any updates?"

"Strand is already there. The prison's on lockdown, obviously. Officers are checking the homes near the grounds,
and choppers are in the air."

"What about the dead COs?"

"One was killed in Gomez's cell, the second in the control room between the block and the sally port, and the
third in a tower."

The last piece of information caused Mace to narrow
his eyes. "How the hell did he get into the tower?"

"You tell me."

"And no one in the block saw anything?"

"Strand moved Gomez into solitary after the interview with your wife. After three days of Gomez howling like a wolf, they moved him into an older building to keep him separate from the skells in solitary."

"Jesus."

"Given Gomez's public declaration last week, I'm concerned he might be a Class L. But we sent his hair samples to Quantico, and his DNA is human."

Mace's jaw tightened. How long would it take for the government to realize DNA was useless to determine if a human being was a Wolf?

Until they capture one alive.

TEN

When the sound of shattering glass somewhere downstairs snapped Sam O'Hearn awake, he thought Billy Jack, the family's bullmastiff, had knocked over something expensive. Then the dog barked, snarled, and barked some more.

"What the hell?" Sam said, wincing at the light coming from the emergency flashlight plugged into one wall.

Debra sat up beside him. "What's that dog doing now?"

A second set of snarls drowned out Billy Jack's, and Sam sat up too. Looking at the alarm clock, he saw 12:00 blinking in red light. He reached for the lamp switch and turned it, but darkness persisted. Downstairs, the snarling grew louder.

"What's going on?" Debra asked.

"Do I look like a fortune-teller?" Sam lifted the phone from its cradle and pressed it against his ear. He heard no dial tone. He tapped the sensor several times, listened again, and hung up. "The power's out, and the landline's dead. Where's your cell?"

Fear crept into Debra's voice. "It's charging downstairs."

Sam stood. "Great."

"Where's yours?"

"On my desk." Sam did PR for clients in New York City from his home office downstairs.

The snarls downstairs turned vicious, with half barks stringing them together. He freed the flashlight from the wall. "Get up."

"Why?" She got out of bed.

Sam grabbed her hand and dragged her to the door. "We're going into Tiffany's room. Maybe she has her cell phone."

They crept into the hallway, illuminated by moonlight shining through the skylight and Christmas lights blinking downstairs. The uproar grew louder and more ferocious, with the banging around of furniture added to the symphony. Debra dug her fingernails into Sam's arm.

Ignoring her, he closed his fingers around the knob of Tiffany's door and turned it. Under normal circumstances, he would have knocked on his sixteen-year-old daughter's door for the sake of her privacy, but he knew she was asleep this late. The door creaked open, and they stepped inside. Sam closed the door, and Debra hurried over to the bed where Tiffany slept. Sam did not lock the door. Why should he? Two animals were fighting downstairs. He guessed that a black bear had somehow broken through a window, and Billy Jack was doing his family duty.

Debra sat on the edge of the bed and shook Tiffany.

"What's happening?" Tiffany said in a groggy voice.

"Where's your cell phone?" Debra said.

"I left it in the car. I was too tired to go get it."

Debra looked at Sam. In the darkness, he could not make out her expression.

"I'm going down there," he said.

Debra stood. "You are *not*."

"I need one of our phones. Billy Jack could get seriously hurt." He loved that dog. "Lock the door after me. I'll be fine."

He opened the door and stepped into the hall. Debra closed the door behind him, and the feeble lock clicked. Sam reentered the bedroom, switched on the flashlight, and drew a metal baseball bat from beneath the bed. Then he switched the flashlight off, walked to the edge of the stairs, and looked down. The steady pulse of the Christmas lights reminded him of police strobes. The lights cast odd shapes over the downstairs floor, then withdrew them into blinking darkness.

Billy Jack continued to snarl and bark, and his opponent issued a growl so deep Sam shuddered. He descended the carpeted stairs with deliberation, grateful the sound of the fighting animals drowned out each squeak. If a bear had gotten inside, what the hell was he going to do? Maybe he should just take Debra and Tiffany out onto the roof below Tiffany's window.

No way. It's too goddamned cold outside.

Halfway down the stairs, he heard a piercing yelp that made him cringe. The yelp came to an abrupt end, followed by dead silence. Sam stood rooted to the spot, his heart hammering. He took a cautious step down and froze at the sound of the creak his weight made. He debated turning around, and in that instant a great black shape slapped the floor at the base of the stairs, eight feet from the front door. Recoiling, he recognized the carcass: it belonged to his beloved dog. Blood poured out of Billy Jack's neck, and Sam believed the fur and flesh had been torn from the dog's skull.

Swallowing, Sam dropped the flashlight and held the bat in both hands, ready to swing. The flashlight rolled end over end down the stairs, like a crippled Slinky. It struck the floor near Billy Jack's head, and its plastic face separated. The two pieces clattered, and Sam drew in a deep breath, debating whether to flee.

A shadow fell over the dog's carcass, and then a black shape blocked his view of the door. He would have mistaken the shape for another shadow had the Christmas lights not cast multiple colors on the beast that stood seven feet tall and as erect as a man, but there was no way in hell that thing was human. Its pointy ears jutted back from the top of its head, and its powerful jaws revealed long canine teeth. Tufts of fur extended from its elbows, and long fingers opened and closed above hind legs with three sections instead of two. If it was a bear, it was the skinniest goddamned bear he'd ever heard of. But he knew it was no bear.

In the blink of an eye, the creature charged up the stairs on all fours, foaming at the mouth, and Sam tightened his grip on the metal bat. He knew he had to make the first swing count, and as the creature leapt forward, snarling at him as it had at Billy Jack, he saw an evil glint in its eyes. He swung the bat with all his might, and it clanged against the monster's head. The beast fell onto the stairs, but it did not roll down them, and Sam raised the bat for an overhead swing. The monster—a werewolf for sure, he thought— lunged forward and sank its teeth into his right ankle. He let out an agonized scream and dropped the bat, which slid down the stairs.

Debra ran to the bedroom door as soon as Sam started screaming, but her hand froze on the knob when the screams stopped. Sensing a presence on the other side of the door, she backed away from it.

"Mom?" Tiffany whispered.

Debra raised her hand to silence the girl. Then she crossed the room to the window facing the backyard. The streetlight on the opposite side of the block reflected blue on the cold glass of the window. She threw the locks and lifted the window, allowing cold air to blow inside. "Get over here."

Tiffany joined her. "What are we doing?"

"Grab some shoes, and get out on the roof."

Tiffany opened her closet door and took out a pair of sneakers.

The doorknob turned.

"Put them on outside," Debra said.

"Mom . . ."

Debra pushed her daughter headfirst through the window and onto the flat roof below. The night sky was bright gray, the moon full and glowing.

Once Tiffany's knees thumped on the roof, Debra leaned forward, intending to crawl after her. Too late: the door exploded off its hinges, shattering into pieces. The snarling beast landed on all fours on the wreckage and jerked its massive head toward Debra, who slammed the window closed. The wolflike creature pulled its lips back, revealing sharp canine teeth that jutted out at uneven angles. It focused on her, and even in the dim light she identified a degree of hatred in its eyes she had never before seen in an animal. It meant to kill her, and there was nothing she could do to stop it.

Trying to distract it from the window so Tiffany could escape, Debra dove over the foot of the bed, and the monster crashed into the wall where she had just stood and unleashed an angry roar. Wedging herself between the wall and the bed, she slid to the floor. The monster snarled and tossed the lower half of the bed aside, exposing Debra within a triangle of floor space. Lying on her back, she scooted under the bed, one of the wooden slats inches from her face. The monster heaved the mattress and box spring off the bed frame, exposing her once more.

Debra screamed as it leapt upon the slats and dug its claws into her forearms. It snapped its jaws at her face, and she twisted her head from side to side and drove her knees against the slats beneath her attacker. Hot spittle flew onto her face. The monster flung the slat protecting her face away, then buried its muzzle in her head, driving its teeth through her flesh, gristle, and bone, its teeth clattering against hers, scraping her gums and coming to a stop that severed her tongue. The pain kept her from passing out, so she was conscious as she choked on her own blood.

The monster tore away another slat, then seized her breasts in its claws, an act of aggression that terrified her with its human intent. Still gagging on blood, she jerked her trunk and pounded its furry thighs as it peeled her torso like a banana. Pain exploded throughout her body, and blood splashed her face in waves. Even as her vision darkened and her consciousness faded, she willed her limbs to continue moving. Every second she fought bought Tiffany extra time.

Don't die . . . don't . . . Tiffany . . .

Her arms flopped to her sides.

Tiffany scraped her knees on the roof as she dropped from her bedroom window. Rolling onto her back, she pulled on her sneakers. Her mother appeared to be ready to follow her when the door smashed open and a large black furred animal sprang into the room. Tiffany uttered a small cry drowned out by the creature's roar.

Her mother slammed the window shut and faced the creature, and Tiffany rose on unsteady legs. Her mother leapt toward the bed, beyond her view, and the monstrous animal slammed against the wall so hard that Tiffany took a step back from the window. She saw the beast's face in the glass, though she was certain it could not see outside. It was no animal; it was a monster. The bed moved back from the wall, and then the screaming started.

Tiffany backed across the roof, turned at its edge, and stared at the L-shaped, wraparound deck below, illuminated by moonlight. Wind whipped her nightgown around her legs, and she trembled. Inside the house, her mother's screams continued. Where was her father?

Probably killed by that thing, whatever it is.

The distance to the deck was too great to jump. She kneeled on the roof, then swung her legs over the edge, scraping them on the gutter. She lowered her body until her armpits pressed against the gutter, her fingertips clawing at the roof's composite surface. Then she let go, tipping her head back so her chin didn't bang against the gutter. It took only seconds for her feet to slam down on the wooden deck, and then she backpedaled to the steps and toppled into the backyard, where water soaked through her nightgown to her buttocks. Working her way up on her elbows, she gaped at her window. The silhouette of a thick black head with pointy ears blotted out the light.

Fear seized Tiffany's throat like a vise. She rolled onto her knees, soaking them, and got to her feet, her wet nightgown clinging to her entire backside. Above her, the window opened. What the hell was that thing? She staggered forward, then broke into a run, circling the deck to the gate of the six-foot wooden fence that surrounded the property. The monster snarled above her. Ignoring it, she threw the latch on the gate, swung the gate open, and hurried through the opening. She closed the gate, pivoting as the latch dropped into place, and ran along the side of the house. The gate rattled behind her, and claws scraped the concrete walkway below it. Tiffany ran faster.

Rounding the corner of the two-car garage, she wanted to ring the front doorbell and see if her father would answer, but she knew stopping meant death, so she sprinted across the lawn at a diagonal angle. The monster howled behind her, a defiant cry that filled the night. The houses in the isolated neighborhood were spread far apart, and she knew she would never reach the nearest neighbors before the monster overtook her. There were no sidewalks, and she jumped over the drainage ditch that separated her house from the hilly road and landed on the asphalt. She ran into the middle of the road, praying a car would come. Hopefully it wouldn't be speeding at sixty miles per hour.

The beast's claws scratched the pavement behind her, and she veered to one side of the road. Her chest ached from sucking in cold air, and she tasted copper. The sound of the scrabbling claws grew louder. She told herself not to look behind her or she might trip. She pumped her arms faster, focusing on the streetlight in the distance.

Tiffany felt something hot and moist on her ankles. Pain flared in the Achilles tendon of her left ankle, and for a moment she imagined a scissor had cut it. The result was the same: she pitched forward onto the road, skinning her palms and chin on the pavement. A weight pounded on her back, driving the wind from her lungs, and she knew it was all over for her and she would not even be able to fight back. She was sure her father and mother had fought to the last possible second.

Salivating on her shoulders, the monster straddled her and rolled her over. Tiffany gazed at the vicious eyes and elongated snout of a muscular wolf that stood like a man. She knew this creature was neither man nor beast but a cocktail of the two. The monster leered at her, its cunning expression sending waves of nauseating fear through her body. It licked its sharp teeth with a long tongue, then plunged its jaws down over her neck, rending her flesh and spilling her blood. She didn't even get to scream.

ELEVEN

Mace made the drive to Ossining, New York, in just under an hour. Traffic was light, but he took it easy driving along the Hudson River at night. Ten minutes shy of Sing Sing Correctional Facility, he pulled over when the police officers at a checkpoint flagged him down. Rolling down his window, he showed his ID to the officer who approached his vehicle. "I've been called to the scene."

The officer pointed a flashlight at Mace's ID, read it, and checked Mace's face for a match. "Yes, sir. You know the way?"

"I've been here before." *Too many times.*

The officer stepped back, and Mace resumed his journey. He drove uphill, the road flanked by trees, and as he crested the hill the prison came into view, spotlights in the towers sweeping the grounds. A police helicopter circled the area, aiming a spotlight of its own at the trees. Mace followed a forked road to a security booth where he showed his ID to two serious-looking corrections officers.

"I'm expected," Mace said. "Where will I find Warden Strand?"

The CO handed a clipboard to Mace. "Park at the visitors' center. You'll see activity on the grounds. Someone there will tell you where to go."

"One of my detectives should be close behind me: Karol Williams. Let her in."

"I'm not authorized to do that on your say-so, Captain."

Mace signed the registry and handed the clipboard back. He hated traveling where he had no jurisdiction. The coiled razor-topped gates of the Cyclone fence parted, and he drove onto the prison grounds, illuminated by work lights. Corrections officers and police officers swarmed in the yard to his left. He wanted to get out there, but he followed the instructions and parked at the visitors' center.

Mace got out of his SUV. Emergency response vehicles were spread out around him. Scanning the terrain, he spotted a cluster of Ossining POs and COs and headed in their direction. When he reached them, he showed his ID. "Is Strand over there?" Mace said, gesturing across the yard to where a dozen men stood next to crime scene tape and a forensics team shot photographs.

"Yeah," one of the COs said.

Mace crossed the yard. As he neared the men, he saw Jim Mint and Warden Strand standing together. The corpse of a CO lay within firing range of the forensics team's cameras. A pair of detectives stood by as well.

"I can't believe you actually beat me here," Mace said.

Jim and Strand turned at the sound of his voice.

"I got the call," Jim said. "The situation needed to be contained."

Mace didn't like the sound of that. "What's happening?"

"Gomez killed two COs inside," Strand said. "Then . . . *something* killed this one. He was stationed in that tower."

Mace felt the muscles in his jaw tightening. "How did it happen?"

"Warden Strand was just about to show me some security footage," Jim said.

"A private screening?"

"Very."

Strand looked pale and shaken.

"First I want to see Gomez's cell."

It took Mace a moment to get his bearings when Strand led them to building two, where a PO and a CO stood watch outside. Mace looked at the weathered building opposite the walkway. It appeared to be marble and shimmered in the moonlight despite the grime on their surface.

"I always thought this block was closed," Mace said.

"It was," Strand said. "We reopened it when Gomez proved to be difficult in solitary confinement."

"Why wasn't I notified?" Mace said. "I'm the arresting officer."

"Which is why you were called about Gomez's escape. You don't need to know what goes on inside these walls."

"He told me and the FBI," Jim said. "I didn't think it was important enough to mention to you."

Mace refrained from voicing further displeasure as they entered the old building.

Strand's cell phone chirped, and he took the call.

Mace stared at bloody footprints on the floor. He kneeled beside one.

Paw prints, he thought. Giant paw prints. He looked at Jim, whose eyes glistened with fear.

"Send him in," Strand said. He pocketed his phone. "Eric Hollander is here."

"My counterpart in the FBI's New York office," Jim said.

"I suppose we should wait for him," Strand said.

"I want to see that cell now," Mace said.

Strand gave a questioning look to Jim, who nodded.

Their footsteps echoed as they approached the entrance to the control room, guarded by another CO and PO. They gave their names to the PO, who recorded them on a clipboard.

"If either one of you has a weak stomach, I recommend waiting out here," Strand said. He opened the metal door.

Inside the control room, spattered blood marred every surface within a ten-foot radius. The tattered remains of a human corpse lay strewn over the console and on the floor.

Gagging, Jim covered his mouth.

Mace stared at the gore. He had seen crime scenes like this before. It resembled the handiwork of Janus Farel, the Manhattan Werewolf. Gomez had stepped up his game.

"Criminy," Jim said in a strained voice.

Mace zeroed in on the torn remnants of a CO's uniform soaking up blood. "How many officers were stationed in here?"

"Just one," Strand said. "Alex McBryde. The other uniform belonged to Jose Alvarez, who was stationed inside the cell block. His corpse is nude. Gomez must have tricked him into opening his cell door somehow. That's against procedure."

"Is Alvarez's body in the cell?"

"Yes. He made a radio call for medical assistance, said something about Gomez's heart. Gomez must have taken him by surprise, then put on his uniform. Wearing that, he tricked McBryde into letting him into the control room. When the medical team arrived, Gomez was gone and Alvarez and McBryde were dead."

Mace's body felt numb. "How did Gomez get off the grounds?"

"We think he scaled the wall," Jim said. "That's how the third CO got killed."

"*Something* scaled the wall," Strand said. "We have video surveillance of it."

Mace felt Jim studying his reaction. "Who's seen that video?"

"A guard in another control room saw it live, then my deputy and I played it back. A guard stationed in the closest tower saw what happened as well."

Four witnesses, Mace thought. Neither Jim nor Strand addressed the elephant in the room. "Who saw this mess?"

"The medical team, the CO and the police officer outside, and the Ossining detectives," Strand said.

"How many in the medical team?"

"Two, just like any EMT would have."

Ten witnesses. "What about the forensics team?"

Strand spoke in an even, guarded voice. "They haven't gotten this far yet. I thought it best that they start out front and stay there until you arrived."

"No one comes inside without your permission. Keep those forensics boys away." Mace turned to Jim. "We need to get Hector Rodriguez and Suzie Quarrel out here."

"That might be a jurisdictional issue," Jim said.

"It shouldn't be. They're assigned to the task force. We have federal weight behind us. Get them out here so they can be the ones to examine the corpses. Otherwise, the FBI is going to seize them from the local coroner, and we won't know anything until they want us to."

"The FBI's taking these stiffs no matter what," Jim said.

"That's fine. Forensics won't tell us anything we don't already know. But if we collect these remains now, we're preventing even more witnesses from seeing the evidence. I assume we're going to try to contain this?"

"Of course."

They stepped around blood spatters on the floor, and Strand opened the door to the cell block. As they crossed the block, Mace scanned the catwalk above them and the empty cells. They stopped at one with its door open. Inside the cell, Alvarez lay dead on the floor. Jelly leaked from the ruptured eyes in his sockets. Gomez's prison blues were on the floor beside the corpse.

"There's hardly any blood here compared to the control room," Jim said.

"Gomez didn't want to get any blood on Alvarez's uniform," Mace said. "His plan wouldn't have worked if the uniform had been soiled."

Strand frowned. "You plan to cover this up?"

"We plan to contain the details," Jim said. "Let's go see that surveillance footage."

They walked back to the control room, where two men in black suits and dark blue trench coats gazed at the gore.

"Hollander, I presume?" Mace said.

Hollander, a thick man Mace's age, mustered a tight-lipped smile. "FBI Deputy Regional Director Hollander, Mace."

Mace didn't like being recognized by people he had never met, something he'd had to live with since apprehending Gomez in the first place.

Hollander gestured to his dark-skinned subordinate. "This is Special Agent Walter Grant. That's quite a show outside. Is there more?"

"We were just about to watch some surveillance footage," Jim said.

Hollander glanced at the camera above the door to the control room. "All because Gomez wouldn't stop howling."

"It was having an adverse effect on the other inmates,"

Strand said.

"Then why not remove *them*?"

"This prison holds two thousand felons. We don't put them in solitary confinement without good reason. Reintroducing them into gen pop would have been dangerous. This seemed an acceptable solution. Neither one of your offices objected."

Hollander's expression soured. "I don't think we had the full picture. Can we see the footage?"

Strand gestured to the door.

Hollander turned to Grant. "Let's get our own forensics team out here."

"We've already called ours," Jim said.

Hollander gave him a patronizing smile. "Good thinking."

Strand closed the blinds in his office, shutting out the bright lights in the prison yard, and sat at his desk. The other men stood around him.

Strand used a remote control to turn on the wide-screen TV mounted on the far wall. He touched his keyboard with trembling fingers, and the monitor blossomed with light. Using a touch pad and clicking on buttons that appeared onscreen, he brought up multiple images from security cameras. "Let's take this in sequence," he said in a quiet voice.

A single image filled the monitor and the TV: a wide-angle view of the cell block they had just visited. A corrections officer ran over to a locked door.

"That's Alvarez," Strand said.

The CO spoke into his radio, then unlocked the door. Mace watched the scene play out with grim resignation. Thirty seconds passed, then the CO emerged from the cell and ran toward the control room.

Strand froze the image. "That *isn't* Alvarez." He enlarged the image twice. "It's Gomez. He cut his hair after his interview with Cheryl."

"You think the interview was a setup for his escape?" Jim said.

"He went nuts on the air to guarantee he'd be sent to solitary confinement."

"But he had no way of knowing he could get himself relocated to that old building," Hollander said.

Mace looked at the warden. "How many COs are stationed in the regular solitary wing?"

"The same: one man in the block, another in the control room."

"So Gomez could have escaped just as easily if you'd kept him there?"

"I wouldn't say that. He could have gotten out of the control room as easily, but he would have had more men to deal with to escape the building."

"Has Alvarez been assigned to that block since you transferred Gomez there?"

"Yes, four nights. He worked one shift in another block the day before the transfer. He was supposed to be off tomorrow."

"Could Gomez have known that?" Jim said.

"I don't know how. We don't allow any talking with inmates confined to solitary."

Jim faced Mace. "Then why tonight?"

"There's a full moon, and Alvarez was on duty. He needed a Hispanic guard to switch places with."

"The Full Moon Killer," Hollander said. "He lived up to his name tonight."

Strand brought up an image from inside the control room, and they watched as Gomez entered. "This is what I wanted you to see. McBryde lets Gomez into the CR, then realizes he's made a mistake."

The Transformation occurred in seconds: Gomez's legs grew longer, adding a full foot to his height. Black fur jutted out from his exposed skin. A canine muzzle grew out of his face. His fingers became claws. He lunged at McBryde. Lupine jaws engulfed McBryde's head. The beast forced the man to the floor and dug into him with teeth and claws. McBryde flailed his arms as fountains of blood erupted from his body.

"Jesus," Hollander said.

Mace recalled when Janus Farel had transformed before him. The metamorphosis had been just as sudden.

The Wolf tore off the remains of the uniform he wore and stood erect like a man. Then it strode toward the door, out of camera range.

"There are three more," Strand said in a shaky voice.

An image of the Wolf running on all fours through the entrance of the building filled the screen.

"It's so fast," Jim said.

The image switched to an exterior shot of the Wolf skulking in the shadows along the edge of the building.

"It knows where it's going," Hollander said.

"It's . . . cunning," Jim said.

The final image filled the screen: a long shot of the Wolf scaling the wall and tower. When it reached the top, a CO faced it. A moment later, the CO plummeted to the ground, and the Wolf vanished over the top of the wall.

"We captured all its movements until it escaped," Strand said, his voice tightening.

"Are there video copies of this footage?" Hollander said.

"Just digital files."

"I want all of them turned over to me."

Strand gave him a cool look. "I don't answer to you."

"On the contrary. You'll receive notification from your superiors to cooperate fully with me within minutes." Hollander turned to Walter Grant. "Make the call."

Nodding, Grant exited the office.

"How many people have seen either this footage or that creature?" Hollander said.

"Three besides myself," Strand said.

"I hope they're still on-site."

"Yes."

"Keep them in separate waiting areas. Grant will provide them with paperwork to sign and a verbal warning to keep quiet. You'll have to do the same."

"Someone will talk," Mace said.

"Not in this economy."

"Maybe someone will make them an offer they can't refuse."

"Grant will make clear how unwise that would be."

Strand rose. "You knew about this. *All of you* knew about this. You knew how dangerous Gomez was, knew what he really is. You should have relocated him somewhere else or warned me to keep more COs on him. Instead, you allowed his incarceration to go on like he was a normal human being. Because of your inaction, three good men are dead."

Mace felt a pang of guilt. "We didn't know—any of us. When I interviewed Gomez two years ago, *he* didn't know."

"But you suspected, didn't you?"

"Yes. After that interview and certainly after my wife's TV interview with him."

Strand glared at Jim and Hollander. "And you did nothing. You just let me sit on him with blinders on."

"We had no proof," Jim said. "The genetic sample we took after his TV appearance last week shows no abnormalities."

"You should have sent him to Guantanamo."

"We needed to be careful," Hollander said. "After his outburst, we couldn't do anything that would show we gave his words credence. Besides, Gomez has rights."

Strand's face turned scarlet. "He's a goddamned werewolf!"

Hollander stepped forward. "Check yourself, mister. The only thing that matters right now is that we apprehend this lunatic before anyone else gets killed and that we keep his animalistic nature under wraps. You can help us, or we'll find someone else who can."

"The Department of Corrections might have something to say about that," Strand said.

"All it takes is one call," Hollander said. "That's how important this is."

Strand reined himself in. "You mean keeping the truth from people?"

"I mean preventing panic."

"There are others like him out there, aren't there?" Strand looked at Mace. "The Manhattan Werewolf?"

Mace waited for Jim to step in.

"Tony can't discuss this any more than the rest of us can," Jim said. "Including you."

The phone on Strand's desk rang, and he answered it. "Yes?"

Someone knocked on the door.

Lowering the phone, Strand stared at Mace. "Williams is at the gate."

"Send her in," Mace said.

"She's clear." Strand hung up. "Come in."

A state trooper strode into the office. "We just got word of three killings in Croton-on-Hudson. The first officer said it looked like a bear did the work."

"How far is Croton-on-Hudson from here?" Mace said.

Strand paled. "Ten minutes."

TWELVE

Rhonda sat up in bed when she heard Karol leave the apartment.

Run like a dog when Mace snaps his fingers, she thought.

She went into the bathroom, turned on the light, and stared at her reflection in the mirror. Her face had become famous since her abduction and infamous since her rescue. She couldn't go anywhere without being recognized. She felt cooped up—caged like a wild animal. She needed to get out. Opening the medicine cabinet, she searched its contents and located a pair of scissors. She took a deep breath, then raised the scissors to her hair.

Snip.

Clump by clump, her hair filled the sink. Then she put the scissors away and replaced them with a razor. Ten minutes later, she studied the reflection of a whole new person.

Now she needed different clothes. Returning to her room, a half office really, she rummaged through the articles of clothing that had been donated to her by members of the pack. She set aside a pair of jeans, a denim jacket, and a thermal top. She inspected the jacket, then took it in both hands and tore off one sleeve with ease.

Ten minutes later, Rhonda emerged from the building. No one paid her any mind. She crossed the street to where three Hispanic boys loitered outside a bodega. One of them spat on the sidewalk. Another made a loud kissing sound as she passed them. The third said something in Spanish, and the other two laughed. They reeked of marijuana.

Come on. Follow me, Rhonda thought. *I dare you. You won't know what hit you.*

The boys remained at their corner, and Rhonda explored the Bronx at night. She wandered the streets, taking in the tall concrete residential buildings and inhaling the scents of the city. She pretended she had no destination, but she knew exactly where she was going.

On the outskirts of Pelham Bay Park, Rhonda crossed the cracked parking lot of a garage and followed its chain-link fence into a field, the full moon providing a sheen of illumination. A dog's sudden bark from just a few feet away caused her to flinch, and when she turned a Doberman lunged at the other side of the fence. Tensing her body, Rhonda told herself she was in no danger and bared her fangs at the dumb animal. She emitted a low growl that sent the dog away, whimpering.

Penetrating the darkness, she reached a graveyard of rusted vehicles, mostly buses and construction equipment, arranged to form corridors. Her sneakers crushed broken glass, and she peeked through the spaces between the stacked vehicles, searching. Orange light flickered in the distance, and she made her way in its direction, drawn like a flying insect to a lightbulb. She spied four figures highlighted by flames rising from a metal barrel between them: two males standing and two females sitting side by side on a seat that had been disengaged from a car. All four were her age.

T-Bone was stocky and wore his hair in a dyed blond fade. A gold tooth gleamed in his mouth when he laughed. He shoved a taller boy, a dark-skinned Dominican called Lincoln because his hair resembled a stovepipe hat. Lincoln emitted a high-pitched squeal as he staggered back, and T-Bone raised his forty of Olde English to his lips. The wind blew their familiar scents toward Rhonda, who approached them without fear.

Raina leapt to her feet, and the others followed her gaze to Rhonda. Diane stood up as well. They wore trendy clothes designed to resemble street fashion, with strategically placed tears, patches, and brand names.

Rhonda felt the warm light of the fire on her features as she drew closer. A faint growling rose over the crackling of the fire, and she turned to Raina. "Drop your hackles, bitch."

Raina took a step forward and jabbed at the air with

one hand. "Who the fuck are you calling bitch, you skank?"

Rhonda smiled. "Watch who you're calling a skank . . . bitch."

Raina drew her lips back in a quivering snarl.

"Chill, Raina." The fifth member of the party stepped out of the shadows. Daniel: tall and thin, with light brown hair and fuzz on his chin. He zipped his fly, then sniffed the air. "She's one of us."

Rhonda kept smiling.

"Who you belong to, girlie?"

"None of you recognize me?" Rhonda said.

"Oh, shit, I know her," Diane said. "That's Rhonda Wilson. We had trig together."

Raina narrowed her eyes. "So?"

"You chopped your hair," T-Bone said. "You look all punk rock and shit."

"I thought you were in witness protection," Lincoln said.

Rhonda stood as close to the barrel as she could without getting burned by the flames. "No, but Gabriel's got me staying with a Wolf cop."

"I'm sorry about Jason and your parents," Diane said.

"You didn't kill them." Rhonda gestured at the twinkling lights of the city. "They did."

"I thought the Brotherhood was going to kill you for sure," Diane said.

Rhonda's nostrils flared. "I was too tough for them."

Daniel moved around the barrel and looked down at her. "What are you doing here?"

Rhonda shrugged. "I need to be with my own kind. My own age."

"She wants to join us," T-Bone said with a grin. "We're the shit."

Daniel kept staring at Rhonda's eyes, the flames crackling beside him. "Is that right? You want to join us?"

Rhonda glanced at the others. They had all been outcasts in school, but at least they had stuck together as Wolves. She and Jason had socialized with more studious classmates—humans. "And be a drug dealer?"

"It's what we do."

T-Bone held up a joint. "You'd better toke up and show us you're not a narc."

"I'll pass," Rhonda said. The last thing she wanted was something that would dull her pain. Her pain fed her anger, and that was all she had.

"We're just small-time," Daniel said. "We move what we need to in order to support ourselves. And all we deal is weed."

"I bet Gabriel doesn't know that."

"I don't care what Gabriel knows. We do our own thing."

Rhonda liked his answer. "Maybe I'll give you a shot."

"Please," Raina said.

"You have to pass an initiation test first," Lincoln said.

"Like what?" Rhonda said.

"You have to sleep with one of us."

Rhonda snorted. "You expect me to pledge myself for life to one of your sorry asses?" She looked at Raina and Diane with skepticism. "Not likely."

"You have to do something to prove yourself to us," Daniel said.

"Fine." Rhonda gestured at Raina. "I'll kick her ass."

"I hope you try it, skank," Raina said.

Rhonda raised the palm of one hand. "Pull in your claws, sister. I would never hurt a fellow Wolf. I'm loyal to the cause. I was just joking."

Raina huffed and T-Bone puffed.

"I don't have to prove myself to any of you," Rhonda said to Daniel. "I've done more than all of you combined."

"Like what?" Daniel said.

Rhonda raised her right hand. "They tortured me for days. One of them chopped off my arm with a sword, and I regenerated it. Have any of you ever done that?" She faced T-Bone and Lincoln. "One of their bitches tried to fuck with me, so I killed her. I tore off her head and threw it at a camera so they'd see it up close." She turned to Diane and Raina. "Have any of you ever killed a human? I don't think so." Both females looked away, and she turned to Daniel. "I've tasted human blood, and it went down nice and smooth."

"She's crazy," Raina said.

Daniel's gaze never wavered from Rhonda. "You're right. You have nothing to prove. If you want to join us, you're in."

T-Bone waved his joint before Rhonda's face. "Try some. It's harsh."

Rhonda shook her head. "That's not my speed."

"How about some of this?" Lincoln took a bottle of Jim Beam from his back pocket and unscrewed the cap.

"Sure, why not?"

Lincoln handed the pint to Rhonda, who raised the bottle to her lips and tipped her head back, allowing the bourbon to slosh into her mouth. Lowering her head and the bottle, she swallowed the alcohol, which burned and sweetened her throat at the same time, and heat spread through her chest. "Thanks." She returned the bottle to Lincoln.

Diane stood before her. "Welcome to the gang."

Raina took her place in the welcoming line and raised one hand. "I guess we got off to a bad start. No hard feelings."

Rhonda clasped Raina's hand. "Yeah, no problem."

"Let's get fucked up," T-Bone said.

THIRTEEN

K arol ran into Mace, Jim, and Hollander as they exited the administrative building of Sing Sing.

"We may have a second crime scene," Mace said over the dull roar of a helicopter overhead. "I'll ride with you."

"Copy that," Karol said.

The four law enforcement officers crossed the bright prison yard together.

"Jim Mint, Karol Williams," Mace said.

"Of course." Jim shook Karol's hand. "I saw you 0020at the funeral today."

But you didn't bother to introduce yourself then, Karol said. "It's good to meet you, sir." "And this is Deputy Regional Director Hollander," Mace said.

Karol smelled ambition and power all over Hollander. "It's a pleasure to meet you," she said.

Hollander shook her hand. "Nice work in Newark."

"Thank you."

They reached the parking lot.

"I'll go with you," Hollander said to Jim.

Karol climbed into the front seat of her SUV and admitted Mace into the passenger side. She took her GPS from the dashboard, and Mace gave her the address of the crime scene, which she programmed.

"Those two seem cozy," she said, pulling out.

"It's just as well. If they didn't ride together, we'd probably be paired off with them instead. That's a little too much micromanagement for my taste."

"What's happening?"

"Gomez turned into a Wolf and killed three corrections officers while escaping. Now we have more bodies at this second location."

Karol's hair prickled. "Does anyone here know he became a Wolf?"

"They have it all on high-def."

Karol tightened her grip on the steering wheel. "Oh, my God."

"Hollander confiscated the footage, and his lackey is reading the riot act to the witnesses. But the FBI has what it wants: uncontestable proof. Gomez just did more damage to your kind than Janus Farel and the Brotherhood combined."

They stopped at the gate, presented their credentials, and signed out. The gate rumbled open, and Karol drove out of the prison. Jim and Hollander followed in Jim's vehicle. The headlights of Karol's SUV illuminated trees ahead.

The helicopter crossed the field beside them, flying low to the ground.

"I need to get in touch with Gabriel," Karol said.

"No, you don't. No calls to him ever. If the FBI takes over this investigation, they may start monitoring our calls. Who knows? They might be doing so already. Gabriel will hear the news soon enough—what news they make public anyway. He'll figure out the rest. Right now we're under a microscope. For your own safety, you've got to be a cop before anything else."

Karol chose not to argue. "What do you think the conversation's like in the other car?"

"They're debating containment and what steps need to be taken if Gomez isn't caught by sunrise."

"Here come the National Guards again."

"Some of them never left."

The feminine voice of the GPS issued directions, and Karol followed the river upstate.

"This is a nightmare," she said.

"I know."

"Do you?"

"I'm worried about my wife."

"I'm worried about my entire species. I thought things would calm down after Newark."

"Let's hope we catch him fast."

Karol stared at the road ahead. "Sleepers are the worst. Because they've had no instruction, they have no sense of our society or our rules. By the time they figure things out on their own, they're usually wild animals."

"I caught Gomez before. He was crazy, not in Janus Farel's league. The Full Moon Killer was no Manhattan Werewolf, but that's because he didn't know what he had inside him. Now . . ."

"He might be worse than Farel?"

"That's my fear. Janus played games with us because he was cunning. The coupling of Gomez's insanity with Wolf abilities frightens me."

"I was a rookie when you caught Gomez, and I was still a PO when Farel did his thing." She wanted to mention that Willy had been her rabbi but held back. "How's Cheryl taking the news?"

"She's fine for now. I have a patrol car stationed outside the house. How's Rhonda doing?"

"I'm worried about her. She's angry and bitter and keeps having nightmares."

"I don't blame her."

"Neither do I, but she won't let me help her." Karol decided not to tell Mace about Rhonda's new hatred of mankind.

Flashing strobes appeared in the distance, and the GPS announced their arrival. Mace squinted at the emergency vehicles ahead: two white police cruisers and a black SUV. Ahead of the emergency vehicles, a civilian smoked a cigarette while leaning against his truck. A police officer in standard blues waved them to a stop and approached the vehicle.

Karol lowered her window and showed her shield. "I'm

Detective Williams, NYPD, and this is Captain Mace."

The officer shone his flashlight inside the SUV. "Do you have ID, sir?"

"Get that light out of my face." *Small-town cops.*

The officer lowered his flash beam.

Mace produced his shield and rotated it so it reflected light in the officer's eyes.

"All right, proceed." The officer stepped back.

Karol raised her window. "A little touchy, aren't you?"

"I'm not ready to go back on a sleepless schedule. There ought to be a law."

Karol pulled up behind the other vehicles and parked. Flares had been positioned on the ground around a corpse. Mace and Karol got out, and Jim's SUV stopped behind them so the officer could check their credentials.

Mace stared at the mangled corpse in the middle of the road. Body parts lay strewn about both lanes, connected by strokes of dark blood that glistened in the streetlight. The carnage reminded Mace of Janus Farel's murder spree.

A squat PO with a sloped forehead walked over to them. "I take it you're the experts from the city?"

"That's right," Mace said.

"I'm Sergeant Mendelo." He pointed at the corpse. "The victim appears to be a teenage girl. Tiffany O'Hearn, we think."

"Why do you think so?" Karol said.

Mendelo gestured at a house across the street and two hundred yards up the road. "The O'Hearns lived there. We've got an adult male vic downstairs and an adult female vic upstairs, both in the same condition. This one climbed out an upstairs window, dropped off the roof, and ran around the house to the road. There were three members in the family, and we've got three bodies."

Jim parked his SUV, and he and Hollander joined them.

"That guy in the truck up ahead passed her in the road and called it in," Mendelo said.

Mace walked along the street in the direction of the house. "He didn't kill her here." He followed a long, wide trail of blood to where it stopped outside the circle of illumination provided by the streetlight.

"Did you say *he*?" Mendelo said. "Because this wasn't a *he*; it was an *it*."

"He killed her here and dragged her body into the light."

"Why?" Mendelo sounded confused.

"He wanted her body to be seen." Mace looked at the house across the street. Yellow light spilled through the glass pane of the storm door. "Was that front door open like that when you found it?"

"Yeah, it was."

"He wanted her to be seen, and he wanted us to know he was inside," Karol said.

"This was a bear or something," Mendelo said. "There's no way it was that escaped convict you're looking for. This was a wild animal, not a serial killer."

"How many times have you investigated killings by wild animals inside people's homes?" Mace said.

"None," Mendelo said.

Hollander took out his smartphone. "Get that chopper

over here to Croton-on-Hudson. Bring the dogs too."

"That won't do any good," Mace said.

"Why not?" Hollander said.

"Because Gomez has already doubled back by now. He wants us to believe he's heading upstate, but he's only ever had one destination, and that's the city."

"We need to catch him before he gets there, then."

"How do you propose doing that?"

"We'll set up checkpoints."

"Where? All he has to do is make it to one of the outer boroughs, and then he can skip right into Manhattan."

"So we shouldn't try?"

Mace sighed. "No, try. But we need to plan for what happens when he slips through the net."

"How the hell is a bear going to sneak into Manhattan?" Mendelo said.

Hollander stared at Mendelo, then his name tag. "Special Agent Walter Grant will be here shortly. Neither you nor any of your men may leave until he's briefed you, and no other personnel may enter this crime scene. I'm exercising jurisdictional control." He turned to Mace. "I think your forensics team already has its hands full at Sing Sing, so I'm turning this over to my people."

Mace felt his grip on the situation loosening, and he wondered if he should care. He looked at the silver Hyundai in the driveway. "Let's go inside."

At the door, Mace, Karol, and Hollander put on shoe covers and latex gloves. Jim gave Mace a helpless look, and Karol handed him covers and gloves from her pocket.

"I don't have shoe covers, either," Mendelo said.

"You've already been inside, right?" Mace said.

"Me and my men."

"You've probably already contaminated evidence," Jim said.

Mendelo's eyes showed fear. "This isn't a homicide. It's an animal attack."

"Join your men at the perimeter," Hollander said. "Get additional support here to keep spectators and media away. Close the entire road down for half a mile in each direction. If there are any leaks, it's on you."

Mace entered the foyer and surveyed the carnage on the floor and the stairs.

"There's no way these Keystone Kops didn't fumble the ball going upstairs," Karol said.

Mace climbed the stairs, moving from side to side to avoid the blood and tissue. Upstairs, he faced a bedroom with a missing door. Moving through the doorway, he stepped around the shattered pieces of a wooden door and gazed at the bloody remains of an adult whose chest had been torn open and arms had been pulled off. Blood dripped from the ceiling, and cold air entered through an open window overlooking a flat roof.

"Jesus," Jim said.

Mace looked at the open window, then the light switch.

Karol studied the mess, her nostrils flaring. "So Croton PD thinks a bear got inside, killed the husband, came up here and killed the wife, and then what? Followed the daughter out that window, climbed off the roof, and chased her into the road?"

"The animal attack won't hold water even as a cover story," Hollander said.

Karol went back into the hall. "Bloody animal tracks go into the master bedroom."

Mace followed Karol into the bedroom with Jim and Hollander right behind him.

"Those prints sure look like they *could* belong to a bear," Hollander said.

Karol opened the closet door, and Mace peered in at the walk-in closet: the rod on the left held a man's clothes, the rod on the right a woman's.

"Gomez killed the husband downstairs, then came up here and killed the wife," Mace said. "The daughter fled out the window, and Gomez followed her. He chased her into the street, killed her, dragged her into the light, then came back in through the front door."

"Why?" Hollander said.

Mace noticed Karol biting her lip. "He turned back into human form and stole some of the husband's clothes."

"So he's walking around out there on two legs?" Hollander said. "He couldn't have gotten far."

Mace went to the two-car garage and peeked inside. "There's a silver Hyundai here, nothing else. A one-car family with a teenage daughter?"

Hollander took out his phone and pressed a button. "This is Deputy Regional Director Hollander calling from the crime scene in Croton-on-Hudson. I need to know how many vehicles are registered to family O'Hearn at this address." He repeated the address and looked at Mace, waiting. "Right, stay on the line." He lowered the phone. "The Hyundai in the driveway is registered to the wife. The husband's got a black Explorer."

"He's already far from here," Mace said.

Hollander brought his phone to his lips. "Put out an APB on that vehicle. The driver is armed and dangerous, and anyone who encounters him should use extreme caution and call for backup." He ended the call. "What does he want in Manhattan?"

Mace held his gaze. "Me. My wife. The ADA who prosecuted him. A tabloid reporter who wrote a book about him."

"All on our little island."

FOURTEEN

Gomez drove the Explorer along back roads with the headlights off. He didn't need them; he had perfect night vision. He drummed his fingers on the steering wheel and tapped his foot on the gas pedal, his senses ablaze. Warm blood tickled the back of his throat. The O'Hearn girl had tasted good. Sam O'Hearn's clothes were large on him, but he didn't mind. He did mind the man's scent all over the articles.

He drove through any wooded areas he could, speeding toward the New York–Connecticut border. When the GPS told him he was getting close, he turned south. He did not intend to travel to New York City this morning; he knew the pathways into the city would be under watch, and the police would soon realize he had taken O'Hearn's vehicle.

Especially if they called Mace already, he thought. The

cop's ability to get inside Gomez's head and anticipate his next move had led to Gomez's incarceration in the first place. Gomez would never forget that little fact.

"Valhalla in 1.8 miles," the GPS announced.

No one and nothing awaited Gomez in Valhalla, which was just a name on a map to him—a map he had spent two years studying, ever since Mace had spoken to Gomez about the Manhattan Werewolf. Mace's visit had solidified in Gomez's mind his kinship with the night stalker and had led to the deep self-examination and discovery of his true nature.

Gomez circled the outskirts of the hamlet, the GPS coaxing him toward busy streets. He went in the opposite direction, the device recalculating his approach. It took him an hour to find the house instead of thirty minutes. The colonial mansion overlooked a horse stable, a barn, and a garage. Gomez had read about its owner, Savana Silvestri, a widow who donated a great deal of money to local charities, including an orphanage. Savana lived alone, although the newspaper article Gomez had read featured a photo of the woman with her college-age granddaughter.

Gomez turned into the long driveway and allowed the SUV to crawl forward between the corral fences at a snail's pace. He reached a fork and took the left branch, traveling toward the barn. A light appeared in the sky, moving closer: a helicopter.

Searching for me, Gomez thought.

His instincts told him to step on the brake pedal, but he allowed the car to continue instead. The distant roar of the chopper masked the sound of the Explorer's engine as he passed the house. No lights came on. The helicopter veered to its left and turned around as Gomez reached the barn. He switched the dome light off, opened the door, and got out. The faint chiming of a car alarm irritated him, even though he knew Savana Silvestri could not have heard it from the house even if she wasn't eight decades old.

Standing between the car and the barn, Gomez scanned the property. Trees of all types peppered the lawn. He inhaled the cold air, feeling alive and aware of himself. Everything made sense to him now. Swinging the barn doors open, he gazed inside at a riding lawn mower and other devices used for lawn maintenance. There was more than enough room for the SUV.

He went outside, slid behind the wheel, and gave the vehicle just enough gas to push it into the barn. He lowered the windows, killed the engine, got out, and closed the barn doors. Then he lay down in the backseat. His belly was full, and he was exhausted from running from Sing Sing to the O'Hearn home. He closed his eyes and slept.

Standing in the foyer of the building on Mott Street, Ken Landry entered his code into the alarm keypad and opened the door to the lobby. Candice Smalls entered behind him, and they traded smiles.

"I didn't expect you for another hour." Landry held the inner door open for her.

"Why, because I'm a woman?" Candice entered the lobby.

"No, because I told you not to come in for another hour."

"When Tony sounds the bugle, I answer the call."

The door closed behind them, and they walked to the elevator.

"Tony told us Gomez is a Class L," Candice said.

"I remember."

The elevator opened, and they boarded the car. Landry pressed the fourth-floor button, and the door closed.

"Six people dead," Candice said. "Gomez is on a mission. The Manhattan Werewolf picked them off one at a time until the dragnet closed in. Gomez is going for the high score right off the bat."

"This is going to get a lot of attention because of the connection between Gomez and the Brotherhood of Torquemada," Landry said.

"The crank calls should start early."

The elevator stopped, and they got off. Landry opened the door to their headquarters with his key card and followed Candice inside. The overhead fluorescents came on as they triggered motion detectors, a recent modification.

"Every day I'm a little more impressed with our Batcave," Landry said as they passed the unmanned reception desk.

"I'll be impressed when the heat comes on before we get in." Candice set her bag on her desk and booted up her computer.

A ringtone came from Landry's pocket: the theme music to *The Taking of Pelham 123*. He answered his phone and looked at Candice while he listened to Jim Mint. "Yes, sir. We'll be ready." He shut off his phone. "That was Mint.

We can expect four clerks from downtown at shift start to help deal with the calls."

Leaving her coat on, Candice logged on to her computer. "Hallelujah."

Carl awoke without assistance from an alarm clock and jumped out of bed in a rare burst of excitement. He staggered over to his computer and tapped the touch pad, which always took a few minutes to warm up, then hurried into the bathroom to relieve himself.

Rubbing his hands together when he came out, he dropped into his desk chair and brought up the website for the *Post*. The home page for the daily newspaper teased him with the headline: Full Moon Killer Escapes from Prison.

A photo of Gomez beneath the headline showed him as he had appeared during his interview with Cheryl Mace. Carl's pulse quickened as he digested the news of Gomez's escape. He scrolled down the page in search of his piece on the Brotherhood of Torquemada and found nothing.

"Son of a bitch," he said.

Dressing in the same clothes he had worn the day before, he left his apartment and took the stairs to the street. It was a two-block walk to the nearest newsstand, and he shivered in the morning cold. The sun had only just begun to rise. The Indian man at the newsstand watched him pick up the print edition of the newspaper, which had the same cover as the online version.

Carl handed the man a twenty. "Give me a pack of Marlboro Lights," he said.

The man gave Carl the cigarettes and his change, which Carl pocketed. Then Carl searched the newspaper for his article. He didn't find it anywhere. It hadn't been buried; it hadn't been printed at all.

Tucking the newspaper under his arm, he lit a cigarette and smoked it on the way back to his building. Inside his apartment, he slammed the door and hurled the newspaper at the floor. Then he took out his phone and pressed autodial.

"Yeah?" John Beaudoin sounded half-asleep.

"Good morning, John. *Did I wake you?*"

"Who's this?" He sounded more awake now.

"Where the hell is my story?"

John sighed. "Did you see the front page? You got bumped."

"I saw it. What I didn't see is a reason why my piece wasn't a perfect sidebar for the Gomez story."

"Come again?"

"Gomez told the world he's a werewolf on live TV, and my piece was about the Brotherhood of Torquemada using the Blades of Salvation to execute werewolves. Could the timing be any more perfect?"

"Listen. Your story is ridiculous, but it has value. Just not today. I'm not above sensationalism, but fearmongering is another story. Some nut out there is likely to take this a little too earnestly, and the next thing you know we'll have civilians shooting each other. I'll run your damn story when things cool down a little."

"You know what you lack? Imagination! No wonder the

newspaper business is dying."

"I'm sorry things didn't work out the way you wanted, but we're running the piece and you're getting paid for it. Now, if you want to see your name in print so badly, give me something timely on Gomez. You're the expert, aren't you? Dig deep until you come up with something."

The line went dead.

"Don't hang up on me," Carl said as he wound up his arm to throw the phone at the wall. Thinking better of it, he set the phone down.

John was right: he was the expert on Gomez, other than Tony Mace. There had to be some way he could turn this to his advantage. But he couldn't stop thinking about the Blade of Salvation.

Cheryl sat on the sofa, bouncing Patty on one knee while switching between Manhattan Minute News and the other local news channels on TV. She lost count of how many times she saw Tony and Karol supervising uniformed police officers inspecting vehicles at checkpoints.

A knock at the door caused her to check the clock—8:00 AM. She didn't expect Anna for another hour. She stared at her daughter, then held one finger to her lips and made a shushing sound. Then she set Patty aside and stood up. In the dining room, she removed her purse from atop the computer hutch and approached the door. Her heart beat faster. Sliding her hand inside the purse, she curled her fingers around the rubber grip of the .38 revolver and pressed her ear against the door.

"Mrs. Mace?" Anna said.

Cheryl exhaled and took her hand out of her purse. She unlocked and opened the door and let Anna inside.

"Good morning," Anna said.

"You're early." Cheryl closed the door and twisted the locks.

"My father told me to come now. He spoke to Captain Mace last night. Captain thought you'd like some company."

"Oh." Tony had neglected to mention that to her, but she was glad he had arranged for Anna to come when she did. "Thank you. He was right."

Anna entered the living room, and Cheryl put her purse on top of the hutch, out of Patty's reach.

"Hello," Anna said to Patty, who giggled.

Cheryl joined them.

"Dada! Dada!" Patty pointed at the television.

"Was Dada on TV?" Anna said.

"Unfortunately," Cheryl said. She picked up the remote control and lowered the volume.

"I've got her if you need to shower," Anna said.

Cheryl smiled. "Do I look that bad?"

"I didn't mean it that way."

Cheryl's phone rang, and she answered it.

"How are you?" Tony said.

Cheryl crossed the room. "Tired. You?"

"Well rested. Karol and I took turns power napping in her SUV."

"What are you, partners now?"

"We are today."

Cheryl pulled back the curtain. The police cruiser still idled at the curb. "Patty was excited to see you on TV."

"You weren't?"

"It all feels too familiar."

"We've never dealt with a prison escape before."

"Are you calling to tell me you caught him?"

"I'm afraid not. The dogs haven't been able to pick up his scent, and a vehicle owned by the second set of victims is missing."

"When will you be home?"

"Dinnertime?"

"I'll believe that when I see it."

"I asked Eduardo to have Anna come early."

"She's here now."

"Good. And the unit?"

"Waiting and ready."

"I'll see you as soon as I can. Try not to worry."

"I'll do my best."

"I love you."

Cheryl closed her eyes. "I love you too." She hung up and faced Anna. "I think I'll take that shower."

FIFTEEN

When Gomez awoke, every muscle in his body burned with pain. He lifted his head from the backseat of the Explorer and felt as if someone was sawing through his neck with a serrated knife. Wincing, he lay back. The simple act of shifting his body sent a tidal wave of agony roaring through his lower back and stomach muscles, and he stifled a cry.

With his eyes widening like twin moons, he stared at the ceiling until his breathing returned to normal. He had experienced pain on those mornings following his partial Transformations in Sing Sing but nothing like this. The act of using his Wolf Form was much more traumatic to his infrastructure than assuming its shape.

With great deliberation, Gomez set his feet on the floor, grabbed the back of the driver's seat, and pulled himself into a sitting position. Sweat formed on his brow despite the cold. His lower lip quivered, and it felt like he'd been shot in the gut. With tears in his eyes, he reached around the seat and retrieved the gallon of purified water he had taken from the O'Hearns' refrigerator. Unscrewing the cap with trembling fingers, he raised the plastic container to his mouth. He guzzled the water until his throat was too cold for him to continue, then looked at the half-empty container, capped it, and returned it to the front seat.

He slumped sideways and went to sleep.

The front door buzzed, and Candice looked up. The monitor on her desk showed a heavy man and a short woman with a blonde pixie cut standing outside the door to the task force squad room. She glanced over her shoulder at Landry, who held a landline pressed between his ear and shoulder, then stood and passed through the short corridor leading to the reception area, where she opened the door.

"*Hola*, Candice," Hector Rodriguez said. He stood in the hall with Suzie Quarrel, his Crime Scene Unit partner. He held a cardboard box.

"There are no bodies here," Candice said.

"We didn't come for any bodies. We've been collecting stiffs all night."

"Then what did you come here for?"

"The Chinese food."

Candice snorted. "You can have it. I got sick of it after

a week."

"We're reassigned here temporarily," Suzie said.

"By who?"

"Jimmy Mint," Hector said.

Candice raised her eyebrows. "Really? I knew we were getting some clerks, but aren't you overqualified?"

"We're not clerks," Suzie said.

"In case you've forgotten, we're genuine detectives," Hector said. "We were told to report here and detect. At least when we're not bagging werewolf burgers."

"I hope you're not bringing your work with you," Candice said. "But if you are, this place is cold enough to refrigerate the corpses."

Suzie chuckled, and Candice led them into the squad room. "You can pretty much have your choice of desks." She pointed at two desks that faced each other in the center of the space. "Williams sits there, and Willy sat across from her."

Hector moved to one of the cubicles. "Not that I'm superstitious, but I think we'll set up over here."

"Agent Shelly sat there."

Hector looked at the vacant seat. "Damn, this whole place is cursed. No wonder you're recruiting from other departments."

Landry hung up his phone. "We're recruiting you because you've already sworn to secrecy. Like the rest of us, if you want your pension, you'll go where the big boys send you."

Hector shrugged. "That's cool. I don't mind playing *Dirty Harry* instead of *CSI*."

"More like *Buffy the Vampire Slayer*," Suzie said under her breath.

"So we're going to help capture the Full Moon Killer, and then we're back to our meat wagon, right?"

Smiling, Landry took his turn at shrugging. "We have an ongoing assignment beyond Gomez. As far as I can tell, you're here for the duration."

Hector chose a seat. "Like I said, cool."

"Welcome aboard."

Hector set his box on top of his desk, and Suzie moved to the desk beside him.

"Look at the bright side," Candice said. "You already know what fucked-up shit you've stepped in. At least we don't have to haze you with wolfsbane or anything."

Mace and Karol sat side by side at the conference table in the NYPD mobile command center. Grant and Jim sat on the opposite side, and Hollander sat at the head of the table. In the rear of the trailer, two POs wearing headsets worked at stations equipped with wide-screen monitors and glowing maps. A sergeant stood at the front of the unit with his arms crossed, staring at another monitor, and the driver remained in the front seat of the wide cab.

"It's been ten hours," Hollander said.

"City hall is all over the commissioner's ass because of the traffic delays," Jim said. "You can guess whose ass the commissioner is all over."

"That's where federal jurisdiction comes in handy," Hollander said.

"Craig Lindberg is giving the press corps the official version of Gomez's escape in an hour. I should be there."

"That should be short and vague," Mace said.

"Do you have a better suggestion?" Jim said.

"Nope."

The door opened near the front of the mobile command center, and Kathy Norton ascended the steps. Mace felt a surprising sense of relief.

Norton showed her ID to the sergeant, then carried her laptop over to the conference table. "I came straight from the airport. I wasn't expecting to go through checkpoints."

"We're keeping them in effect for another fourteen hours," Hollander said.

Norton looked at each seated person. "I gather you've had no luck?"

"All six bodies are on their way to Quantico," Grant said.

"Special Agent Norton, Special Agent Grant," Hollander said. "You two will be spending a lot of time together from now on."

Norton shook Grant's hand. "Pleased to meet you."

"Same here."

Hollander rose. "Deputy Chief Mint and I have meetings to attend. You all know your assignment. Let's catch this animal before any more lives are lost, then get busy identifying the rest of them."

Mace made sure he didn't look at Karol as the group filed out of the mobile command center. Cold wind assailed them as they moved to their respective SUVs, facing Manhattan.

"Do you have a ride?" Mace said to Norton.

"I'm all set. I'll see you at the squad room."

Mace got out of his SUV in the Fifth Precinct parking lot and waited for Karol, Norton, and Grant. Karol had driven him back to Sing Sing from the O'Hearn crime scene. Now she joined him first.

"Why don't you take an early lunch after we see what's what?" Mace said. "We've already had a full night."

Karol held his gaze. "I won't argue. What about you?"

"I'll grab something at the office. You take care of what you have to, though."

"Thanks."

The FBI agents had the same stiff walk and wore shades.

"We're just a couple of blocks away," Mace said to Grant.

"I know."

They didn't speak as they walked through Chinatown. At the building on Mott Street, Mace entered his code into the keypad and held the door for the agents. They rode the elevator to the fourth floor, and after Mace used his key card to open the door, they stood at a desk in the reception area.

An Indian woman in a khaki clerical uniform sat at the desk, speaking into a headset. No one had sat there since the task force had been formed. Multiple phone lines lit up. "Please hold for the next available detective," she said into the phone, then pressed the Hold button.

"I'm Captain Mace. You are?"

"Nadira Endri." The woman offered her hand. "I'll be your weekday daytime clerical officer."

That means three or four people will be filling the spot in total, Mace thought.

Nadira gestured at her monitor. "Right now I'm trying to cross-reference the reports on what happened in Newark while answering these calls."

Mace introduced Karol, Norton, and Grant.

"Pleased to meet you." Nadira pressed another button and spoke into her headset. "NYPD special task force, how may I direct your call?"

Mace led the way into the squad room. A telephone rang unanswered while Hector, Suzie, Candice, Landry, and three additional clerks handled other calls.

"Captain Tony," Hector said. He had a phone pressed against his ear and a grid of the city on his monitor.

Mace squeezed Hector's hand and nodded at Suzie. "Thanks for the help."

"We didn't have a choice," Suzie said. "But it's a welcome change of pace, except that I'm a little tired."

"Welcome back, Kathy," Candice said to Norton.

"Thank you," Norton said.

Landry hung up his phone. "Crackpots! I don't know what it is about the full moon."

Mace raised his voice. "I'd like you all to meet Special Agent Walter Grant. He's been assigned to work with us."

Landry stood and shook Grant's hand. "Walter."

"Walt is fine."

Norton gestured to Shelly's old desk. "Here's your parking spot."

"Thanks." Grant set his laptop case on top of his desk.

"All calls related to Gomez are being forwarded to the front desk," Landry said. "We're getting tips left and right, none of them useful."

"Gomez isn't in the city yet," Mace said. "He'll wait until we let our guard down."

"We haven't been able to get ahold of Carl Rice, but I left a message for him."

"He's probably out looking for Gomez too. Or his next book deal."

Carl sat in his rented car across the street from the Mott Street headquarters of Mace's task force, with the engine running for heat. He had videotaped Mace, Williams, and the two suits entering the building twenty minutes earlier, and now he sat up as Williams exited the building and headed in the direction of the Fifth Precinct.

"Going somewhere, Detective?"

Setting his camcorder down, he merged into traffic and drove around the block, praying he wouldn't lose Williams. Back on Mott, he saw her in a mass of people congesting the sidewalk. He followed her to Elizabeth Street, where she entered the parking lot of the Fifth Precinct station house. He double-parked at the corner and picked up the camera, using its zoom to locate Williams getting into an SUV that resembled the others parked among the police cruisers.

When she pulled into the street, he set the camera down and wrote her license plate number in his notepad, then followed her to First Avenue, which she took to the FDR Expressway.

"The Bronx is a long way from Kansas, Toto," he said fifteen minutes later. He almost lost track of her in the heavy traffic, then caught sight of her exiting at Jerome Avenue. He followed her at a discreet distance, taking greater care to be inconspicuous than he had earlier. Several turns later, she pulled over to the curb near a Korean delicatessen. He didn't bother to pick up the camera.

"Damn it," he said.

Karol didn't put quarters in the meter because she didn't have to, a perk of her position. Who could afford parking fees on a cop's salary? Inside the deli, she passed a short line. After selecting a premade sandwich, she joined the line. The Korean woman at the register made eye contact with her.

"I need to speak to your husband," Karol said.

The woman nodded. "Five dollars."

Karol paid her.

"Wait at the end of the counter."

Karol moved to the end of the counter and dug into her sandwich while she waited.

A Korean man dressed in stained white work clothes

came out of the back room. He rounded the counter so she wouldn't have to raise her voice.

"You have something for me," she said. "And I have something for you."

Carl watched Williams exit the deli with half a sandwich in one hand. She got into her SUV, started the engine, and merged into traffic.

"What the hell are you up to?" Carl followed her around the block. She headed toward Manhattan, and Carl frowned. A growing sensation in his gut told him something wasn't right.

Soon they reentered Manhattan, and Williams led him back to the Fifth Precinct parking lot. Double-parking again, he watched her exit the lot and walk toward Mott Street.

Something is very wrong with this picture, Carl thought. *Who drives all the way to the Bronx for a sandwich?*

After recording the time in his notepad, he did a U-turn and headed back to the Bronx.

"Deputy Chief Mint is in a meeting, Captain Mace," Mint's receptionist said. "Would you like his voice mail?"

Norton entered the office.

"No, just tell him I called." He hung up. "Settled back in?"

"Sure." She threw one thumb over her shoulder. "Let's

step out for a minute."

Mace's gaze darted to the back of Grant's head. "Okay." Exiting his office, Mace leaned close to Landry, who scribbled notes in a pad while speaking on the phone. "I'm stepping out for a minute."

Landry nodded, and Mace followed Norton through the squad room and reception area and to the elevator, which they boarded. Norton pressed the button for the third floor, and the elevator descended and shook. Mace opened his mouth to speak, but she shook her head so he closed it. They exited the elevator into a hot, noisy sewing shop where scores of Chinese women sat side by side at stations. A few women glanced at them, but no one approached them.

"No one can hear us here," Norton said.

"I don't think anyone speaks English."

"Things are crazy in D.C. This has mushroomed into something huge. FBI, CIA, and Homeland Security are all in on the action—even the Pentagon."

"That doesn't surprise me," Mace said. "If they accept the existence of Class Ls, they're not going to sit around waiting for them to be discovered. They're going to strike first."

"Believe me when I tell you that offices are being set up around the city—around the country—to monitor this situation. Our task force might be on the front line, but a network of these agencies knows every move we're making, and we don't even know who or where they are."

"Hollander and Mint . . ."

"We may have brought down the Brotherhood of

Torquemada, but there are other brotherhoods above us."

"Grant?"

Norton shrugged. "He may be a straight shooter, but they wouldn't have brought him in if they didn't want him to report on what we're doing."

"Why are your own people spying on you?"

"Why are yours spying on you?"

Mace pictured Nadira and the other clerks who had been assigned to the task force.

"You have to assume every inch of the squad room will be bugged if it hasn't been already."

"Why the lack of trust?"

She gave him a frustrated look. "You tell me."

"They're not buying our story about what went down in Newark."

"They may have found fur on the warehouse floor."

"According to our story, someone came along and took the swords after we left. The fur could have gotten on the floor then."

"Maybe it's too pat. Maybe they don't believe we'd have left the swords. Regardless, they don't trust us."

Mace worried about Gabriel. "You're not changing your story, are you?"

"No, how can I? But none of us can, or we're all finished. I'm talking treason, not just unemployment. I'm not worried about you, and by extension your wife, but what about Rhonda and the others?"

"I don't know. Karol says Rhonda's overwrought."

"You've got to tell Williams to talk to her. Every move

we make, every syllable we utter, we have to use caution. And we have to be in agreement about something else: we know nothing about Karol's identity, and whatever she shares with Gabriel is on her, but you and I are to have zero contact with him. Gabriel and his people have their agenda, and we have ours. I'm sympathetic to their plight but not enough to go to Leavenworth over."

Picturing Cheryl and Patty at home, Mace sighed. "Agreed."

"We have to do our jobs. Gomez has to be caught or killed before his nature becomes public—preferably killed. I'm sure they would love to get their hands on him alive. If Joe Public finds out what Gomez is, this country is going to change for the worse. The world will change. Werewolves will be the new terrorists."

"Let's pray that's not what we turn them into."

SIXTEEN

Savana Silvestri crossed the wide entry of her home to the inside door, which she opened. In the foyer, she opened the paneled outer door.

A Mount Pleasant police officer in navy blues stood on her wooden porch. The black cruiser behind him had a yellow lightning bolt painted on its side. Mount Pleasant policed Valhalla, which had a population of less than thirty-five hundred people. The officer smiled. "Mrs. Silvestri?"

"Yes?"

"I'm sorry to disturb you, but I guess you heard they had a prison break over at Sing Sing. Rodrigo Gomez escaped."

"Yes, I saw it on the news." Savana left the TV on all day, even though she watched very little of it. She preferred keeping her house in order to getting fat.

"We're making all the locals aware of the situation,

especially you folks out in the boonies. If you see anyone or anything out of the ordinary, be sure to give us a call."

"I will. Thank you."

"Have a nice day." The officer turned and strode down the steps to his cruiser.

Savana closed the door and went inside. Cold air lingered around the doorway. Parting a curtain, she watched the cruiser drive off.

In almost thirty-five years of living in the colonial house, she could not recall the police visiting her before. She had been a widow for six years and had given away most of the savings of her husband, who had owned a bottling company in the hamlet. She had kept only enough to live comfortably and maintain the house. At eighty, she felt lonely. Her son and daughters had moved away long ago, and only her youngest granddaughter, Callie, who attended college at SUNY Purchase, visited her.

She passed the living room, then the entrance to the darkened dining room, and stopped at the threshold to her spacious country kitchen. Slowly, she turned back the way she had come, then crept toward the dining room. Something had felt wrong in there. She moved into the darkness, and her body stiffened.

A naked man sat at the table, his dark eyes reflecting light at her. With her heart pounding, she groped along the wall and flipped the light switch. The man, who had short dark hair and Hispanic features, smiled. Savana recognized him from the news: Rodrigo Gomez, the escaped convict. She saw in his eyes that he knew she recognized him.

Turning to flee, she heard thumps on top of the table. Gomez smashed into her back, and she cried out as she fell to the floor, his weight crushing her. What if he had broken one of her ribs? She stretched her arms before her, hoping to claw at the carpet and crawl away, even though she knew she could never escape. Then the weight upon her back vanished, and Gomez rolled her over. Ignoring his manhood, which swung above her face, she gazed at the crouching killer's features.

"Don't worry, grandma. I'm not going to eat you." Gomez pulled her upright so that her gaze met his. "Your meat is probably too tough and grizzled anyway." His breath reeked.

Gomez shoved Savana into one of the dining room chairs. "But that doesn't mean I'm not going to kill you. I probably will. But I'll keep you around long enough so you have a chance to change my mind."

Savana swallowed. "What do you want?"

"What does any man want?" He looked around the room. "Shelter. Food." He stroked her wrinkled cheek. "A good woman by his side."

She turned her face away, and he chuckled.

"Who's this handsome devil?" Gomez picked up a framed photo on a shelf.

"My husband, Henry," Savana croaked. "He went to the store. He'll be back any minute." Maybe Henry could still save her . . .

Gomez set the photo down. "You're lying. Your husband's been dead for six years. I didn't stumble in here by accident. It's just you and me on this cold winter's day."

"Would you mind putting some clothes on?"

He turned his body toward her. "I'm not going to rape you. I'm no rapist." He smiled. "I'm not even a man."

Savana remembered Gomez's live TV interview one week earlier. She hadn't watched it—she didn't bother with trash television—but she read about it the next day. Gomez believed he was a werewolf.

"I'm so much more than a man," he said. "Now, you're going to take me on a tour of this house, room by room, and you're going to show me everything in it, drawer by drawer, so I can make myself comfortable. Understand? Nod if you get it."

Savana nodded.

"Everything good?" Mace said into his cell phone while he skimmed new reports of Gomez's escape and the murders of the O'Hearns on his computer.

"Affirmative," Cheryl said. "But I can't stop watching the news."

"That will make you paranoid."

"I can't believe I was part of this machine."

"I understand how you feel."

"Any word?"

Jim and Hollander entered the squad room.

Mace straightened up. "No. I've got to go. I'll talk to you later." Standing, he pocketed his phone and went into the squad room.

"Get your task force into the conference room," Jim said. "We need to brief everyone."

Mace glanced at Norton, who registered his curiosity but avoided reacting.

"I need all detectives and special agents in the conference room," Mace said in a raised voice.

Karol rose first, followed by the other detectives and the FBI agents. Inside the conference room, everyone sat around the table except for Hollander, who connected his laptop to the PowerPoint projector.

"The hunt for Gomez has obviously sidelined your primary objective." Hollander looked at the faces around the room. "We'll get Gomez one way or the other. Continue taking the calls and looking into leads, but don't allow Gomez to consume all your time. He's one man—or one Class L. Your priority is still to identify any and all Class Ls in New York City. That's why we"—he gestured at Jim— "have brought in extra people to assist you."

Mace bit his tongue. Replacing fallen comrades wasn't bringing in extra help. It was maintaining the status quo. The only additional people they had were the clerks.

"Preliminary testing shows Gabriel Domini's DNA is human. That's unfortunate. You still have to bring in his brother, though. It's entirely possible that Raphael Domini is a Class L." He addressed Mace. "I want the file on their sister, Angela, reopened. I don't like that she disappeared when she was so connected to the Manhattan Werewolf murders."

Mace avoided looking at Karol.

"The bureau now has a confidential informant with detailed information about both the Brotherhood of Torquemada and the Class Ls."

Father Tudoro, Mace thought. He had watched Norton and a team of feds take Tudoro into custody at JFK.

"This informant has connected several dots we uncovered going over the Brotherhood's laptop, which you recovered in New Jersey."

Mace had lobbied Jim for access to the data contained in the laptop to no avail.

Hollander tapped at his keyboard, and the face of an olive-skinned man with curly black hair filled the screen. "According to our source, this man is a Class L. His birth name is Frank Ninotos. For the last several years, he used the alias Elias Michalakis. He was the leader of a cell of Class Ls based in Greece. In Piraeus, the same members of the Brotherhood you extinguished in Newark kidnapped one of the Class Ls in Ninotos's cell, secured explosives to his corpse, and dumped the body outside the Class Ls' hiding place. The explosion killed every member of the cell but Ninotos, who disappeared."

Hollander pecked at his laptop again. A surveillance photo showed Ninotos in an airport. "Three weeks ago, Ninotos flew into Philadelphia under the name Panos Mircouri. We've been unable to trace his movements from that point on. If he's still using that name, it hasn't turned up in any credit card purchases or hotel registries. The timing of his arrival coincides with that of the Brotherhood, and we believe he came here because they did, perhaps to warn other Class Ls.

"For the purpose of our mission, Elias Michalakis is his primary alias. Special Agent Norton will provide you with a list of his other aliases. If he's in New York, we want you to find him. He's as important as Gomez. One other thing: our informant insists that all three Dominis are Class Ls. If he's right, I don't know how Gabriel Domini fooled our test unless the hair sample was tampered with."

"I clipped that sample in front of Captain Mace," Candice said in a frosty tone.

"And I sealed the envelope according to protocol," Mace said.

"Bring Gabriel Domini in and administer the test again," Hollander said. "Get urine and blood samples too."

"He may find that request excessive."

"I don't care what objections he has. He's our best lead. When you get him in here, make sure he tells you the location of his brother and sister. And since he claims he isn't hiding, keep him under surveillance. According to our informant, the Brotherhood took Rhonda Wilson prisoner because she was a Wolf. Jason Lourdes was the collateral damage, not her."

Below the table, Mace clenched his fists. "Wilson gave us hair samples, and the corpses of her parents were human."

Hollander stared at him for a moment before answering. "That's true. All the DNA tests we've conducted at Quantico verify that Wilson is human and her parents were too. That doesn't change our informant's sworn statement."

Mace didn't want to put himself on the line for Rhonda if he could avoid it.

"I'd say that calls the veracity of our informant into question," Norton said.

"I agree," Hollander said. "For now. But we have to keep tabs on Wilson. Why don't we have a current address for her?"

"We do have an address for her," Karol said. "A sublet on Staten Island."

Masking his surprise, Mace couldn't help but look at Karol.

"I entered it into the database this morning," she said.

"Good," Hollander said. "Don't lose track of her. I don't like that our two most likely Class Ls tested human."

Savana crept up the squeaking wooden stairs, her gnarled hand sliding up the banister. Still naked, Gomez followed her. His feet made little noise, even though he weighed more than she did, but his breath came in short, wet rasps, like that of a dog. She had already showed him where she kept the car keys, which seemed to be his primary interest. She knew he wouldn't leave her in peace, that he intended to kill and probably rape her.

For the first time since Henry's death, she felt good that he was no longer alive: he would have done something foolish and tangled with this killer, and something bad would have happened. At least he had gone peacefully in his sleep.

This man is going to kill me.

The thought played over and over in her mind.

At the top of the stairs, she opened a bedroom door. "This was my husband's extra room. I guess you could call it his study."

Gomez shoved her with the base of one palm, and she staggered inside. She caught herself against a bookcase filled with leather-bound editions of literary classics. Henry had received one a month for ten years through a subscription service.

Gomez entered the sunlit room and studied the framed certificates on the far wall. "Your husband was a man of accomplishments."

Savana did not answer him.

Gomez walked to where she stood and scanned the book titles. "He appreciated the classics."

Savana backed away from him into the middle of the room.

Gomez selected a book and flipped through its pages. "*The Call of the Wild* by Jack London."

She knew this might be her only chance; she just wished she still possessed the speed and grace of her younger years. Pivoting on a heel, she jerked open the top drawer of the desk, pushed aside the Bible, and raised Henry's loaded .32 revolver in both hands. Henry had kept the weapon there for as long as they had been married, and she had continued the tradition. It felt so heavy.

Gomez smiled. Then he snapped the book shut, which caused her to flinch, and returned it to its space on the shelf. He raised his hands. "Don't shoot."

Savana aimed the revolver at Gomez's chest. "What kind of man are you, preying on an old woman?"

His smile broadened. "That's the question, isn't it? I've changed my mind. I think I *will* eat you." He took a step forward.

Savana squeezed the trigger. The gun's roar was deafening in the small room, even with her poor hearing. The recoil almost toppled her, and her wrists ached. The round tore into Gomez's left pectoral. His body jerked to the left, a snarl forming on his lips. Savana fired again. This time, the round burrowed into the ribs on his right side. She fired a third shot, and a cloud of plaster dust puffed from the wall behind her quarry. Gomez turned to her. Taking careful aim, she fired into his stomach, and he fell to his knees.

"That . . . hurt," Gomez said, gasping. When he looked up at her, his face trembled with rage.

Two shots left, Savana thought. She aimed at the man's head.

"Don't do it," Gomez said.

"No jury in the world would convict me."

"Please, mommy. Let's make nice."

"*Monster.*" She shot him again. This time the round disappeared inside his left collarbone. She expected him to scream. Instead, he roared.

Gomez leapt off the floor, diving for her with surprising agility. In the second it took for him to reach her, black fur spread over every inch of his body. A clawed hand swiped the gun away, and as he collided with her, his face assumed a lupine form. Screaming, Savana toppled onto the desk top.

The creature that Gomez had become seized her wrists

in his claws. He spread her arms wide apart and pulled her toward him, roaring in her face. His fur grew longer, his features more wolflike, and Savana smelled death on his breath.

Carl watched the delicatessen from the front seat of the rental car, his camcorder at the ready. Customers entered; customers left. He listened to a news report on Gomez's escape on the radio. However that turned out, at least he knew there was another true crime book in the incident. He had made some scratch off Gomez's name. But why did the son of a bitch have to pull his disappearing act last night and derail his front-page news story?

A truck driver carted stacks of two liter soda bottles inside and exited. Nothing of interest transpired, and he doubted his instincts. His lower back ached.

"Screw this."

He turned off the engine, slid the camcorder into his coat pocket, and got out. Stretching his arms in the air, he looked from side to side and crossed the street. Three customers stood in line at the counter when he entered. He absorbed the interior in seconds: an older Korean woman worked the cash register, and a man—presumably her husband—made sandwiches at the meat counter. A round convex mirror looked down at him from one corner, a video camera from another. He made his way up and down the aisle, pretending to look for something.

He didn't get it. What had motivated Williams to drive

all the way here from Chinatown, buy a sandwich, and drive back? And why had it taken her so long to get the sandwich? There was something about this place. There had to be. He knew it.

Carl passed the refreshments refrigerators. He didn't know how long he would be sitting in that car, and he didn't want his bladder to force him to abandon his post. After circling the entire store, he went to the meat counter.

The Korean man looked at him. "Yes?"

"I'll have a pastrami and Swiss on rye," Carl said.

The man made the sandwich. Nothing about him stood out. He set the bagged sandwich on the counter, and Carl took it to the register.

The Korean woman rang it up. "Six dollars," she said.

Carl handed her a ten-dollar bill, and she gave him change.

"Thank you," she said in a singsong voice.

Carl went outside. *Fuck*, he thought as he returned to his car. He got in and turned the ignition.

"What the hell should I do now?" He stared at the deli, debating whether to return to Mott Street.

Instead, he ate his sandwich and kept watching.

With his furry body covered with sticky blood, Gomez staggered into the bedroom next to Henry Silvestri's den and collapsed on the queen-sized bed. Slobbering saliva, he lay on his back with his knees raised. He hadn't experienced pain from the old woman's gunshots at first, but now each wound burned and throbbed.

Staring at the ceiling with his chest rising and falling, he willed his body to Change. The Transformation into his human form took longer than the Transformation into a Wolf had, and it felt like bottling himself up rather than a release. As he took his weaker shape, the pain decreased. He groaned.

How had he been so careless? He had smelled fear all over Savana. When she pointed the gun at him, his instincts told him he had nothing to fear. When the first bullet tore into his flesh and he felt no pain, he believed himself invulnerable. He knew now that his body must have gone into shock. The pain came minutes later while he feasted on the woman's entrails. Now, with sweat covering his quivering flesh, he glanced at the wounds in his torso.

They had closed.

Gomez pressed his fingers to the wounds, and the pain returned. The wounds did not reopen, and the pain felt good. Blood slicked the bedcovers. Savana's or his?

Taking a deep breath, he Changed again. He had never attempted Transformation into Wolf Form so soon after turning human, and he found the shift easier than expected. He didn't want to be human again but needed to complete the test. Another breath, another change. The regression of his fur tickled his insides. His muscles ached, and the sweat spackling his body cooled, the bloodied sheets clinging to him like a wet diaper. He examined his body. The bullet wounds had become scars.

Gomez laughed, but he felt bitterness for the years he

had wasted confined to his human form. None of his kind had sought him out, and none had shown him the way to his true self. He would teach himself everything he needed to learn, and then he would make the world pay in blood for neglecting him.

SEVENTEEN

After parking his SUV in his driveway, Mace walked over to the motor patrol car at the curb, no longer double-parked. The female officer behind the wheel lowered her window.

"How long have you been here?" Mace said.

"Since shift change at 0400," the officer said. "We're staying on until midnight unless Dispatch wants us to pull overtime."

He looked at her partner, who appeared to be tall and skinny. "If either of you needs to use the restroom, you know which floor we're on. Just call before you come up."

"Thanks," the woman said.

Mace went inside. As soon as he closed the inside door, the first-floor apartment door opened. He expected to see Eduardo. Instead, it was Eduardo's wife, Anita.

"Captain Mace." Anita approached him. She had a tiny figure, and only the streaks of gray in her hair suggested her age. "We've been watching the news all day. This man Gomez, do you think he'll come here? Is that why the police car's outside?"

"It's just here as a precaution," Mace said. "Everyone in the house is safe."

"Will you catch him soon?"

"I hope so."

"Don't worry about Mrs. Mace. I'm home all day, and Anna will be upstairs whenever you like."

"I appreciate that, but I don't want any of you to worry."

"Don't *you* worry. Just stop this man."

"I'll send Anna down." Mace climbed the stairs, hung his coat on a hook, and stepped out of his shoes. When he entered the apartment, multicolored lights blinked on and off in the living room. Sniper greeted him, wagging his tail. Turning the corner, he took in the sight of a Christmas tree decorated with ornaments. Additional lights blinked in the window frames. Cheryl and Anna tossed tinsel onto the plastic tree.

"Dada!" Patty ran toward him, fell, and got up.

Mace swept her into his arms. "There's my girl."

The toddler pointed at the tree. "Tree!"

"I see that. A Christmas tree."

"'Rismas tree."

Cheryl moved before him, and they kissed.

"We needed to do something cheerful, so Anna helped us decorate the tree," Cheryl said.

"Great," Mace said. "Anna, you can go now. I think your mother could use the company. I smelled chicken and hot peppers down there."

"Okay," Anna said. "I have some studying to do. I'll see you all tomorrow."

"Good night," Cheryl said.

Anna kissed Patty's cheek and squeezed her hand. "Good night."

"G'night."

Cheryl waited until Anna had closed the door behind her before asking, "Is there any news that they're not reporting on TV?"

Mace didn't want to tell her the truth, but he knew that if he held back information she would sense it and drag it out of him. "Sing Sing's security camera captured Gomez changing into a Wolf."

"Wolf," Patty said.

Cheryl's posture wilted. "Oh, my God."

"FBI seized the footage and clamped down on the prison employees who saw it."

"That isn't right."

"You're not a reporter anymore, remember? And if you breathe a word of this you'd better get an extremely high-paying job, because I'll be out of mine. Worse, I'll be in jail. CIA, State, and Homeland Security all have an interest in this now."

"Can't you just quit?"

He handed Patty to her. "And lose my pension? I've put up with too much s-h-i-t to lose that now." But the thought of finding something new to do had its appeal.

"You've risked your life—too many times. When does it end? They'll eat you alive without thinking about it twice."

"Don't you feel safer at the moment, knowing I can provide protection?"

Her voice remained firm. "I'd feel safer if you were home all day."

"What am I supposed to do, be a telemarketer?" He stroked her back. "I need to shower."

"Walk the dog first. Come on, Patty. Let's put the star on the tree."

"I told the officers downstairs they can use our bathroom if they need to."

"Wonderful."

Sighing, Mace retrieved the dog leash. "Come on, boy."

Karol heard the soft throb of music when she entered her apartment. After setting her unopened bills aside with the others, she hung her coat in the closet and took off her shoes. In the kitchen, a pizza box rested on top of the stove. She moved the box onto the counter, then made her way to Rhonda's room and knocked on the door.

A moment later, the volume of the music decreased, and the door opened. Rhonda stood before her, her hair shaved close to the scalp on the sides and long on top. She had also dyed it blonde, and she wore a sweatshirt with the sleeves torn off.

"Wow," Karol said.

"I did it myself," Rhonda said.

"I hardly recognize you."

"I need to get out for some fresh air once in a while." Her voice sounded softer than it had all week.

"Did you go out today?"

Rhonda shrugged. "I walked around a little."

"I see you've eaten already."

"There's still some pizza left. Help yourself."

"Thanks, but I'm going to bed. I didn't sleep last night, and I worked a double shift plus overtime. Do you need anything?"

Rhonda shook her head. "Thanks for asking."

Karol took a business card from her pocket. She had taped two keys onto its blank side. "Here."

Rhonda took the card. "What's this?"

"The address of your decoy apartment. It's an attic in an apartment house on Staten Island. Memorize the address. If for any reason anyone asks, that's where you live, but don't go there under any circumstances."

Rhonda turned the card over and looked at the keys. "Am I in danger again?"

"We all are. This is just a precaution."

Rhonda swallowed. "Should I disappear?"

"If you do that now, it will only send up red flags and get me in hot water. But you might want to start thinking about where you'd like to spend the rest of your life. Good night."

"Good night." Still looking at the card, Rhonda closed the door.

Karol went into the bathroom and brushed her teeth, then entered her bedroom and closed the door. She set her phone on the bedside table, shed her clothes, and crawled under the bedcovers. Maybe the living situation with Rhonda would work out after all.

Carl switched on the rental car's ignition again. He had taken to alternating between letting the engine run for heat and turning it off to save gas, but he had to let it run for longer periods of time now that the sky had blackened.

The dashboard clock taunted him with the time—7:19 PM. He had spent most of his day staking out a Korean delicatessen while most reporters in the city followed the manhunt for Gomez, and he had nothing to show for it. The thought of spending the night in his apartment while the inevitable newscasts played caused his muscles to sag. He needed dinner, and he would be damned if he was going to buy another meal from the deli after its owners had wasted his time.

The Korean man who had made his sandwich exited the deli. He wore a winter coat.

"Hello, what have we here?" Maybe the man didn't own the deli. Maybe he was just an employee, and his shift had ended. *What woman works alone at a cash operation in the Bronx at night?*

The man turned to his left and headed up the sidewalk. Carl shifted the car into gear and made a U-turn for the second time that day. He followed the deli owner for half a block, then stopped and waited for the man to get farther ahead before resuming his crawl. Two long blocks later, the man turned right at an intersection. Carl cursed at the one-way street. He sped up to the next intersection, turned right, and circled the long block.

"Come on, goddamn it," he said.

He made one more right-hand turn, slowing down only when he saw the Korean man on the left in the distance. The man turned into a driveway, and Carl pulled into a parking space and looked over his shoulder at the driveway. Two block-like residential buildings sandwiched the Grand Concourse Family Values Community Center. A black metal fence surrounded the center. A woman wearing a long black coat approached the gate, glanced around as if to make sure no one watched her, then opened it, stepped onto the property, closed the gate, and followed the driveway until she disappeared from Carl's view.

"It must be bingo night." Carl switched his camcorder on and set it next to the window, aiming it behind him and turning the screen toward him.

Two more people passed through the gate and walked around the building. Where the hell were these people going?

Carl looked up and down the street. A few silhouettes shuffled through the pools of light cast by streetlights. He put on a ski cap, then slid his camcorder into his coat pocket. He got out of the car, crossed the street, and opened the gate. He crept toward the corner of the building and peered around it. A tall man wearing an army jacket and a red cap stood outside the side entrance.

A sentry? Carl ducked out of sight. *What the hell are they up to?*

Facing the street again, he circled the front of the building to its opposite corner and peeked around it. The fence separating the building from the apartment building next door created a narrow alley. The only light in the alley came from the apartment windows above.

Carl turned on his phone's flashlight and used it to illuminate his way. He sneaked through the darkness, searching for some sign of where the Korean man and the other people had gone. A faint murmuring reached his ears, and a sliver of pale light sliced the cracked concrete walkway before him.

Plywood covered the basement windows, but he noticed a gap in one of the windows. Crouching, he noted the voices came from inside. He pressed one eye against the edge of the plywood, but all he managed to see were shadows on a dingy green floor.

Kneeling on the cold concrete, he wrapped his fingers around the plywood and pulled. The movement created a scraping sound, and he stopped after shifting the wood just three inches. He still couldn't see inside, but he had enough room to squeeze his camcorder through the opening. Lying on the ground, he took the camera from his pocket, flipped its screen open, and set it on the concrete window ledge with the lens aimed inside.

The screen showed about a dozen people standing in the basement meeting room, surrounded by folding chairs.

Most of their heads were cropped from this angle. The sounds of traffic and wind prevented him from hearing what they said.

Carl adjusted the screen and the angle of the lens, framing the people from head to toe. He pressed Record and counted ten men and four women of mixed ethnicities. The Korean man stood in profile, speaking to a Hispanic woman. Carl zoomed in on them, then panned around the room, the automatic focus sharpening blurry figures. All were middle-aged or older. At least two men were dressed in suits and overcoats, but most wore jeans with sweaters or sweatshirts. The whole scene reminded Carl of Alcoholics Anonymous.

A tall man with black hair walked over to a podium in front of a chalkboard and spoke. Carl couldn't make out the man's echoing words. Except for two men who stood behind the speaker, the rest of the men and women sat on folding chairs with their backs to the camera. Carl zoomed out, then zoomed in on the speaker. Carl's heart beat faster. He recognized the man: Gabriel Domini.

EIGHTEEN

Standing at the podium in the meeting hall, Gabriel made eye contact with the representatives of the Greater Pack of New York City. This wasn't the first time he had called them together on short notice, but he believed it might be the last. Micah, his cabdriver, and Joe Sevin stood behind him, and George and Bennett sat in the front row.

"Everyone's here, so let's get started," Gabriel said. "Thank you for coming. I assure you this is an emergency."

Pensive eyes met his gaze.

"First, the Blades of Salvation have been destroyed. They'll trouble us no more, and anyone seeking strength from their symbolism will be disappointed. I also want to make sure everyone knows that George Allen has replaced my brother, Raphael, at my right hand, and Bennett Jones is advising me as well. The Brotherhood of Torquemada has been defeated, but we're in greater danger than ever."

Carl strained to hear Gabriel's words, which proved fruit-less. He hoped the camera's built-in microphone captured the audio.

On the screen, Gabriel and the men standing behind him—bodyguards?—looked to their right, as if distracted by a sudden noise.

Gabriel heard voices in the hallway. A moment later, Jonah, the guard in charge of security, barked like a dog. Gabriel started forward, but Micah clasped his shoulder and proceeded to the door instead, followed by the second bodyguard.

Micah opened the door, revealing Jonah within the door frame, his arms braced against it to prevent entry. Three men stood before him: Raphael, his bodyguard Eddie, and Elias Michalakis, the Greek who had turned Raphael against him.

"Let them in," Gabriel said.

Jonah stepped away from the doorway, and Raphael led his fellows inside.

"What do you want?" Gabriel said. "Have you finally come to your senses?"

Raphael cast his gaze over the council members. "I'm here by my birthright."

"You gave up those rights when you turned your back on the pack," Gabriel said.

"Don't forget we were the ones who located the Brotherhood's hiding place." He faced the seated Wolves. "Or did you neglect to tell them that?"

"The Torquemadans are no longer a threat. We're here tonight to deal with new issues."

"My invitation must have been lost in the mail, *Brother*."

"You and Eddie are welcome. Elias isn't. He doesn't represent anyone in the pack."

"He represents me and my followers."

Gabriel felt the council members watching him. He knew they expected him to show strength in the face of dissention, but he did not wish to argue or prolong the meeting. "Come in then."

Raphael, Eddie, and Elias moved into the room and sat down.

Carl believed one of the three men who had just entered was Raphael Domini, Gabriel's brother, also wanted for questioning by the police. He debated whether to call 911.

After I find out what this is all about, he thought.

"I've called you here tonight because our worst fears have been realized," Gabriel said to the council. "Julian Fortier's killing spree two years ago brought the Brotherhood here. We dealt with them. They're finished, but their actions have raised the interest of the authorities. The police know about us. So does the FBI. That means federal scrutiny. Right now, Tony Mace's task force has been assigned to identify as many of us as possible. I met with them and gave a hair sample for DNA testing. I did this to buy us time, but now that Gomez is following in Fortier's footsteps, the clock is ticking."

"What do you propose we do?" Anne Wong, a council-woman, said.

"I'm afraid we can no longer lie low and hope the danger will pass. As much as it pains me to say this, we need to disband the pack and leave the city."

"You're just going to abandon Father's dream?" Raphael said.

Here it comes, Gabriel thought. "I shared in Father's dream of integration into human society. I took it to a higher level. We have pack members in law enforcement, education, and medicine—even lawmakers. But in joining this society, we've made ourselves vulnerable to exposure. Fortier created the domino effect he wanted. For the survival of this pack and our species, we need to go underground."

Whispers and murmurs rose from the council members, and Raphael glared at Gabriel.

"Where do you expect us to go?" Cecilia Perez said.

"I don't want to know," Gabriel said. "And I don't want any of you to share your destination with even your closest friends or distant family members. If you do, it will just take the capture of one of us to lead to the identification, imprisonment, and execution of others. Go where you feel safe. Canada is suitable for now. With the Brotherhood defeated, Europe is wide open. All your members have invested money in our stocks. Under my orders, we've been liquidating those funds in a careful manner and splitting them accordingly. But you have to make preparations now, and so do your people."

Raphael stood. "You want us all to run."

"I want us all to survive."

"By running."

"It wouldn't be the first time."

Raphael looked around the room. "Maybe some of us don't want to run. Maybe none of us do. We have jobs, family."

A few people nodded.

"We need to put the safety of the species ahead of our own human comforts." Gabriel hoped to appeal to the Wolves in a more subtle manner than Raphael's approach.

Raphael locked eyes with him. "So you're stepping down as leader of the pack?"

Gabriel did not look away. "No, I retain my leadership. And as the alpha, I order the disbandment of the pack."

"You mentioned Mace." Raphael turned to the council members. "Did you tell everyone that he and his wife and the female FBI agent witnessed you and Karol Williams transform into Wolves to defeat the Brotherhood, and you allowed them to live?"

Gabriel felt his temperature rising. "Killing police officers would have only made matters worse."

"And yet now you say we have to fear the very agencies

they work for."

"The Torquemadans blew up cars and buildings. They killed policemen in order to assassinate Wolves, and now they're dead. The fact that our existence hasn't been made public yet is due to Mace's loyalty to us."

"I warned you to kill them."

"I told you then and I tell you now that *I* make the laws, and I say the Maces and Norton are to be left alone."

Raphael spread his arms for emphasis. "You took a chance in letting them live. You risked our safety for their sake, and now you're telling us to upend our lives like criminals and abandon everything we've built."

More people nodded.

"I say you're unfit for leadership," Raphael said.

Gabriel looked at Elias, who hadn't spoken a word. "It saddens me that you've let an outsider come between us."

"Elias led a cell of freedom fighters in Greece. He knows how to counter human violence."

"All his people are dead. That's some leadership."

Elias's features tightened, but he remained silent.

"They were killed by the Brotherhood, just like so many of our kind were," Raphael said. "Now the Brotherhood is finished; you said so yourself. We have to stand our ground, not run like rabbits."

Gabriel chuckled.

"It's a mistake to laugh at me."

"Then don't make preposterous statements. What would you have us do? Fight the government of the United States of America? We're outnumbered by millions. And this isn't the dark ages, *Brother*. Modern man possesses technology our ancestors never had to worry about. Satellites. Heat sensors. Drones. Once they know who we are, they can wipe us out without setting boots on the ground. Our hunters have never been so sophisticated. Any aggressive action taken by us will result in our genocide."

Raphael narrowed his eyes and softened his voice. "You're quick to blame Fortier, the Brotherhood, and Gomez, but your own actions may have brought this scrutiny upon us. Your proposal to disband the pack proves you're unfit to sit at the head of the table."

Gabriel gestured at the council members. "Look around you. Do you see soldiers in this room? *Freedom fighters*? These are working-class men and women with children to raise. They're not going to fight some insane war that we can't possibly win."

"I'm not asking them to; that would be foolish. But I am asking them to stay put, to live their lives among their own kind."

"And who will lead them? You?"

Raphael waited only one second before answering. "Yes."

"You never used to be so ambitious."

"It's the right of anyone in the pack to challenge your leadership."

"You lost that right when you left the pack. Now you're a rogue like Fortier and Gomez. You have no more say in what we do from this point on than Elias does, and I remind everyone in this room that Elias indoctrinated Fortier into his cell and sent him here in the first place. As political advisors go, he leaves a lot to be desired."

Raphael moved closer to Gabriel. "This isn't about Elias. It's about you and your inability to lead."

"Don't do this, Raphael," George said.

"Shut up, old man."

"If your father was alive, this would break his heart."

"Don't use sentimentality against me."

"This is bullshit," Micah said. "You don't get to break from the pack and then try to take over it."

Raphael gave Micah a dismissive snort. "I do if I win this challenge."

"There hasn't been a challenge to leadership since the Greater Pack was united," Bennett said. "No one will follow you just because you picked a schoolyard fight. That's no way to lead in this day and age."

Raphael sneered at Bennett. "Don't be so sure, grocer. I've already reached out to several people in this room. I have supporters."

Gabriel glanced at the council members and wondered which ones considered betraying him.

"I'm calling you out," Raphael said. "If I win, my right to lead will be legitimate."

Micah crossed his arms. "If you beat him, I'll challenge *you*."

Raphael smiled. "I'll enjoy that . . . in one month's time, as stipulated by the law of succession." He turned back to Gabriel. "I always follow the law."

Gabriel saw there was no dissuading his brother. "I have no intention of fighting you."

"Then you forfeit?"

"Never."

Raphael slapped Gabriel. "I challenge you for leadership."

Gabriel's lips parted, and his teeth grew longer. Raphael dove at him, and the two men crashed into the chalkboard.

The council members jumped to their feet and rushed forward.

Carl zoomed in on the action inside the meeting room. He had no idea what was going on or why Raphael Domini had struck his brother, but the clandestine fight had gained his full attention. The people who rose from their seats blocked his view of the brothers. He couldn't tell if they cheered the fighters on, but none of them tried to stop the contest.

The brothers reappeared, clawing at each other, and went out of focus. Blurred, they tumbled into the hallway beyond Carl's view.

"Damn it," Carl hissed.

Ten seconds that felt longer passed.

Two battling figures staggered into camera range, and Carl blinked twice. They wore human clothing, but they didn't belong to the human race. Each stood seven feet tall, his head and claws covered with black fur, jaws opening to reveal long teeth. The creatures snarled at each other, their pointy ears pinned back.

Werewolves, Carl thought. *Fucking werewolves!*

In his excitement, he bumped the plywood that covered the window, and the plywood tipped over, its crash on the cement echoing in the alley. Holding his breath, Carl froze.

Several people in the basement turned in his direction, and an Asian woman pointed at him. "Look!"

Carl lowered the camera and made eye contact with the woman, then he leapt to his feet and fled. As he neared the corner of the building, a high-pitched howling from the basement made the frigid night air seem even icier. Feet pounded the walkway behind him. Carl sprinted across the front lawn and through the gate and slammed it shut with a clanging sound. He glimpsed the sentry from the other side of the building racing toward him, and he charged across the street to his parked car. The gate opened behind him.

Carl ran faster, knowing he would have a hard time stopping. Footsteps pummeled the pavement behind him. He crashed into the car, jerked out his keys, and unlocked the door. His pursuer bore down on him. With his heart pounding, Carl opened the door and left it jutting out at an angle as he jumped into the car. The sentry rammed into the open door and rebounded off it with a howl of pain. Carl shut the door, then activated the locks. The sentry lunged at the window, his face only a foot away, and Carl stared into the man's eyes. The irises expanded, blotting out the whites, and as the man roared his teeth elongated.

Carl jammed his key into the ignition and turned it just as the sentry pounded on the glass, shattering it. Pieces of glass flew around Carl, who shifted the car into Drive. A clawed hand groped the front of his coat. Groaning, Carl stomped on the gas pedal, and the car lurched forward. The sentry clung to him.

As he drove across the street at a forty-five-degree angle, a growl caused him to look to his left. A lupine face surrounded by tufts of black fur snarled at him, lips peeling back to reveal deadly teeth. Carl screamed, and a moment later he plowed into a parked sedan, triggering the vehicle's alarm. The impact hurled the sentry headfirst into the sedan, and Carl slammed into the steering wheel.

Without waiting to see if the beast had been killed, Carl backed the rental car up, then twisted the steering wheel in the opposite direction and stomped on the gas, rocketing the car forward. He heard a wet-sounding bark, then nothing but the alarm behind him. Ahead, the light changed from yellow to red. Ignoring it, he raced into the intersection and peeled left toward Manhattan.

"Look!"

Gabriel released Raphael and shoved him back. Turning, he saw Anne Wong pointing at the window across the basement. A man holding a video camera peered inside. Then he disappeared.

Raphael collided with Gabriel, knocking him to the floor. Raphael snapped his jaws at Gabriel, who forced his head back. Gabriel unleashed a howl, alerting the guards of danger.

George pulled Raphael off him. "Stop it," he said, then Bennett and Elias got into the middle of the fight as well. "We have bigger problems than who's alpha."

Gasping for breath, Gabriel transformed into his

human form. "Everyone, get out!"

The council members ran for the door.

Gabriel stared at Raphael, who remained in Wolf Form.

"We have to leave," Elias said.

With hatred still blazing in his eyes, Raphael turned human.

Micah handed Gabriel his shoes, which he had removed in the hall, and Gabriel sat on a chair and pulled them on.

"This isn't over," Raphael said, plucking a clump of fur from his mouth.

"You're wrong," Gabriel said. "It's all over. We have to make a new beginning. You and I need to work together, not against each other."

Elias gave Raphael's shoes to him, and Raphael put them on.

"You're going to ruin everything we've built," Raphael said.

Gabriel stood. "The house is already coming down around our ears."

Raphael took his coat from Elias. "I'll be in touch." He strode from the building, followed by Elias and Eddie.

Bennett handed Gabriel his coat.

"Outside," Gabriel said.

They hurried into the hallway and up the stairs to the side entrance to the building. Out front, they stood shoulder to shoulder with a handful of council members who remained on the sidewalk while cars drove away. A car alarm blared to their left.

Renny, the sentry, limped forward in human form, clutching his shoes. "I was too late. He got away."

Gabriel scanned the windows of the buildings around them. Silhouettes gazed down at them.

"We all need to get out of here now," Gabriel said.

NINETEEN

Carl weaved between cars as he raced into Manhattan. Adrenaline caused his arms and legs to shake, and he squeezed the steering wheel.

"Werewolves," he said over and over. "They're all werewolves!"

And he had seen one up close. It had almost killed him. He wished he had videotaped the sentry's attack on him, but he knew that if he had, he probably wouldn't be alive now. He found it impossible to shake the image of its long teeth.

What about the Lourdeses and the Wilsons? Detective Williams? His mind raced faster than the rental car. There was still so much to figure out, but he didn't intend to wait to connect all the dots. He had waited too long with his background on the Brotherhood of Torquemada and had been burned because of it.

Twenty minutes later, he found a parking space in front of his building and got out. Inspecting the car for damage, he grimaced at the dents and scratches in its front. A small price to pay for glory. For the first time in his life, he felt like a real journalist.

Carl entered his building and ignored his mailbox. Inside his apartment, he turned on the lights, peeled off his coat, and sat at his computer. He removed the memory card from his camcorder and inserted it into a port on his laptop. As the footage downloaded, he took out his phone and searched for a number. When he didn't find it, he brought up the website for Manhattan Minute News and went to the contacts page, then he keyed in the number he found.

"Manhattan Minute News desk," a woman said.

"I need to speak to Colleen Wanglund. Tell her it's Carl Rice and it's important."

"Just a moment, please. I'll see if she's left for the day."

Elevator music replaced her voice. Drumming his fingers on his desk, Carl watched the progress bar for the download.

"Hello?" Colleen said. Her monotone dampened his excitement. They had attended Columbia and had worked on the *Columbia Spectator* together before following related career paths. He considered her a colleague, and it hurt to realize she didn't hold him in the same regard.

"I've got something big for you," he said.

"Do you know how many times a week I hear that?"

"I'm talking earthshaking this-episode-changes-everything *news*—the story of a lifetime."

Colleen sighed, and he knew she intended for him to

hear that. "What have you got?"

"Not over the phone."

"I was just getting ready to leave for the night. I'll be in tomorrow morning at seven."

The *Post* had already screwed him; Carl didn't plan to take another chance. "That won't do, darling. If you don't air this story tonight, we'll both be sorry. But if you do, we'll make beautiful history together."

Silence.

"How soon can you get here?"

Carl glanced at the progress bar for the download again. "Forty minutes."

"I intend to be drinking hard liquor in thirty."

"What are you in the mood for? I'll bring it."

"Scotch."

"It's a deal. Sit tight." He ended the call, then sprang to his feet and pumped both fists. "Hell, yes, baby!"

Rhonda's bedroom door whispered open because she had oiled its hinges and those of the front door earlier in the day while Karol was at work.

It's not my bedroom, and this isn't my apartment, she told herself. It was as much of a prison to her as her cell in the Brotherhood's Newark base. She had no home.

She took a deep breath, then stepped into the hall and waited. Gazing at Karol's bedroom door, she counted sixty seconds before reaching behind her and shutting the door.

She counted to sixty again, waiting to see if she had awakened Karol, then tiptoed through the dark apartment in her socks. She wore her coat and carried her sneakers.

Rhonda took her time unlocking the front door, then slipped into the building's hallway, deserted and quiet except for the buzzing of the fluorescent lights. She shut the door, wincing as metal rubbed against metal, then locked the door and ran to the emergency stairway. She hurried down two flights of gray concrete before she sat on a landing and put on her sneakers.

Outside, Rhonda breathed in fresh air and ignored the three teenage thugs who loitered near the door, smoking cigarettes and laughing. One of them wore a Taft High School jacket. She glanced in their direction, and they turned quiet. Maybe they knew she stayed with Karol, or maybe their instincts warned them not to mess with her. She didn't care.

When she reached the sidewalk, a police car cruised by her. She didn't care about that, either. Nor did she give a damn about the gang hanging out in front of the bodega across the street. Not a single person dwelling in the night summoned her fear or interest. She liked being outside, away from her temporary prison.

Rhonda walked several blocks to the outskirts of Pelham Bay Park, then followed the chain-link fence separating the garage from the field and the wrecking yard behind it. The Doberman yelped at her from a distance, too frightened to approach the fence. She smiled.

In the wrecking yard, she navigated her way through the

corridors of twisted metal, moonlight glinting on the surface of the decaying vehicles that provided shelter from the wind. The city's traffic sounds faded. Orange firelight flickered along the edges of a rusted van, and laughter reached Rhonda's ears. Making no effort to conceal herself, she strode into the clearing where her teenage friends sat on seats taken from cars and arranged around their barrel furnace.

Friends. The word felt strange. She had never expected to have friends again.

"Look what the moon brought out," Daniel said.

Raina stood first. "Bitch," she said without animosity.

"Skank," Rhonda said.

Raina returned to her seat.

T-Bone pulled on a joint. "You shouldn't be out on a night like this. Gomez likes the full moon."

"I don't sweat him," Rhonda said.

"He's a big, bad werewolf."

"I don't believe in werewolves."

"Who does?" Diane said.

Lincoln withdrew a pint of Jim Beam from his coat. "I know why you came out to play."

Rhonda took the bottle from him, unscrewed its cap, and took a gulp. She handed the bottle back to Lincoln, who slid over on his seat, making room for her.

"Don't sit there," Daniel said. "He's a loser."

Lincoln made a dismissive sound.

"Sit here. It's warmer."

Rhonda felt the others watching her. She had not expected Daniel to make his interest in her known so early.

That made him less interesting to her. Turning to Raina and Diane, she tried to read their eyes. Did she see jealousy, dismay, or just curiosity? "Move over, girls."

Grinning, Raina and Diane slid away from each other, making room for her, and T-Bone laughed.

"Oh no," Lincoln said, laughing.

Rhonda sat between the females and smiled at Daniel. "I like it here."

"Suit yourself," Daniel said, showing no emotion.

"How's business?" Rhonda said.

Daniel's expression didn't change. "I can't complain."

"Heads-up," T-Bone said. "We got another customer."

A short figure, silhouetted in the moonlight, shuffled toward them from the opposite direction Rhonda had come.

Lincoln and T-Bone stood, then Daniel did too. Rhonda leaned forward to stand, but Diane grabbed her wrist and shook her head.

Alpha male mentality, Rhonda thought. *Just like the adults in the pack.*

As the hooded figure neared the barrel, a wide nose and full lips came into view. Female. The wind blew toward the newcomer, preventing Rhonda from detecting her scent.

"What's up?" T-Bone said.

"You selling tonight?" the girl said.

"Who wants to know?" T-Bone said.

The girl pulled back her hood, allowing long cornrows to spill out. "Yolanda."

Rhonda guessed the girl was fourteen.

"I know her," Lincoln said. "She's cool."

"What are you looking for?" Daniel said.

"What you got?"

"Jamaican gold."

"Gimme an eighth."

"Sixty."

Yolanda took her left hand out of her pocket. She clutched folded bills. "That's what I got."

Lincoln crossed the distance between them and collected the cash. He counted three twenties and returned to the barrel. T-Bone turned his back to the fire and tipped his seat. When he turned around, he held a plastic bag containing an eighth of an ounce of marijuana.

Yolanda pulled her other hand free of her pocket and aimed a gun at Lincoln. The flames in the barrel cast orange highlights on the black Glock.

T-Bone and Lincoln flinched at the same time, but Daniel stood cool.

"Hands in the air, bitches," Yolanda said.

Three figures materialized in the moonlight behind her: tall black men with long dreadlocks, each clutching a Glock. Between the four of them, they had Daniel's crew covered. Rhonda's muscles tensed.

One of the men moved into the firelight and studied each of the males. "You know who I am?" He had a heavy Jamaican accent.

"Desmond," Daniel said.

"That's right. You know who I work for?"

"Big Kwamie."

"Good. Now who the fuck are you?"

"Daniel."

"When I heard some punks were slinging Jamaican gold in our turf, I said, nah, that can't be right. No one who lives around here could be that stupid. You live around here, white boy?"

Daniel shrugged.

"I didn't think so." He looked at Lincoln and T-Bone. "But I seen y'all before."

"We're small-timers," Daniel said. "We only sell to our friends. We're not cutting into your action."

Desmond swung his Glock in Daniel's direction. "Who's your supplier?"

Daniel bit his lip. "You wouldn't know him."

"How the fuck do you know what I know?"

Digging her heels into the cold earth, Rhonda dove straight at Desmond. By the time she reached him, she had transformed into a Wolf, and she sank her canine fangs into one of his forearms. Desmond fell screaming to the ground with Rhonda on top of him. Snarling, she shook her head, breaking his arm, and he dropped his gun.

"Oh, shit," Yolanda said.

The other two Jamaicans fired their Glocks at Lincoln and T-Bone, opening holes in their torsos. Blood spilled out of the wounds, and they gasped and collapsed on their seats. Raina and Diane leapt into the air as human females and landed on the earth before the assassins as Wolves. The Jamaicans pointed their weapons at them, but before they could fire, Daniel howled at the moon. They turned in his direction and saw a Wolf where he had stood. Raina and

Diane pounced on them, tearing the men's throats with their teeth.

Desmond beat at Rhonda's side. She released her hold on his arm and sank her fangs into his face, tearing half of it off. Then she forced her muzzle beneath his jaw, fastened her teeth on his neck, and tore out his throat, tasting hot blood. All three men issued strangled gargling sounds.

Yolanda backed up, aiming her Glock at each of the Wolves attacking the Jamaican men. She turned to run, and Daniel sprang after her, driving her facedown to the ground. She tried to crawl away, but he tore into her buttocks, and she screamed.

Rhonda shredded Desmond's chest with her front claws, and when he stopped moving she pushed herself up. She found it difficult to stand with her paws and extended legs confined in her sneakers and almost tipped over. With the sound of her beating heart throbbing in her brain, she reverted to human form, her chest rising and falling and her clothes dripping with blood.

"That's enough," she said to Daniel, who had worked his way up to Yolanda's neck, leaving a wide, glistening trench in her back that separated fabric and flesh. He continued to gnaw on her meat. "I said *that's enough.*"

Daniel bared his fangs at Rhonda.

"We have to get the hell out of here."

Daniel stood erect and reverted to human form, blood and gristle dripping from his lips.

Rhonda turned to Raina and Diane, who chewed their victims with wild abandon. "That's enough, bitches," she said.

Raina and Diane looked at her, then returned to their feeding frenzy.

"Chill!"

The females stopped, shook their heads, then turned human, their faces smeared with blood. They looked at each other, faces two feet apart, and smiled.

Rhonda hurried over to where T-Bone and Lincoln lay. They stared at her in wonder.

"You'll both live," she said.

Daniel joined her.

"We have to get them out of here before the cops show up," Rhonda said. She expected him to rebuke her for giving orders.

"That was *good*," he said.

TWENTY

arl took a taxi to the headquarters of Manhattan Minute News on West Thirty-second Street. He didn't want to be seen getting out of the damaged rental car by anyone who worked there, and it occurred to him the werewolf people might recognize the vehicle from its scratches and dents. Were they looking for him? He doubted they even knew Carl Rice existed, let alone recognized him in the seconds they had seen him through the window.

Inside the lobby, he signed in at the front desk and boarded an elevator, which he rode to the third floor. The Manhattan Minute News bull pen didn't impress him: four people manned desks in a sea of deserted cubicles, two of them speaking in soft voices on their phones while MMN played on two monitors suspended from the ceiling. He felt no excitement, no sense of urgency in the station's hub. He had chosen such a small operation for his launchpad.

At the far end of the space, Colleen spoke to a young man with glasses. Seeing Carl, she glanced at her watch.

"I'm sorry I'm late," Carl said. "It took me longer to get everything together than I expected."

"What a surprise," she said.

"You'll be glad you waited."

"I bet you didn't bring the scotch, either."

"I'm all out, darling."

Before he could hug her, Colleen turned her back on him and led him into her small glass-faced office, which had a view of the city. Awards and certificates covered one wall, and a monitor played MMN on the other.

"You've got five minutes to wow me." Colleen sat at her cluttered desk.

"That's all I need." Carl took out a DVD. "I shot this footage myself."

"I'm on the edge of my seat."

Carl opened the tray of Colleen's Blu-ray player and set his DVD inside it. The machine swallowed the disc, then daytime footage of the deli filled the screen. "This is a deli I staked out today. Seven hours of sitting on my butt."

"Fascinating."

He fast-forwarded to the nighttime footage outside the community center. "I followed the deli owner to this building a few blocks away. It's a community center. Notice all the lights are off. See the people going through the gate? I decided to investigate."

"Why were you watching that deli in the first place?"

"I'd rather not say. There are other aspects to this story I'm still putting together." The basement of the community center filled the screen. "The basement windows were all boarded up except this one. There was a gap in it. I opened it wide enough to fit my camera through for a look-see. There were about a dozen people down there."

"It looks like an AA meeting," Colleen said.

"I thought the same thing." On-screen, Gabriel faced the seated people. Carl tapped the screen. "That's Gabriel Domini."

Colleen put on her glasses. "The funeral director?"

"And co-owner of the Synful Reading bookstore."

"Where's the audio?"

"I'm not a freelance cameraman. I shot this with a flip-screen camera. I couldn't pick up what they were saying."

"Nice job."

Three men entered the basement. "The guy in the middle is Raphael Domini. Not one law enforcement agency has produced a motivation for a European terrorist organization to travel to the US and target the businesses of these two men."

"But you've got the answer?"

"The historic Brotherhood of Torquemada used swords called the Blades of Salvation to execute people accused of witchcraft and being werewolves during the Spanish Inquisition. The only mention I've found of this is in a book called *Transmogrification in Native American Mythology* by Terrence Glenzer, the first victim of the Manhattan Werewolf two years ago."

"I remember. The police found one half of a broken sword in Glenzer's safe," Colleen said.

"And they recovered the other half of that sword in Central Park on the night those cops were killed."

"The Manhattan Werewolf is still out there," Colleen said.

"Maybe he ran away when the National Guards came to town like people say, or maybe someone killed him."

"Like the Brotherhood of Torquemada?"

"That very well could be the case. I believe Pedro Fillipe, who was also killed in Central Park that night, belonged to the Brotherhood."

On-screen, Raphael lunged at Gabriel.

"Trouble in *la familia*," Colleen said.

"You have no idea."

The brothers disappeared from view.

"Are you pitching me a news story or a reality series?"

"You tell me."

Two figures leapt into view on the screen, and Colleen did a double take. "What the hell?"

"This is real. *Those* are real."

"What is this, a dogfight?"

"What dogs walk upright and stand seven feet tall?" Carl froze the picture. "Those are the same shirts the Dominis were just wearing." He resumed play, and the werewolves snarled at each other.

"This is a hoax. It has to be. Those are special effects."

"No, dear. I was there. Those are living creatures."

"The other people aren't even afraid," Colleen said.

"Because they're all the same."

"Wolves?"

"Werewolves."

An Asian woman turned to the camera and pointed straight at it. She said something, and the camera angle shifted to the ground.

"That's where I got into trouble. They chased me to my car. One of them broke my window and held on to the door while I drove off. I saw it up close. I looked into its eyes. This is no hoax; these things are real. I barely escaped with my life."

Colleen stared at the blank screen. "Werewolves . . ."

Carl leaned over her desk. "I can't prove it, but the Manhattan Werewolf was one. You remember the stories when that Indian got killed? That was across the street from Synful Reading. Tony Mace was in charge of that case, and he was on the scene. He must have told the NYPD brass what he saw, and that's why they shuffled him off to Floyd Bennett Field and the K-9 Unit. Then the Brotherhood came to town and went after the Dominis in a way that couldn't be covered up, so the big shots pulled Mace out of mothballs because he was the only person who knew the truth."

Colleen blinked. "Tony."

"Everything connects to him, and you got caught up in it. So did I. And now we're sitting on the story of the century."

Colleen opened a desk drawer and took out a bottle of scotch and two glasses. "Why bring this to me?"

"The networks will never buy it. In their eyes, I'm trash, nothing but a yellow journalist who turns out dime-store true crime books." He gestured at the newsroom. "But you need my brand of sensationalism."

Colleen handed him a drink. "Do I?"

"Hell, yes. Plus, you want to know why the Brotherhood chloroformed you and kidnapped Cheryl."

With her eyes never leaving him, Colleen gulped her scotch. "What do you want?"

"I want to report this story on TV. I want to do all the follow-up work. I want to do live remotes, and I want a weekly half-hour interview show to call my own."

"You want to be an on-air personality."

"Who else do you have?" Carl raised his voice. "Cheryl isn't coming back. Michael O'Hear? He's the opposite of sensational. You need this as much as I do."

"This could backfire. We could be laughingstocks. I could lose my job."

"No guts, no glory. Gomez is out there. He's part of this too. Someone is going to break this story. I'm begging you—let it be us."

Colleen tapped her fingernails on her desk. "Play it again."

Rhonda followed the others into the three-bedroom apartment where Lincoln lived. Daniel supported Lincoln, and Diane and Raina held T-Bone upright between them.

"Mom works the night shift, and my sister's got her own crib now," Lincoln said between gasps.

"Stop that heavy breathing," Rhonda said. "I had my arm cut off, and it grew back. You guys will be fine."

Lincoln detached himself from Daniel and fell into an armchair. "Set T on the couch."

Diane and Raina deposited T-Bone on the sofa. He grimaced.

Lincoln pulled up his bloody shirt and gazed at the wound in his torso. "It doesn't look so bad."

"Of course it doesn't," Rhonda said. "Our bones are rock hard. The bullet never got past your ribs. The act of Transformation heals the tissue. I guess you never paid attention in Sunday school."

Diane and Raina went into the kitchen and returned with two chairs, then went back for two more.

Rhonda took off her coat and draped it over a chair. "Don't get comfortable yet. We have to wash the blood out of these clothes." She peeled off her bloody shirt. Blood caked her chest. When she removed her bra, the clean surface of her breasts stood out against the crimson around them.

The others gaped at her.

"Don't be shy, boys and girls. We may not have to worry about the cops, but we do have to worry about your parents, starting with Lincoln's mother."

Daniel took off his coat, then his shirt, and kicked off his shoes. Diane and Raina removed their coats and tops. Rhonda finished stripping first and went to the couch and started undressing T-Bone. Daniel joined her, and Diane and Raina helped Lincoln out of his clothes. The uninjured Wolves stood nude before Lincoln and T-Bone.

"Try not to get blood on the furniture," Lincoln said to T-Bone.

"Do you have a washer and dryer?" Rhonda said.

"Yeah, but they're small." Lincoln scratched around his wound. "Damn, it itches so bad."

"Because your skin is healing, dummy." Rhonda turned to the others. "Let's wash these off in the bathtub before we stick them in the machine."

In the bathroom, they ran water over the clothes and watched the blood swirl around the drain. Then they loaded the clothes into the washer. They took turns showering and washed the tub again.

"Now we have to wash the towels," Raina said.

"So do it," Rhonda said.

"What now?" Daniel said back in the living room.

"Let's have an orgy," Lincoln said.

Rhonda set a towel on the sofa beside him and sat on it. "No, I think we'll watch the news."

TWENTY-ONE

Carl entered the Manhattan Minute News studio with Colleen. A grid of ceiling lights shone down on the two-person desk with a bright green screen behind it. Two cameramen stood behind large broadcast cameras. Michael O'Hear looked up from the desk with raised eyebrows.

"Michael, I'm sure you know Carl Rice," Colleen said.

"Yes, I do," Michael said with obvious disapproval.

"I love your work," Carl said in an insincere tone.

Michael stood. "What's he doing here?"

"I work here now," Carl said. "We're colleagues."

Michael looked at Colleen with disbelief in his eyes, and she nodded.

Carl stepped on the set and gestured to the seat Michael had just vacated. "Do you mind sliding over one? This is my segment."

Michael moved over to the other seat and shot Colleen a confused look.

"Introduce Carl as a contributing editor," Colleen said.

"All right." Michael stretched the words out, articulating his displeasure.

Carl sat in the primary seat, then leaned over to Michael. "Wait until you hear this story. You're going to love it."

"I'm sure I will."

A short woman wearing a headset and holding a clipboard came over and held out one hand. "Hi, I'm Julie, your director."

Carl shook her hand. "Pleased to meet you."

Julie turned to Colleen. "I just read the copy for the teleprompter. Is this for real?"

"Yes," Colleen said.

"Okay, then, let's get started." Julie retreated to the shadows in the rear of the studio. "Camera A, you're up. Camera B, stand by."

"Remember what I said," Colleen said to Carl.

Carl beamed. "Let's make history together."

Colleen joined Julie.

"And five, four, three, two, one," Julie said.

The light on camera A glowed red.

"Welcome back to Manhattan Minute News. For those just tuning in, I'm Michael O'Hear, and it's now my pleasure to introduce you to Carl Rice, who joins us tonight as a contributing editor."

"Camera B," Julie said into her headset.

The light on camera A faded as the light on camera B

flared. On the monitor, the medium shot of Michael cut to a two-shot that included Carl.

"Thank you, Michael." Carl turned to camera A.

"Camera A," Julie said.

"When you see this exclusive Manhattan Minute News report, you might mistake it for a fictional story, but I assure you that is not the case. I was an eyewitness and the cameraman, and I stand by its authenticity."

"Camera B close-up," Julie said.

Colleen watched Carl's head and shoulders fill the monitor.

"Two weeks ago, New York City came under attack by a group of Europeans who called themselves the Brotherhood of Torquemada."

"Roll images," Julie said.

Photos of two teenagers filled the screen.

"These terrorists beheaded Jason Lourdes, age eighteen, in the occult bookstore Synful Reading and abducted Rhonda Wilson, also eighteen. Lourdes and Wilson were employees at the store . . ."

Still nude in Lincoln's apartment, Rhonda sat forward on the towel on the sofa. She had not expected to see Jason and herself on the news station. She loathed Carl Rice for writing *Rodrigo Gomez: Tracking the Full Moon Killer* and *The Wolf Is Loose: The True Story of the Manhattan Werewolf.*

"Hey, that's you," T-Bone said.

"No shit," Raina said.

"Quiet, both of you," Rhonda said in a flat tone.

Photos of Jason's and Rhonda's parents appeared.

"Over the next several nights," Carl Rice said in a voice-over, "Lourdes's parents and Wilson's parents were executed, their homes destroyed. Some of the victims were decapitated by swords."

Rhonda parted her lips and tried to hold back tears.

"The Domini Funeral Home and Synful Reading were destroyed in bombings," Carl said. "Both businesses were co-owned by these men." A photo of Gabriel and Raphael, dressed in suits, was shown. "Gabriel Domini and his brother, Raphael."

Carl Rice came back on-screen. "The Dominis have a sister, Angela, wanted for questioning by police regarding the murder of John Stalk, a tribal policeman. Stalk traveled to Manhattan from upstate New York during the hunt for the serial killer known as the Manhattan Werewolf. He was killed on the fire escape of a building across the street from Synful Reading. Witnesses claimed Stalk was killed by a 'large animal covered with black fur.' Angela Domini disappeared after the incident and has not been heard from since."

"Tony, wake up."

Mace rolled over with a groan. "What is it?"

Cheryl had already turned on the overhead light and the TV. Carl Rice appeared on-screen, sitting behind the Manhattan Minute News desk. "It looks like Colleen gave

Carl a job, and he's spilling everything."

Mace sat up and rubbed sleep from his eyes. He stared at himself on the screen.

"The man in charge of the Manhattan Werewolf investigation for the New York Police Department was Captain Anthony Mace, who had previously brought to justice Rodrigo Gomez, the Full Moon Killer, who escaped from Sing Sing Correctional Facility last night."

Gomez's mug shot appeared next to the photo of Mace.

"Mace wasn't so lucky with the Manhattan Werewolf, who was never apprehended." Carl returned to the screen. "Mace was put in charge of a joint NYPD and FBI task force assigned to capture the Brotherhood of Torquemada."

Photos of the Brotherhood of Torquemada appeared, forming a rogues' gallery. Mace bristled at the sight of Valeria Rapero.

"Mace was allowed to remain on the task force even after the Brotherhood abducted his wife, Cheryl Mace. His task force located the Brotherhood's Newark, New Jersey, hideout, and in a pitched battle, killed the terrorists. Cheryl Mace and Rhonda Wilson were rescued."

Mace's cell phone rang, and he answered.

"Are you watching this?" Jim said.

"I'm trying to."

"Call me back."

Mace shut the phone off and found himself staring at a familiar building.

"This is the Mott Street building that houses Mace's task force. Until now, its location was a secret."

"Damn it," Mace said.

Carl returned to the screen. "What no authorities will admit is the Brotherhood's purpose for being in the United States in the first place or why they targeted the Domini, Lourdes, and Wilson families."

Cheryl raised one hand to her mouth.

"As detailed by the late historian Terrence Glenzer in his book *Transmogrification in Native American Mythology*, the Brotherhood of Torquemada was formed during the Spanish Inquisition, and the men who wielded the Blades of Salvation were charged with executing men and women accused of witchcraft . . . and lycanthropy: in plain English, werewolves."

"Oh, my God," Cheryl said.

Mace's expression turned grim.

"It is no secret that I'm an acknowledged expert on both Rodrigo Gomez and the Manhattan Werewolf, and I've strived to bring to light the secrets of both of these killers," Carl said. "Tonight I bring you evidence of why the Brotherhood of Torquemada came to our country and why its members targeted two of our citizens, Gabriel and Raphael Domini."

Grainy footage of a dark building appeared.

"Acting on a tip, tonight I staked out this building. The Grand Concourse Family Values Community Center in the Bronx. The building appears to be closed, its windows dark, but I discovered clandestine activity in its basement."

"What the hell?" Mace said.

"A meeting made up of residents of our fair city. Who

are they?"

An image of people in a basement froze, and a red circle formed around the head of one man. An enlarged screen capture of the man appeared next, recognizable despite the grain.

"This is Gabriel Domini."

"Oh no," Cheryl said.

Mace swallowed.

As the footage resumed, three more men appeared. The image froze again, and a circle appeared around the head of another man, followed by an enlarged screen capture of him.

"And this is his brother, Raphael Domini."

The footage resumed, and Raphael and his companions took their seats. Gabriel spoke to the people sitting before him.

"I wasn't able to record audio of what was said at this meeting, nor did I hear it myself, as I filmed the activity from outside through a window. What I can tell you is that I witnessed the most frightening occurrence that I have ever seen in my life. This footage has been edited for time."

On the screen, Raphael lunged at Gabriel, and the seated people jumped to their feet and blocked the view of the brothers.

"I repeat that this footage is genuine. It is not a hoax."

Mace got out of bed, his eyes glued to the screen. "Jesus Christ."

Cheryl uttered a small cry at what happened next.

Carl's triumphant face returned to the screen. "Ladies and gentlemen, you have now seen what I witnessed earlier tonight. A man who stood guard at the community center chased me to my car and broke one of its windows after I got into it. I barely escaped with my life, and because luck was on my side, I'm able to provide you with the truth: creatures formerly reserved for fairy tales and horror movies actually exist. They walk among us in human form, and our police force and federal authorities are aware of their existence. I believe the Manhattan Werewolf was one of them, and Rodrigo Gomez may be one as well. Was the Brotherhood of Torquemada a threat to our population, or were they heroes vilified by the law enforcement agencies and the media? I won't rest until you know the full story."

The camera cut to a two-shot of Carl and Michael O'Hear.

"Back to you, Michael," Carl said.

A medium shot of Michael's pale face filled the screen. "Thank you for that . . . tantalizing report, Carl. We'll return after this break."

Cheryl muted the volume on the TV and faced Tony. "He just outed everyone."

Mace's cell phone rang, and he answered it.

"You've got another long night ahead of you," Jim said. "I'm stationing a patrol car outside that community center to keep people away. Assign your people to dig up the dirt on that place, and contact whoever runs it. I'll leave it to you and Norton to visit that TV station."

Jim hung up, and Mace called Landry. "Switch to Manhattan Minute News."

"I'm already on it. I was about to call you."

"Get the address on that community center, and send Candice out there to find out what she can."

"Should I send Karol with her?"

Mace considered the question. "No, send Grant. I want you to record MMN for an hour. They're bound to repeat the segment."

"Got it."

Mace hung up.

"I'll make you a sandwich to go," Cheryl said.

Rhonda couldn't believe what she had just seen.

"Wow," T-Bone said. "That was some serious shit."

"Gabriel must be having a cow," Daniel said. He turned to Rhonda. "What do you think?"

"I think nothing will ever be the same again," Rhonda said. "And I think I'm in big trouble."

Sitting on the living room sofa of the safe house on the Upper West Side with George and Bennett, Gabriel muted the volume on his television. Micah sat in an armchair next to the sofa.

"Now we know who saw us," Bennett said.

"So does everyone else," George said.

"So stupid," Gabriel said. "After all these years . . ."

"It was Raphael's fault," George said.

"If we'd posted one more guard on the other side of the building . . ."

A cell phone chimed. George took out his phone,

checked the display, and answered. "Go ahead."

Gabriel stood. "Rice was always a thorn in our side. I underestimated how much damage he could do."

"What could you have done?" Bennett said. "Ordered him killed?"

Gabriel said nothing.

George hung up. "That was Minjun Kim. He recognized Rice from earlier today. He came into his deli and ordered a sandwich like any other customer. Kim didn't think anything of it. Rice must have followed him to the center."

Micah stood as well. "But why was Rice watching the deli in the first place?"

"Karol went to the deli to tell Kim what was happening with the task force," Gabriel said. "That's why I called the council meeting. Rice must have been watching the police in Chinatown and followed her." He turned to George. "Call Kim back. Tell him and his wife to pack their essentials. They have to leave the country tonight before the police trace Rice's movements."

"They have a daughter in NYU," George said.

"She has to leave too. They're to tell no one where they're going." He turned to Micah. "Take them to my sister's in Canada. Anne was visible in that video as well. She and her family have to go. After that, every member of the council and every Wolf who was in that center. Rice drew a connection to Rhonda too."

"You're going, right?"

Gabriel shook his head. "I have to stay here to make sure everyone has what they need to escape."

"That's unwise," Bennett said. "After that report, you'll be wanted for more than questioning."

Gabriel gestured at the walls. "I'll be safe here or in one of our other safe houses."

"If you're going to coordinate things from closed walls, you can do that in Canada," George said. "Bennett and I will be your liaisons."

"You and Bennett are leaving, and long-distance communication is out of the question. It has to be me here."

Micah moved forward. "What about Raphael? He knows the locations of all the safe houses. Will you be safe from him?"

Gabriel drew in a breath. "Raphael has other things to worry about. We all do."

Gomez sat on the sofa in Savana Silvestri's living room. His muscles still ached, but after several hours of sleeping he felt better. He picked up the remote and activated the widescreen TV.

"Good evening, and welcome to Channel 2 News," a handsome male news anchor said. "I'm Clifford Chancer. Tonight we lead with a story that's causing an uproar in New York City."

When the news story had finished, Gomez unleashed a wild roar and leapt over the coffee table. He seized the TV, raised it over his head, and hurled it to the floor, shattering its screen. Then he picked up the wreckage and threw it at the wall.

TWENTY-TWO

Snowflakes landed on the windshield of Mace's SUV as he parked near the corner of West Broadway and Duane Street. He got out of the vehicle and took a quick reading on the apartment building: modern looking but unassuming. Anyone passing by would mistake it for just another collection of high-priced condominiums.

"Good evening, sir," the doorman said as Mace entered the revolving door.

Inside the spacious lobby, the lights on a tall Christmas tree blinked on and off near a fireplace.

"May I help you?" the man behind the counter said.

"I'm here to see Kathy Norton."

"Your name?"

"Tony Mace."

The man picked up the house phone. After a moment

he said, "Miss Norton, Mr. Mace is here." He waited. "Very good." The man disconnected. "Miss Norton says you can go on up, Mr. Mace. Unit 6D."

"Thanks." Mace crossed the lobby, ascended two steps, and boarded an elevator. On the sixth floor, he located the correct door and rang the bell.

The door opened, and Suzie Quarrel stood before him in a long button-down shirt. Mace tried to hide his surprise.

"Come on in."

Mace followed her inside.

"Kathy will be right out. She's fixing her hair." Suzie picked up a pair of slacks and pulled them on. "Crazy shit, huh?"

"I'll say." Mace looked around the apartment. He knew the tasteful furniture came with it, and he wondered what view was beyond the closed curtains of the floor-to-ceiling window.

"Landry called. Me and Hector are on standby. No bodies to collect yet."

Not yet, Mace thought. "You'd better sleep while you can."

Suzie gave him a perfunctory smile. "I'll do my best."

Norton exited the bathroom, dressed in a customary black suit, hair in a ponytail. "Welcome to Tara."

"This is some place."

"It's a hotel for professionals. FBI has a whole bunch of units like this for visiting higher-ups and special Special Agents." She went into the open kitchen, opened the refrigerator, and returned with a power drink. "Want one?"

"No thanks. I wolfed down a sandwich on the way over here."

"Let me guess: roast beef?"

Mace smiled. "Rare."

"You've got to change those eating habits now that you're getting older." Norton opened a closet door and took out her winter coat. "See you later, Suze."

"Later."

Mace and Norton exited the apartment together and walked to the elevator.

"Next thing I know, I'll find out Landry and Candice are having an affair."

Norton smiled. "Maybe they are."

They boarded the elevator.

"Hollander's on his way to meet with the governor," Norton said. "He wants to know what's going on, and we don't want him coming to the city or doing anything else that might lend credence to Rice's story."

"Is Jim on board with that?"

"It doesn't really matter, does it? Let's be honest. This thing just got too big for the shots to be called anywhere but D.C. We can play our roles, but the decisions are being made two hundred miles away."

They exited the elevator and crossed the lobby.

"Do you think they'll shut us down?" Mace said.

"No, that would also lend credibility to Rice's story. Everything needs to appear status quo; any sudden waves will rock the boat. I'd say you have a short window to produce results before someone else becomes point man."

"I don't feel like I'm on point now. Why did I have to learn from you that Hollander is heading to Albany?"

"It's my agency. You're a cog in your machine. I'm a cog in mine."

They passed through the revolving door, and Norton shivered.

"Did Suzie know before you told me?"

Norton frowned. "Of course not. Don't overestimate my relationship with her. You and I are partners."

"Are we?"

"That's why you picked me up, right? So we can talk in private?"

"Face time is important."

"You're learning."

"I have a good teacher." Using his remote control, Mace unlocked the SUV's door for Norton, who climbed inside. He circled the front of the vehicle and got in on the other side, then started the engine and pulled out.

"For better or worse, I put my entire career on the line when I went along with your version of what happened in Newark," Norton said.

"I know. Hopefully current events will keep our bosses too busy to look any deeper into what went down."

Mace's phone rang, and he checked the display. "Speak of the devil." He pressed the phone's screen. "Go ahead, Jim. Kathy Norton is with me."

"What are you, carpooling? Your budget isn't that tight."

"I thought we could save time by coordinating before we reached the station," Mace said.

"I'm on my way to meet with the mayor's people. This is every bit the shit storm you would expect. Our position is that this is all a hoax. Do you understand?"

"Roger that."

"Hollander's got a federal judge signing a warrant for that footage now. Do you want to wait for it before you go in?"

"I'll take my chances with Colleen. We go back a ways."

"Suit yourself. Just don't leave without that footage. Do you have someone standing by to review it?"

"Landry's heading to base now."

"We can't put an APB on the Dominis without it looking like we're taking this seriously. It's on you to bring them in. We want them alive."

Mace gritted his teeth. "Understood."

"Keep me in the loop." Jim hung up.

Norton looked at Mace. "I hope Gabriel has the good sense to run."

"He won't."

"What makes you think so?"

"He won't abandon his people any more than I would mine. Besides, he knows that if he runs, he may get caught. He's got to lie low."

"Are you in communication with him?"

Mace shook his head. He trusted Norton—he *had* to— but he also felt the need to protect Gabriel. There was no telling what damage sharing too much information could cause. He could never forget Norton was a fed. "They're nuts if they think they can cover this up."

"They're not going to cover it up; they're going to discredit it," Norton said. "There's a big difference. Rice makes a pretty easy target."

"I almost feel sorry for the poor bastard."

"Why wouldn't you? I read his books. He's made you out to be a bona fide hero."

"I never asked for that. I never wanted it."

"I have *got* to see that TV movie."

Mace chuckled. "Anyone who sits through that thing deserves a medal." He paused. "Why are you doing this? Why go out on a limb?"

Norton stared straight ahead. "Why are you?"

"Because I know the truth about these people. All they want is to be left alone. And if Gabriel hadn't helped us that night, Cheryl would be dead. I owe him too much."

"I joined the bureau because I always wanted to be a cop, and being an FBI agent is being the ultimate cop. No offense."

"None taken."

"I made up my mind what I wanted to do after 9/11. There are people out there who want to destroy this country. There are people *in* this country who want to destroy it. Gabriel isn't one of them. The Brotherhood of Torquemada was a genuine terrorist threat, and Shelly was killed by them. I have to believe my partner's death was worth something."

Mace couldn't help but think of Patty and Willy. "We're navigating a minefield."

"There's an elephant in this vehicle."

"Karol."

"We did what we could to protect her, but what now? She's one of them, and she's in the heart of this. As long as she knows what we're doing, so does Gabriel."

"I'm counting on that."

"As long as we both know what's going on here."

"She's a cop and a good one."

"But she's Class L too. You heard Mint: they want a Wolf alive. They don't care who it is. If she's exposed, we're exposed. Maybe she needs to run and take Rhonda with her."

Mace pulled over to the building that headquartered Manhattan Minute News. "I'll make that suggestion to her, but she's as committed to protecting the Wolves as Gabriel is."

"All of this commitment spells trouble."

Mace switched off the engine and reached for his cell phone when it rang again. He saw the phone number for the task force on the display and pressed the screen. "Go ahead, Ken."

"Candice and I are at base," Landry said. "I recorded the repeat of Rice's segment so I can get started before you get here."

"Good work."

"The eleven o'clock broadcasts picked up the story, which has been uploaded to YouTube and Vimeo by multiple people. The clips are getting hits. This has gone viral. There's no shutting it down."

"We'll see you soon." Mace pocketed his phone and got out.

Norton joined him on the sidewalk, and they entered the building, where they showed their IDs to the attendant at the security station. Mace had seen the man many times before when he had visited Cheryl at work.

"We're here to see Colleen Wanglund or anyone else in charge at MMN," Mace said.

The attendant reached for a phone with a confused expression. "Yes, sir. Just one minute."

"You can tell them we're on our way up, but we don't need their permission," Norton said. "Let's go, Tony."

Colleen and Carl stood at the end of the bull pen as Mace and Norton entered the Manhattan Minute News office.

"Hello, Tony," Colleen said.

"Colleen, this is Special Agent Norton."

Colleen nodded to Norton, then looked back at Mace. "How's Cheryl? We miss her."

"We want the broadcast copy and Carl's unedited footage."

"You can't have it. It belongs to Manhattan Minute News."

"We have warrants on the way," Norton said. "Are you going to make us use them, or are you going to cooperate?"

"I'm a firm believer in freedom of the press," Colleen said. "It's my lifeblood."

"Do you care to comment on my report while you're here?" Carl said. "Maybe we could do a live interview right now."

"We want that footage," Norton said. "And we expect you to answer questions about how you came by it."

Carl smirked. "Sure, I'll answer whatever questions you have, as long as we can shoot it."

"That isn't going to happen," Mace said.

"Where shall we speak? At Mott Street?"

Mace's phone rang. Landry again. "Excuse me." He stepped away. "Go ahead."

"We've got four fresh stiffs in a wrecking yard in the Bronx," Landry said. "They were all torn apart. It looks like Gomez has landed. I called Hector and Suzie in to work their magic."

"I want Karol there on point," Mace said.

"Copy that."

Mace returned to Norton's side.

"Good news?" Carl said.

"Yes." Mace gestured at a man with short hair walking over to them. "Our warrants are here."

TWENTY-THREE

Karol awoke to the sound of her phone's ringtone. The clock beside the lamp showed 11:26 PM. Dragging herself to an alert state, she sat up and answered the call without bothering to turn on the bedside lamp.

"It's Ken. We've got a monsoon of activity."

Any news was bad news these days. "I'm listening."

"Carl Rice went on TV and showed video of our HQ and Gabriel and Raphael Domini turning into Wolves at some meeting in the Bronx."

Oh no, Karol thought.

"We've also got four stiffs in a wrecking yard not far from your place. Hector and Suzie are heading to the crime scene now. Tony wants you on point."

"Copy that. Text me the address?"

"As soon as we hang up. Don't forget to clock in."

Karol hung up, turned on the light, and dressed. Then she went into the living room, turned on the TV, and sat at her computer. She logged on to the NYPD website and signed in. As a member of the task force, she didn't have to leave her weapon at work. Carl Rice's report came on Manhattan Minute News, and she watched it in dumbfounded silence. She had never seen footage of Wolves before; as far as she knew, none existed. But there were Gabriel and Raphael, fighting in Wolf Form on television for everyone to see.

A strange ringing filled the house: one of the burners Gabriel had given her. She returned to her bedroom and took the call.

"Have you seen it?" Gabriel said.

"Just now."

"Rice followed you to Kim's deli this afternoon. He must have stayed and followed Kim when he left."

Karol felt as if she had been slapped. "Oh, God, no. It's my fault?"

"Whose fault it is doesn't matter. There's plenty of blame to go around. Rice didn't name you in his report, but he's going to. You have to run tonight."

"I just got called to a crime scene. Gomez killed four people not far from here."

"Forget it. Let someone else handle it. I want you gone. Kim's already left town with his family."

Karol swallowed. "Even if Rice connects me to the deli, he can't prove I'm a Wolf. There's nothing they can do to me."

"They can make you disappear and torture you until they learn what they want."

"Right now, I'm your only source in NYPD. You need me where I am. The whole pack does."

"You could become a liability at the drop of a hat."

"You'll have to trust my instincts. I'll know when I need to go, *if* I need to go."

"Unfortunately, Rhonda's in your care. Rice's report stopped just short of branding her a Wolf. People will reach that conclusion anyway."

Rice is the problem, Karol thought. Then she dismissed the thought as quickly as it had formed. "If Rhonda runs, it will be an admission on our part."

"Either way, your new relationship with her spells trouble."

"I have to go. I'll be in touch."

"Throw this phone away."

"I will."

Karol glanced at Rhonda's door. She cared about the young woman despite her petulant attitude, which Karol understood. In the kitchen, she wiped her fingerprints from the burner phone, then put on her coat and gloves and slipped the burner into one pocket and her cell into the other.

Outside the building, she ignored the teenagers loitering near the door. One of them howled like a wolf, and the others laughed.

Mace and Norton sat in a conference room with Colleen and Rice while they waited for the footage to be produced for them.

"Why do you even want this footage?" Carl said. "Aren't you just going to deny its authenticity?"

"There's no such thing as werewolves," Mace said. "But your broadcast made other assertions regarding the Brotherhood of Torquemada. That makes it relevant to our investigation."

Carl pointed at Mace. "There was nothing in that report related to the Brotherhood that you didn't already know."

"We'll be the judge of that," Norton said.

Mace looked at Colleen. "I'm surprised at you for running that report. It was irresponsible. If people believe what they saw in that footage, it could cause a panic."

"If it was such bad reporting, why did all the other channels pick it up?" Carl's voice grew louder. "No one is shying away from the truth. It's a new day and age, courtesy of yours truly."

"I have to agree with Carl," Colleen said. "There were no edits in that footage. We checked it out thoroughly. It was valid reporting."

"When Cheryl worked here, that story never would have reached the air. I think you've lowered your standards. Do you honestly believe the men who chloroformed you and kidnapped Cheryl were chasing werewolves?"

"I don't know what to believe anymore," Colleen said. "I only know that what's on the memory card is real."

"Why were you staking out that delicatessen in the first place?" Norton said to Carl.

"I don't have to answer that. Freedom of the press. I don't have to name my sources. I *won't* name them."

"We'd like you to come downtown to answer some questions," Mace said.

"Downtown to your task force?"

"You know the address."

"I'll consider your offer in the morning. I have a lot of communications to send first."

A production assistant entered and set two DVDs on the table. "Here's the broadcast version, and here's the unedited footage."

"Thank you, Brian," Colleen said.

After Brian exited, Norton slid a pair of documents across the table. "Please sign these, and I'll note your compliance with the warrants."

Mace looked at Rice. "May I speak to you alone for a minute?"

"Two years of dodging my calls, and now you want to talk?"

"I let you into my office yesterday."

"I don't have an office yet."

"You can use mine," Colleen said.

Carl rose and held the door open for Mace. "After you, Captain."

Mace exited the conference room and entered Colleen's office. Carl followed and closed the door. They remained standing.

"What's on your mind?" Carl said.

"I won't waste your time. I just want to make sure you're cognizant of how many people were killed by the Brotherhood of Torquemada."

"So? You and your people killed them all."

"Did we? What makes you so certain?"

"Even if you didn't, terrorists love publicity."

"For the sake of argument, let's say that Gabriel and Raphael Domini are what you say they are. Do you think *they* love publicity?"

"I think you just warned me that werewolves might have something against me."

"I didn't say anything about werewolves. I only want you to be careful, okay? Seriously. I've seen too many bodies."

"If Gabriel and Raphael pose a threat to me, you'd better arrest them."

"According to your story, we have a lot more people to worry about than them. I'd hate to be the one to tell my wife if something happened to you. I'm offering you police protection."

Carl burst into laughter. "Oh, really? You mean police spies, don't you? Thanks for the offer, but I think I'll pass. Say hello to Cheryl for me. Tell her I said barred windows don't suit her."

Mace turned and left.

Karol dumped the burner phone in a Dumpster ten blocks away from the wrecking yard, then circled back to the crime scene. She saw four police cars parked around a garage and recognized the Crime Scene Unit van that Hector and Suzie drove. She parked her SUV, got out, and showed her shield to a PO near the crime scene tape. A dozen spectators stood on the sidewalk across the street, even at this hour and with nothing to see.

"Back inside the yard," the PO said.

Snow fell as Karol walked around the garage to the field bordering Pelham Bay Park. On the other side of the fence a Doberman crossed the pavement, then stopped in its tracks and turned tail. Karol had grown accustomed to strange reactions from dogs ever since she had been a child.

Flares burned on the ground at the mouth of the wrecking yard, and another PO stood watch there. Karol showed him her shield and followed more flares between rows of stacked vehicles until she reached a clearing. Hector and Suzie measured a blood spatter near a smoldering rusted barrel. On the perimeter of the scene were two POs and two DATF detectives. Snowflakes descended onto the corpses on the ground and turned red.

"Hola, Karol," Hector said. "I guess they called in the hometown home girl."

Karol entered the perimeter. "I see four vics."

"One female and three males," Hector said. "The female was just a girl, thirteen or fourteen."

"Who were they?"

Hector aimed a thumb over his shoulder at the DATF detectives. "According to these guys, they ran with Big Kwamie's gang."

Karol stared at a man whose head had almost been chewed off, his dreadlocks splayed out on the ground around it like the petals of a flower. "Jamaicans."

"Maybe our boy Gomez likes his *gonja*," Hector said.

Karol crouched at the man's side, her nostrils flaring as she sniffed around his corpse. She smelled Wolf scent, but it didn't belong to Gomez. She didn't recognize it.

"What are you doing?" Hector said to her.

"I'm trying to empathize with the vic. Maybe I can understand why the perp killed him."

Hector glanced at the moon in the cloudy sky. "Yeah? You can do that? I think we all know why Gomez killed him."

Karol rose and crossed to another corpse. This one belonged to another man with dreadlocks, but he had only half a face. His right forearm had been snapped in two and relieved of its flesh. His chest had been ripped open and his throat ripped out. A Glock lay on the ground, spattered with blood. She kneeled beside the dead man, and it took only seconds for her to recognize the scent lingering around the wounds.

Oh, my God, she thought. *Rhonda*.

TWENTY-FOUR

Carl and Colleen sat in Colleen's office after Mace and Norton had left.

"Do you want to go out for that drink now to celebrate?" Carl said.

"To celebrate or mourn my career?" Colleen said.

"Your career isn't over, darling. It's just beginning."

"Stop calling me that. It's reverse sexual harassment. I think I've made a colossal mistake."

"Learn to live with regret and bask in success."

Colleen gave him a serious look. "Why were you staking out that deli?"

"I'd rather not say yet." Carl stood. "It's part of my next big story, information to be revealed when this one dies down a little."

"Oh, God." Colleen poured herself a drink.

"I'll see you tomorrow. What time shall I come in?"

"Let's say noon. But call first, in case we've both been fired." Colleen gulped her scotch.

"I've got a contract." Carl draped his coat over one arm. He turned in the doorway. "Do I get an office?"

"No, you get Cheryl's old cubicle."

"I'll take it. I think we should do a live remote from the community center. In the daylight, of course." Carl whistled as he walked through the newsroom and kept whistling as he waited for the elevator. Then his cell phone vibrated in his pocket, and he took it out. "Hello, John," he said in a cheery voice. "What can I do for you?"

"Why haven't you returned my calls?" John Beaudoin said. "I've been trying to reach you for two hours."

The elevator door opened, and Carl boarded it. "I'm sorry, but I've been busy. What's doing?"

"I want you to rewrite your article to include your little adventure tonight. Congratulations. You've made the front page. We're running your story as is, with a transcript of your broadcast."

"Which broadcast are you referring to?"

"Do you want to play games, or do you want to make this work?"

"I love playing games, but I like working more." The elevator door opened, and he walked through the lobby.

"I'd like fifteen hundred words by noon tomorrow."

"How about three o'clock? I have an engagement in the morning, and I have to report to MMN at noon. Three will still give you plenty of time to make the afternoon edition."

"I guess I don't have any choice."

"No, you don't. And fifteen hundred words is fine, but I want fifteen hundred words every week."

"A column?"

"It's that or nothing."

"Agreed, you extortionist. With one provision: if this story of yours is proven a hoax, the deal is off. Capisce?"

"I'll expect a contract before I deliver my piece."

John hung up.

Laughing, Carl exited the building and hailed a taxi.

Mace drove uptown to the Bronx.

"Rice is a real charmer," Norton said beside him. "What did you say to him?"

"I offered him police protection, which he declined."

"You don't think he's in danger, do you?"

"From Gabriel's people? No way. But I don't know Raphael, and now Gomez is in town."

"If any of them kill him, it will only convince people he was right."

"Then we'd better keep the arrogant sleazeball alive."

Parked emergency vehicles appeared in the distance.

"Who's working this?" Norton said.

"Hector, Suzie, and Karol." He switched off the engine and got out, then showed his ID to a PO, who nodded toward the wrecking yard.

A pair of police officers carried a gurney toward them

from the field.

Mace raised one hand. "Just a minute."

The POs stopped.

Mace unzipped the body bag, allowing snowflakes to land on the features of a teenage black girl. "Jesus." He zipped the bag again.

The POs carried the gurney away.

"Let's not forget what we're dealing with," Norton said.

"I never do."

A Doberman unleashed a series of loud barks from a few feet away on the other side of the fence. Both of them flinched before resuming their trek.

"What was it like facing Janus Farel?"

Mace felt snowflakes melting on his cheeks. "It was the scariest thing I've ever done in my life."

"Worse than what we faced in Newark?"

"We faced men and women in Newark. The only Wolves there helped us."

"Until Raphael and his mini-pack showed up. I don't mind telling you that scared me. They could have torn us apart."

"Seeing them is scary; fighting them is worse. I still have nightmares about Farel. I don't ever want to fight one of those things again. It was a miracle I survived. They're strong, fast, and ferocious."

"I did see Gabriel and Karol in action."

"You can't imagine what it's like to have one of them in your face. Pray you never do."

They entered the wrecking yard.

"And yet you want to save them," Norton said.

"I owe Gabriel my life. So do you. Never forget that."

"Gabriel and Karol, yes. What about the rest of them?"

"They're benevolent."

"How can you be so sure?"

"Because Gabriel and Karol say they are."

"Have you met any others?"

"One. Gabriel's sister."

"And where does she fit on the Domini scale of benevolence?"

"She saved my life too."

"It sounds like you've been lucky."

"Maybe."

The glare of work lights brought them to the crime scene. Three bodies remained on the ground.

Hector came over to them. "It's our boy, all right. It has to be. These bodies are just like the ones from the Manhattan Werewolf case and like two of the three at Sing Sing."

"Four of them," Norton said. "All armed?"

"Nines all around," Hector said.

"Who found the bodies?" Mace said.

Karol walked over to them. "A neighbor reported gunshots coming from this area."

Mace noticed Karol appeared shaken. "Any line on the victims?"

"DATF says these are Big Kwamie's boys," Hector said. "This may have been a drug spot."

Mace frowned. Why would Gomez attack drug dealers in the Bronx?

"May I speak to you alone, Captain?" Karol said.

"Sure." Mace turned and led Karol back the way he had come. Once out of earshot of the other cops, he faced her. "What's on your mind?"

"Gomez didn't do this."

Mace raised his eyebrows.

"His scent isn't on any of those bodies. It was Wolves. As many as five of them. But Gomez wasn't one of them."

"Do you recognize any of the scents?"

Karol shook her head.

"That doesn't make any sense. Gabriel wouldn't order an attack like this. It wouldn't make sense for Raphael to, either."

"Maybe it was self-defense. Maybe they were in the wrong place at the wrong time."

"Anything else?"

Karol seemed hesitant. "It's my fault Rice got the footage. I went to that deli in his report to relay a message. Rice must have followed me from the squad room."

"We just picked up Rice's unedited footage."

Karol stiffened. "If I'm on it . . ."

"I know."

She hesitated. "Is there any chance it can disappear?"

"It's only a copy. The footage still exists."

Karol's features wilted. "Will you give me a heads-up what you find on it?"

"I'll do my best. Maybe you should consider running now."

"I can't do that."

"Can I ask why?"

"I can't tell you."

"You might want to pack your bags to be safe. Tell

Rhonda to do the same. Even if you escape this, she may not. It's just a matter of time before we have to bring her in."

"Can we go to the station now and watch that footage?"

"That's my plan. Maybe you should stay here. I'll call you. Even if you're not on it, Rice still knows you went to that deli."

"I know. But if he doesn't have proof . . ."

"I hope you paid for whatever you bought there with cash."

"I did."

"Let's get back to work."

Mace got into his SUV and waited for Norton to join him. Then he started the engine. "Karol says Gomez didn't do this. She picked up the scent of other Wolves but not his."

"That's some superpower she has."

"Maybe she's wrong."

"You weren't sure whether to tell me, were you?"

"If the bosses find out there's more than one Wolf hunting humans, they'll declare open season."

"Then we'd better leave Karol's super sense out of any reports."

Mace pulled away from the crime scene. "Do you want me to take you to your vehicle or straight to the squad room?"

Norton fastened her seat belt. "Straight to the squad room, so we can check out this footage. Our operation won't be crippled if I don't have wheels. I can ride with you, right?"

"Right," Mace said. "We're in this together."

Carrying two folded newspapers under one arm, Mace entered the reception area with Norton. The lights had been left on.

"An empty reception desk again," he said.

"That may have to change soon, with all these unplanned night shifts."

They hung their coats and entered the squad room. Landry sat in the conference room, viewing the MMN broadcast on the largest TV.

"How's it going?" Mace said.

"I've identified someone else," Landry said. He reversed the footage, played it at normal speed, then froze the image when Raphael entered with two companions. He tapped at the keyboard, superimposed a rectangle around one of the men, hit Enter, and a face filled the screen.

"Elias Michalakis," Norton said. "Minus the beard."

"Then we've confirmed he's in New York," Mace said. "Good work."

Norton set one DVD on the table. "We need to go through this one next. It's Rice's unedited footage of his stakeout. Go through every second of it with a fine-tooth comb."

"I've always wanted to do that," Landry said. He swapped out the DVDs, and the Korean deli appeared on-screen.

"See how long this section is," Mace said.

Landry fast-forwarded it. "Jesus, he was there for a long time. Why?"

"That's what we're going to find out," Mace said.

The image darkened, and the community center appeared. Landry stopped, reversed direction, and stopped again. "Forty-three minutes of deli business."

"Okay, start with that," Mace said. He opened one of the newspapers he had bought outside. "The *New York Daily News*." A grainy color screen capture of Gabriel and Raphael battling as werewolves covered the front page. The headline read, Manhattan Werewolves! He tossed the paper onto the table and opened the second tabloid. "The *Post*." Almost the identical image graced the second newspaper cover, with the headline, Werewolf City!

"It's just like old times," Landry said.

"Has Candice checked in?"

"We tracked the chain of title on the community center, but it's a nonprofit. I don't think we're going to get ahold of anyone before business hours. Right now, she and Grant are sitting on their duffs."

Mace turned to Norton. "Dig up Carl Rice's address, and tell them to go watch his building. Just so they know, I went them there to make sure he's safe, but he doesn't know it. They're not to be seen unless they want to wind up on the news."

"Check." Norton went to her desk.

Mace's phone rang. "Stay on that footage. It's important."

"Right," Landry said.

Mace wandered into his office and closed the door as

he took the call.

"I want an update," Jim said.

"Landry's going through the footage now."

"Did Rice give up any additional information?"

"No, he's playing everything close to the vest. My gut says he's sitting on something, probably to keep the story alive."

"I don't think there's any danger of this dying. What's with the DOAs in the Bronx?" Jim said.

"Four dealers who ran with Big Kwamie got themselves taken apart," Mace said.

"So Gomez is in town, right?"

Mace sat at his desk. "It appears so."

"That isn't really an answer. Were those dirtbags killed by Gomez, or do we have other Class Ls to worry about?"

Mace heard the tension in Jim's voice. "It has to be Gomez."

"Good, because I don't want to ratchet this situation to another level of crazy. What's the word on the Dominis?"

"Gabriel isn't home, and Raphael hasn't been at his residence in weeks."

"In other words, they're gone with the wind. What about the Korean deli owner?"

"We're looking as best as we can with the number of people we have."

"Jesus, this boat is sinking fast."

"We identified Elias Michalakis in Rice's footage. He's one of the two men who entered the community center with Raphael."

"Fucking A. We can tie Michalakis to the Brotherhood; we know they were looking for him. And now we can tie him to the Dominis. Put out an APB on all three of them. We can bring them in without breathing a word about werewolves."

"But if we use the footage to link Michalakis to the Dominis, we're acknowledging the footage is real."

"Goddamn it. All right, then: put out an APB on Michalakis alone, but make it known that Gabriel and Raphael are wanted for questioning. We can't tiptoe around these guys anymore."

"Right," Mace said.

"We've got a new bad guy. Hopefully we'll get all four of them."

TWENTY-FIVE

Lincoln and T-Bone remained lying down while the other teenagers dressed in their laundered clothes.

"I have bloodstains on my sweater," Diane said.

Rhonda examined the brown splotch. "That could be anything. At least you can walk around and get fresh clothes."

"My muscles hurt all over," Raina said.

"Fuck you, girl," Lincoln said, wincing.

"Your muscles hurt because you hardly ever Change," Rhonda said. "Weekend retreats and summer vacations aren't enough. I remember what it's like. Every time you Change is like the day after running a marathon." She turned to Lincoln. "You and T-Bone are healing fast. You'll heal faster the next time you Change."

"We should freaking Change *now*, then," T-Bone said.

"Suit yourself. But I wouldn't recommend it. I'd let

those bullet holes completely scar over first."

"What are we going to do about the cops?" Raina said. "We can't stay here forever."

"We can go to my pop's place in the morning," Daniel said. "He works all day. Then we can bounce back here when it's time for him to come home."

"That's only going to work for so long," Rhonda said. "Don't worry about the cops. They'll think Gomez killed those guys. We have a bigger problem. How long will it be before whoever sent those guys . . ."

"Big Kwamie," Daniel said.

". . . sends more soldiers after you?" She looked each of her fellows in the eye. "How hard do you think it will be for him to find out who was selling weed in that wrecking yard? He already knew you were there. What do you think it will take for one of your customers to rat you out? An ounce of product? A half ounce? Guys like Kwamie don't play around. They're going to come after you and your families with guns blazing."

"Our families can take care of themselves just like we did," T-Bone said.

"Maybe. But we're not indestructible. We can be killed with enough firepower. Sooner or later, they'll break out Uzis and AKs. What if they use explosives? And even if your parents take care of them, what's the risk? By morning, the whole city will know about us, and half the population will believe we exist. If your folks are forced to defend themselves, they might be discovered. Then what? Do you think the government's going to let them go about their lives? We'll all wind up in concentration camps or worse."

"What do you think we should do?" Daniel said.

"This isn't my problem. Nobody on those streets ever bought weed from me."

"What do we *do*?" Raina said.

"You have to take Kwamie out."

The teens turned to Daniel.

"Will you help us?" he said.

"Sure," Rhonda said. "What are friends for?"

Mace's phone rang, and he checked the display: Cheryl. He had meant to call her earlier but had run out of time. "Hi, babe."

"Are you coming home?"

"I plan to, maybe in a few hours."

Landry appeared at the door, and Mace beckoned him forward.

"I don't like being alone," Cheryl said.

"I know. This will all be over soon."

"I hope so."

"Go to bed. I'll be back soon."

"I love you."

"I love you too." Mace hung up and looked at Landry.

"There's nothing interesting in the first half of that footage, skipper. Just customers coming and going. Unless we want to assume they're all Class Ls."

"No one we know?"

Landry shook his head.

"Okay, then." Mace stood. "Keep working on the rest of the footage. I'm going to meet up with Karol and see if we can track down Kwamie. Head home when you're done."

"Seriously?"

"There's nothing else to do, and we have a busy morning ahead of us. Tell Candice and Grant to go home if Rice is tucked safely in bed." Mace walked into the squad room, where Norton worked at her computer. "Wrap it up, Kathy. I'm rendezvousing with Williams. Send me anything you can find on Big Kwamie in the Bronx, then go home."

Norton gave him a questioning look.

"There's nothing else the three of us can do now."

Karol watched two POs load the last of the bodies into the meat wagon. Suzie Quarrel lit a cigarette at her car nearby.

Hector came over to Karol. "We're taking these stiffs to the morgue. As soon as next of kin is notified, the FBI will send them to Quantico. This is a babysitting job for us. What about you?"

"I guess I'll go home," Karol said. She watched them get into their cars and leave. Then she walked to her SUV. Her phone rang as she got in. She checked the display. Mace.

"Williams," she said, holding her breath.

"Landry went through Rice's footage. He identified Elias Michalakis as one of the men with Raphael Domini, but there are no other leads."

Karol exhaled. "Are you sure?"

"Positive. I'm on my way to the Bronx. I figured you and I could look in on Big Kwamie."

Karol wanted to check in on Rhonda, who had not returned her calls. "That sounds good. I'm leaving this crime scene now. Why don't you pick me up at my place?"

"Will do."

She hung up, then started the SUV's engine and drove through the Bronx. Snow continued to fall. She wondered if she would have to run.

After parking her vehicle, Karol walked to her apartment building. Her wet rubber heels squeaked on the lobby floor. In the elevator, she closed her eyes. She missed Willy. The door opened, and she headed to her apartment. Inside, she knocked on Rhonda's door.

"Rhonda?"

No one answered.

"Rhonda, are you home?"

She knew the answer even before she opened the door.

Mace saw Karol standing in the lobby of her building when he pulled over to the curb. She opened the door and walked in his direction. Her gait was stiff, and she seemed dazed. He unlocked the passenger door, and she climbed in beside him.

"Congratulations," he said. "I'm happy for you."

Her eyes appeared glassy, as if she had been crying. "Thanks, but we both know I'm not out of the woods yet.

Rice followed me to the deli. It's just a matter of time before he spills his guts."

"One problem at a time," Mace said.

"What I can't figure out is why he stayed at the deli when I went back into the city. Nothing happened that could have tipped him off that the deli was a relay station for messages."

"Say the word, and I'll go see Kwamie alone. You can go underground with Rhonda."

"I can't."

"Why not?"

She hesitated. "I'm the only conduit to Gabriel right now. I have to be the eyes and ears for him and the rest of the pack."

"You mean a spy."

"I can't pretend otherwise."

"Let's go find Kwamie. The database says he owns a nightclub on Jerome Avenue."

"I know the place."

Mace selected the coordinates he had programmed into the GPS before leaving the station and drove away. "What can you tell me about Michalakis?"

"Nothing detailed. He headed a small pack in Greece until the Brotherhood took them out. We thought they'd all been killed, but Elias showed up right after the Brotherhood killed Jason Lourdes and kidnapped Rhonda. He created a rift between Gabriel and Raphael, and now he's playing on Raphael's team. Some of us believe he's pulling Raphael's strings."

"So he's the instigator," Mace said. "Can you think of any reason why Michalakis would want those dealers killed?"

Karol looked away. "None. An attack like that threatens the entire pack."

"You said as many as five Wolves were involved. That suggests organization, not a rogue berserker like Farel or Gomez. If Michalakis is pulling Raphael's strings, he may have had a reason to have those four killed. Gabriel sure didn't."

Karol said nothing.

"The feds and the brass are hot to prove the existence of Class Ls and to learn as much about them as possible. They want Gabriel and Raphael brought in, but they want them alive. We can only imagine why. Now that Michalakis is in the mix, I'm wondering if it will buy Gabriel time if we bring him in instead."

"Alive, Michalakis poses a threat to my entire species."

"That's why I want to bring him in dead. Let them cut him open and poke around all they like if it means the rest of you can get away."

"You're talking about murder."

"Laws apply to men and women, not Wolves. Will you help me find Michalakis?"

"If I stay, I'll help you find him, but I won't help you kill him."

Kwamie's Spot came into view. No one stood in line to get in.

"He named his club after himself," Mace said as he searched for a parking place. "It must not be much of a club. No one's fighting to get in."

"Why are we bothering with this?" Karol said.

Mace parked the SUV. "Everything we do has to follow protocol. Four gangbangers turn up dead. We have to show we're investigating. We can't have it seem like we're writing it off as just another werewolf attack, can we?"

They got out, crossed the street, and approached a tall, brawny black man with a shaved head. Mace attempted to move around him.

The man stuck out one arm. "Hold it."

Mace took out his ID and held it close to the man's face. "Police business. Tell Kwamie to meet us so we don't waste time looking for him."

The bouncer stepped back, and Mace and Karol entered the club. They climbed half a flight of wide stairs covered in red carpeting, then passed through one of three sets of double doors. Purple light filled Mace's eyes, and rap music assailed his ears. Couples gyrated on the dance floor, and a DJ worked in a glass booth two stories above.

"Do you want me to speak to the bartender?" Karol said above the deafening noise.

"Just wait."

Two minutes later, a tall man in a Day-Glo green zoot suit circled the floor, followed by two men in black suits. All three of them had dreadlocks. Kwamie wore sunglasses. He looked down at Mace, then lowered his shades for a better look at Karol. "What y'all want with me?" he said in a deep voice with a Jamaican accent.

Mace raised his ID.

"So? What you want? This is my place."

Mace gestured to the doors. "Can we go where there's less noise?"

Kwamie made a show of looking Karol up and down. "Be quick about it."

Mace turned his back on Kwamie and exited with Karol at his side. Once on the other side of the doors, they waited for Kwamie and his bodyguards, who looked even taller in the light.

"I'm Captain Mace, and this is Detective Williams."

"Captain from where? I never heard of no Captain Mace in the Bronx."

"We're not based in the Bronx."

"Then I think you got no jurisdiction here."

"My jurisdiction is the whole city."

Kwamie raised his eyebrows. "So? Talk."

Mace handed him a stack of photos. "Do you recognize this crew?"

Kwamie flipped through them. "Jamaican brothers, could be possible. Look around." He used the corners of the top three sheets to poke at the bottom one. "Not this one, though. We don't let no children in here."

"We were told they were your crew," Karol said.

Kwamie smiled at Karol. "Who told you a lie like that?" He put the photos together and held them out. "One of these people? It don't look to me like they talking to no one.

You know their names?"

"Not yet," Mace said. "They weren't carrying any ID, so we haven't identified the bodies. They were a hit squad. Who do you think they would want to take out in a wrecking yard? And who would send assassins out to deliver a message?"

Kwamie looked befuddled. "I don't know. There be some mean motherfuckers out there."

"Drug kingpins, you mean?"

Kwamie nodded in an exaggerated manner. "Mm-hm. Not a respectable businessman like myself." He motioned to the bar. "Why don't you two have a drink on the house?" He held out the photos for Mace to take.

"No, thanks." He nodded at the photos. "You can hang on to those. I think someone sent a message to *you*."

The mountains of Kwamie's face fell, and Mace and Karol descended the stairs to the exit.

"Hey, Captain!"

Mace and Karol turned.

"Maybe the werewolves killed those bad fellas." Kwamie burst into booming laughter.

Mace closed the SUV door and started its engine. "Charming fellow, I hope vice takes him down soon."

"Or someone else," Karol said. "Now that he's lost some of his muscle, the vultures may start circling."

Mace turned on his wipers and pulled away from the curb. "So . . . are you really sticking around?"

"For now, yes."

"Would you mind filling out the report on this house call from home?"

"Sure, why not."

Mace pulled into his driveway and killed the engine. The lights were on downstairs as well as in his own apartment. He got out carrying two coffees in a cardboard tray and a box of snacks and carried them over to the patrol car parked on the street.

The PO sitting behind the wheel lowered his window. "How's it going, Captain?"

"It's been a busy night." Mace handed the coffees and snacks to the driver, who passed them to his partner.

"Thanks. Last night of the full moon, huh?"

"Yeah. You guys stay warm. You won't take a break unless another car spells you, will you?"

"No, sir. You're covered."

"Thanks." Mace heard the car window rise as he climbed the front steps.

Sniper greeted Mace as soon as he entered the apartment, and Cheryl came out of the bedroom as he closed the door. Mace kneeled and petted the dog, then stood and kissed his wife.

"You don't have to walk him," she said. "Anna did it at eleven."

Mace glanced at his watch and shrugged. "He could stand another walk."

"Forget it. I don't know how long I have you, so you're keeping me warm."

"I'm giving myself four hours of sleep and time for a shower."

She walked him to the bedroom, and Sniper followed. "How's it going?"

He shrugged. "We're doing the best we can."

"How's Carl?"

"Blinded by success. It's pretty frightening to see."

"I saw four gangsters were killed in the Bronx. The report seemed really sketchy."

"It wasn't Gomez. No matter what you might hear on the news, nothing suggests he's in New York City."

They entered the bedroom. Patty slept in the middle of the bed, drooling.

Mace unbuttoned his shirt.

Cheryl rubbed his back. "It's good to have you home."

He slid an arm around her waist. "This will all be over soon."

"Will it?"

"Either we'll catch Gomez and Gabriel's people will get away, or I'll find myself back on Floyd Bennett Field."

Cheryl draped her arms around his neck. "Would that be so bad?"

Mace drew in a breath. "For you and me and Patty? No.

But this is bigger than us. I feel it in my bones."

"Maybe the survival of an entire species is too big a responsibility for one man."

He forced a smile. "I'm not alone."

"No, you're not." She kissed him. "Let's go into the living room."

TWENTY-SIX

Mace parked in the underground garage of the Bonaventure Hotel and entered its opulent lobby. He gave his name at the front desk, and the clerk directed him to a conference room on the second floor. A few minutes later, he joined Jim and Hollander.

"Déjà vu," he said as he closed the door. It had been only a matter of weeks since he had met with Jim, Norton, and Shelly in a similar room in the same hotel and had accepted the offer to head the task force. A copy of the *Post* lay on the table.

"Did you get any sleep?" Jim said.

"Enough." Mace took a seat.

"What have you got for us?" Hollander said.

"Minjun Kim, the owner of the deli, disappeared. So did his wife and daughter. The deli is padlocked. We're running down employees of the community center who could have unlocked that basement door. So far, we've been unable to reach one Mildred Ramirez, who worked at that community center, but it's early yet."

"Wonderful." Jim gestured at the paper. "I assume you saw this?"

"Terrence Glenzer is going to become a best-selling author posthumously. Maybe Rice will get to write a new introduction."

"The governor will refute Rice's report at nine, and the mayor will do the same at ten," Hollander said. "Their tone will be dismissive to say the least. At eleven, several people who have worked with Rice will call his judgment into doubt. These folks will make themselves available to the cable news shows throughout the day. Columnists across the country will denounce him in the afternoon editions of newspapers. By then, no one will touch him."

"So we're resorting to a smear campaign," Mace said.

"Six murders were committed between midnight and 5:00 AM by people who swear their victims were werewolves or claimed they were themselves werewolves as a defense," Jim said. "One hundred and forty calls were made to 911 by citizens who say their neighbors and coworkers are werewolves. And New York Senator Jack Prince is making noise about calling for senate hearings looking 0069nto the investigation of the Brotherhood of Torquemada."

"We're making sure Prince quiets down, or he'll suddenly find himself dealing with an investigation into his campaign finances," Hollander said.

"Craig Lindberg has his hands full," Jim said. "He'll address the press corps at noon. NYPD will brand Rice's claims sensational fearmongering and will focus on real crimes. At this time, the entire department will engage in the hunt for Gomez, and the FBI will do the same for Michalakis. Our goal is to make their faces as visible as those from Rice's video. Once Rice's sanity has been called into question, they will be the *only* faces anyone cares about."

Good luck, Mace thought. "I see one flaw with this strategy. Rice has already implicated Gomez as a werewolf, and someone else may recognize Michalakis in that footage."

"It's all in how the message is delivered," Hollander said.

Mace made a mental note to exercise extreme caution if he ever had to cross Hollander. "And if any more transformations are made public, we'll all have egg on our faces."

"We have to make sure that doesn't happen."

"Where does this leave my team?"

"We're maintaining that your focus is still on wrapping up the investigation into the Brotherhood of Torquemada," Jim said. "We've had to station two POs outside your base to keep reporters away. They've been briefed on what to say. While the department and bureau turn this city upside down looking for Gomez and Michalakis, I want you and your people to find Gabriel Domini."

"What do you want us to do then?"

"Report his location to us. We'll take care of the rest."

Mace wanted to argue that Gabriel hadn't broken any laws, but he knew that wouldn't help Gabriel or himself. "What about Raphael?"

"We'll find him when we find Michalakis," Hollander said.

"I'm still short on manpower. What about those detectives you promised me?"

"That's impossible now," Jim said. "We need to make a show of putting these detectives on the street. If we divert manpower to your task force, it will not go unnoticed. Your hunt for Domini has to be under the radar."

"How do you intend to capture our Class Ls when you find them? I fired six shots into Janus Farel at point-blank range, and it didn't even knock the wind out of him."

"So you say," Hollander said. "According to your report, Farel 'willed himself to die' after you stabbed him with that broken sword. It's more likely the bullets just took their time getting the job done. Since his body wasn't recovered, we'll never know."

"I hope you're not willing to gamble cops' lives on a theory. If you corner them with firearms, they *will* transform and cops *will* be killed."

"Glocks are more powerful than revolvers," Jim said. "We'll have tactical teams and choppers standing by with enough firepower to win Nam, plus animal tranquilizers and gas."

"I should be coordinating this."

"Thanks to Rice you're too visible now, and we don't even have any leads," Jim said. "We're playing a waiting game."

"Bring Rice in for questioning," Hollander said. "Let him see your operation is still bare bones."

Mace didn't like being used as a public relations tool.

"Do you have a problem with that?"

He shook his head. Let them think that was in response to Hollander's question.

"When this is all over, you'll still be a hero for bringing down the Brotherhood of Torquemada," Jim said. "The task force was a success. This just got too big too fast."

"Is there anything else?" Mace said.

"Yes," Hollander said. "Make sure Agents Norton and Grant are kept in the loop on everything."

"Of course." Mace stood and exited the room. As soon as he reached the elevator, he called Landry.

"I'm at the office now, boss," Landry said.

"Tell Candice and Grant to bring Rice in for questioning at 0900."

"What if he doesn't want to come in?"

"He won't refuse our invitation." Mace boarded the elevator. "The bosses want us to make capturing Gabriel our priority. They're not saying so, but they're shutting us down soon. Now that Rice has named us New York City's werewolf hunters, we're just a decoy operation."

Landry paused. "Is that so bad if they do close our doors?"

Mace thought about it. "No."

Raphael came downstairs into the living room of his Long Island safe house. Elias sat on the sofa, drinking coffee and watching the morning news. Leon and David sat in chairs doing the same. The closed curtains prevented sunlight from entering.

"Do we have breakfast?" Raphael said.

"I'll get you something," Eddie said.

Raphael sat. "Anything new?"

"The morning shows are treating Rice's story like a joke," Elias said. "This could blow up in the face of Manhattan Minute News, but it isn't going down without a fight." He switched the channel to Manhattan Minute News and raised the volume.

A middle-aged black man with wire-rimmed glasses spoke to a reporter. "I know what I saw on TV. You can call them what you want, but those were werewolves."

A young white man with horn-rimmed glasses replaced him. "Yeah, I saw it a hundred times. I've got it saved to my hard drive."

"Do you think it's real?" the female reporter said offscreen.

"I don't believe in monsters, but that looked real to me. And those two Domini guys were there. I believe everything the story said about the Brotherhood of Torquemada. It all makes sense."

A black woman in her thirties got her turn. "I saw it. I don't care what you say; there's no way that was real." She shook her head. "People around here are acting crazy. It's Christmastime, not Halloween."

Another middle-aged man spoke. "Yes, I believe it. Maybe they weren't werewolves, but they sure weren't human, and don't tell me that was just another dogfight in the Bronx. Did you see the size of them? It was scary. It isn't safe around here."

The image shifted to an Asian woman sitting at the

Manhattan Minute News desk. "And there you have it, diverse reaction this morning to our exclusive report from Carl Rice that shows *something* no one's seen before."

Elias muted the volume. "Even people on the street know your name."

"We never should have gone to that meeting," Raphael said in a tight voice.

"You're the one who insisted on seizing power according to pack rules."

"The timing was bad. Gomez's escape changed everything."

"No doubt. But last night was your only chance. If you hadn't gone, Gabriel would have dissolved the pack. Your only mistake was being so aggressive."

Raphael's voice turned even. "He was so calm, so damned agreeable. I hate when he uses logic. I wanted to make him lose control."

"Would you have killed him?"

"No. He's my brother. But I would have beaten him to within an inch of his life so no one would have doubted who deserves to lead the pack. It doesn't matter now, does it?"

"Of course not." Elias gestured at the TV. "With all this attention, New York is the last place on earth for our kind to flourish."

"They'll be leaving in droves or lying low and avoiding contact with each other."

"Do you blame them? No one ever attempted a pack this size before your father. It was grandiose but impractical."

"He had a vision," Raphael said with admiration.

"But a faulty one. Gabriel's mistake was expanding it."

Raphael exhaled. "Where will you go now?"

Elias smiled. "I'm not going anywhere. I have no place *to* go." He sat forward. "We can't have the Greater Pack of New York City because it's falling apart, but we can still have a pack. Our species still needs to survive."

Raphael's voice softened. "Who will follow me after this? I've endangered everyone."

"Will you run to Canada like the others? Or France or Italy?"

"My place is here."

"Others will stay too." He turned to Leon. "Will you still follow Raphael?"

"Sure," Leon said.

Eddie came out of the kitchen with a plate of eggs and bacon.

"How about you, Eddie? Will you follow Raphael if he asks you to?"

Eddie handed the plate to Raphael. "Raphie's my bro. Where else can I go now?"

Elias returned his gaze to Raphael. "So there are at least four of us. We'll find others, including females. We'll build our own pack."

Raphael felt skeptical. "And live happily ever after, with the government on our tail?" "That will never be the case. But we can make our people safe at least."

"How?"

"This man Mace turned out to be trouble, just like you predicted," Elias said. "It's because of him and your brother that the government is aware of us. Don't ever forget that. We need to know what the police know about us before we can do anything else."

"Karol Williams is the only Wolf on the force, and she's solid with Gabriel."

"Then we'll have to grab her."

Cheryl scooped mush into Patty's mouth. The toddler spat it out and giggled. Cheryl wanted to scold her, but she couldn't suppress her own laughter.

"Let's try that again," she said.

The landline rang, and Anna walked into the kitchen. "Do you want me to get that?"

"No. Would you mind taking over here for a minute?"

"Sure." Anna crouched before the high chair and took the spoon. "Come on, precious."

Recognizing the number on the cordless phone, Cheryl answered and went into the living room.

"Thank God you picked up," Colleen said.

Cheryl's body tensed. "Why wouldn't I?"

"I think I've made a terrible mistake. I need a friend to talk to."

"You know I'm here for you." Cheryl pulled back the curtain on the front window and glanced at the police car parked below. At least it had stopped snowing.

"I'm catching a lot of flak for running Carl's story last night."

Cheryl let the curtain fall back into place. "So why did you run it?"

"Did you see the footage?"

She had been able to think of little else. "Yes."

"It was fucking sensational. Our overnights were through the roof. How could I say no to that opportunity?"

"Other networks would have, or Carl would have gone to them."

"Touché but they all covered us."

"They're laughing at you."

"I know."

"I'm sorry if you're getting blowback on this, but you should have known better."

"It's horrible. The station owner called me last night, then again this morning. God knows what I'm going to find when I go into the office."

"Are you planning to put Carl on the air again?"

"I don't have any choice. I promised him a contract."

"Oh, Colleen . . ."

"He caught me at the perfect time. My life has been crazy too since that night, and trying to keep this ship afloat without you . . ."

Cheryl tightened her grip on the phone. "Don't blame this on me."

"Of course not. Oh, honey, I would never do that. I just feel so *helpless*. You're the only one I can turn to."

Cheryl took a breath. "How can I help?"

"Please believe that I wouldn't even ask if it wasn't important."

"Spit it out."

"It would really solidify my position and put Carl's story in a more positive light if you would consent to be interviewed for MMN."

"You've got to be kidding."

"You haven't spoken to the press about what happened that night or what those guys in the Brotherhood were like—what they wanted from you—or how Tony rescued you. That kind of human face could really—"

Cheryl hung up.

TWENTY-SEVEN

Karol awoke feeling drained of her emotions. She took a long shower and forced herself to eat a full breakfast. She would glance at the clock, then at Rhonda's bedroom door. So this was what it felt like to be a parent. First she had lost her mate, now her surrogate daughter.

She's not my daughter. She's a troubled kid I feel sorry for.

Karol picked up her phone and called Rhonda again.

"Hi, this is Rhonda. Leave a message."

Recorded before her abduction by the Brotherhood of Torquemada, Rhonda's voice sounded so innocent and carefree. Karol had listened to the outgoing message during Rhonda's absence before she had met her and decided to offer her a place to stay.

On the TV, camera flashes highlighted the features of Governor Gramm as he addressed a roomful of reporters in

Albany. "I have a statement to read, and then I'll take a few questions. Last night at approximately 10:15 PM, Manhattan Minute News ran a report that purported the existence of fantastic creatures in New York City and suggested that police and federal authorities have known about these creatures and covered up an investigation of them. The report exploited recent terrorist attacks in New York by trying to connect the activities of the Brotherhood of Torquemada to these creatures that appeared in an amateur video presented by Carl Rice. Needless to say, as any rational person would conclude, this report was a hoax. Carl Rice is not a journalist but the author of two sensational true crime books. I believe he perpetrated this hoax to generate publicity for these books and to enable him to write another one.

"Regardless of Rice's motivation, it was irresponsible and unprofessional of Manhattan Minute News to air this unbelievable fiction. The calamity caused by this TV station's failure to meet even the minimal standards of broadcast journalism has already wasted time and manpower in the New York Police Department when its members are engaged in several serious investigations. I intend to meet with the attorney general as soon as possible to discuss whether charges can be filed against both Rice and Manhattan Minute News."

"Strong stuff," Karol said. The power brokers were wasting no time dismantling Rice's story. She knew there was no chance in hell the state would prosecute MMN or Rice, but the threat of doing so would pressure MMN to cut Rice off at the knees.

A reporter asked the governor a question.

He raised one hand in a dismissive gesture. "I don't know what Carl Rice was thinking. He obviously didn't consider the panic he could cause among people who should have known better. My understanding is that the NYPD is focused on apprehending Rodrigo Gomez and the FBI is concentrating on Elias Michalakis, who may have ties to the Brotherhood of Torquemada and is believed to be at large in New York City. I can't comment on either investigation." He pointed across the room. "Next question."

Elias Michalakis had just been thrown to the wolves.

Karol finished dressing and left for work. She had considered taking the day off to look for Rhonda, but she had to put the needs of the pack ahead of those of one angry young woman. The exodus would be in full swing, and she could best help Gabriel and the council members by staying in the loop at work.

She headed toward her SUV around the corner. Had Rhonda walked this same path? There was no way for her to pick up the scent in this wind, and the frigid air caused her nostrils to flare. Although the sun had risen, a layer of frost covered her vehicle, and she used her coat sleeve to wipe it from the driver's side window.

Karol didn't notice the black van until it pulled up beside her and she saw its reflection in the glass. The side door of the van opened, and a man sprang out at her; she recognized Leon as he pressed a cloth over her mouth and nose. She tried to struggle, but she inhaled chloroform that burned her nostrils and slowed her motor functions.

"Take it easy," Eddie said.

Darkness crushed her as Eddie pushed her inside the van and she struck the cold metal floor.

Mace, Norton, and Landry worked on laptops in the conference room. The cubicles in the squad room sat empty.

"It's quiet without those phones ringing," Landry said.

"No more crackpot calls," Norton said.

Mace drummed his fingers on the table. "Michalakis left virtually no trail from his arrival in Philadelphia until now."

"He's a trained terrorist," Landry said. "They're good at that."

"Is he? Or is he a survivor of terrorist persecution? Don't forget the Brotherhood of Torquemada hunted him, not the other way around."

"Sooner or later, the people hunted by terrorists make the decision to live normal lives or become terrorists themselves," Norton said. "It's a matter of survival."

"What's the line between a terrorist and a freedom fighter, though? According to the FBI, the Brotherhood termed Michalakis's group a cell, but it was the Brotherhood who took them out with a bomb, and we've labeled the Brotherhood a terrorist group. Can it be both ways?"

"This wouldn't be the first time the US has gotten caught between two groups and had to make that distinction."

"Our guest is here," Landry said.

Candice and Grant entered the squad room with Rice,

who looked amused.

Mace glanced at his watch, then picked up a remote and powered on the TV, which showed Mayor Branson speaking at his podium in the city hall press room, with the Manhattan Minute News logo glowing in the lower right-hand corner of the screen.

"You two clear out," Mace said. "He'll speak more freely if I'm alone."

"You mean you actually expect to get something out of him?" Norton said. "I thought this was all for show."

"You never know." Mace exited the conference room, and Norton and Landry gathered their laptops and followed him. "Hail the conquering hero," Mace said to Carl. "I see you made the front pages today."

Carl grinned. "Did you see my byline in the *Post*?"

"How could I miss it? But the *Times* only mentioned you on its editorial page. Rough words."

Carl's smile tightened. "You can't please everyone." He glanced around the squad room. "Speaking of everyone, where *is* everyone? This place looks like Hitler's bunker. I thought you'd be marshaling the forces."

"I told you our assignment is to investigate the Brotherhood of Torquemada. We're not hunting Gomez or Michalakis."

"There's that name again. He sure came out of nowhere. It couldn't be that the department is trying to distract people from my story, could it?"

"I don't speak for the department; Craig Lindberg does. You can ask him when he gives his press briefing at noon."

"I plan to. Too bad I can't be at the one the mayor's giving right now."

"Oh, do you have credentials for that? Never mind." Mace gestured at the conference room. "We can watch it together in here."

"You're not my ideal date, but you'll do."

"Why don't you hang your coat up and stay awhile?"

"Thanks, but I'm still cold from the chill outside." Carl passed Mace and entered the conference room.

Mace followed and closed the door.

"I assume you get the laptop?" Carl said.

"Good guess."

Carl sat near the door. Mace sat behind his laptop, picked up the remote for the TV, and raised the volume.

"The story's ridiculous, and I won't dignify it with an answer," Mayor Branson said. "Carl Rice isn't even a real journalist, and Manhattan Minute News has damaged its reputation. The police department and the FBI are searching for two dangerous criminals right now, one of them Rodrigo Gomez, who escaped from Sing Sing Correctional Facility two nights ago, the other Elias Michalakis, who they believe has ties to the Brotherhood of Torquemada. An escaped serial killer and a possible terrorist are real monsters, and I don't want anyone panicking over the wild horror tales of a desperate tabloid writer who has run out of material."

Mace muted the volume.

Carl held his smile, but hurt lurked in his eyes. "You couldn't have timed this sit-down better. The mayor and the governor must receive the same talking points from higher-ups."

"They're crucifying you," Mace said.

"I bet you're hammering the nails."

Mace sat back in his chair. "That isn't true. I may not like your methods, and I have no love for the way you turned me into some cheap pulp hero, but I feel for you."

"Oh, really? I can't tell you how much that means to me."

"I don't want to see you get crushed like a cockroach."

"Is that what this meeting is about? You want to save me?"

"Turn off your pocket recorder."

"I'll show you mine if you show me yours first."

"We're not recording this conversation. It's just you and me, off the record."

"That's no fun." Carl took a digital recorder out of his pocket, set it on the table, and turned it off. "My recorder's on the table. Why don't you lay your cards next to it?"

"Tell me what you were doing at that Korean deli."

"That's confidential."

"Don't make me invoke national security."

"Don't make me laugh in your face."

"I need to know."

"Why?"

"I want to make sure no one gets hurt who docsn't deserve it."

"Tune in to MMN at six o'clock, and you'll get your answer."

"You can do better than that."

Carl glanced over his shoulder at the squad room.

"Where's that detective who was Diega's partner until he got killed?"

Mace's stomach tightened. "Karol Williams."

"That's the one."

Mace tried not to show any emotion. "She's a good cop."

Carl leaned forward. "Yes, but is she a good werewolf?"

Mace knew the tension showed on his face now. "She's a good woman."

"She's one of them. She has to be. I followed her from here to that deli, all the way in the Bronx, and do you know what she did? She came out of there with lunch."

"Karol lives in the Bronx. Maybe that deli's her favorite place."

"I was halfway back to Manhattan when I decided to turn around and see what was so special about that place. Do you know it didn't open this morning?"

"Maybe the owners took the day off because of bad publicity. Maybe they were afraid someone might do something crazy after your report, like shoot the place up with silver bullets."

"Or maybe they're getting the hell out of Dodge before an angry mob shows up with torches, or an NYPD and FBI task force breaks down their door with warrants."

"Maybe Williams was there on assignment."

"That would be a neat wrinkle, but according to you, her assignment was filing paperwork on what went down in Newark."

"You can't even prove she was there. She's not in your footage."

"And I bet any security camera footage taken in that deli disappeared with that nice Korean couple. My mistake. But I can offer eyewitness testimony, and I'm going to. Werewolves in the city, werewolves in the NYPD. This adds a whole new level to police corruption, one the public will find worth exposing."

"You're grasping at straws."

"I'm on a train that's picking up speed, and I'm not letting it slow down. Williams is a big piece of the puzzle, and she leads straight to . . . you. How long have you known what she is?"

Sitting straight, Mace drew in a breath. "I deny everything you just said."

"Of course you do. What choice do you have? You have to answer to the king, the queen, and the bishop. You probably think you're a knight, but you have the most limited moves on the board."

Mace stared at the table for a moment, thinking, then looked up at Carl. "What if I give you something else? Will you hold off on dragging Williams into this for forty-eight hours?"

Carl snorted. "It will have to be pretty big to top a werewolf with a gold shield."

Mace held the reporter's gaze.

"Twenty-four hours," Carl said.

"We didn't pull Elias Michalakis out of thin air. He's wanted all over Europe, and he's in your footage."

"The FBI's new favorite terrorist isn't a member of the Brotherhood of Torquemada but a member of the werewolf pack?"

"I don't believe in werewolves, remember? But he's on your footage."

"Where?"

"Find him yourself. Then you can say you found him all on your own."

Carl grinned. "Not bad."

"It's better than not bad. Everyone's trying to discredit you, but the man they're using to distract people only supports your case."

"Twenty-four hours," Carl said.

TWENTY-EIGHT

Mace led Carl out of the conference room. "Candice, you and Grant take Mr. Rice home. It's not like we have patrol cars available to us."

"That's okay. I'll get home on my own," Carl said. "I missed breakfast, and I want to pick up extra copies of the *Post*. Vanity is my deadly sin." He winked at Norton and left.

"Don't let him out of your sight," Mace said to Candice. "One of you follow him on foot, the other by car."

"You drive," Candice said to Grant. "You stick out like a sore thumb with that stiff walk of yours."

"What do you mean?" Grant said as he followed her out.

Landry and Norton came over to Mace.

"Well?" Norton said.

"He gave me nothing," Mace said.

"Does he believe we're just doing follow-up work on the Torquemadans?"

"Not a chance." Mace went into his office and called Karol. She needed every minute she had to run.

Her phone rang, and then an outgoing message came on. "Hi, this is Detective Williams. I can't take your call right now, so please leave a message."

"Karol, this is Mace. Call me back right away. It's important." He hung up.

Come on, goddamn it.

Karol's stomach somersaulted, and she groaned. The smell of grease and gasoline filled her nostrils, and she shivered.

"Wake up, Karol."

Where the hell am I? She remembered going to her SUV and then . . .

She opened her eyes. Raphael loomed over her, a high gray ceiling above him. She sat up on a sofa with bad springs, and her head swam. Dull sunlight shone through glass block windows in a mechanic's garage stripped bare of tools but cluttered with garbage. Leon stood by the entrance, Eddie by the exit. Elias Michalakis lurked behind Raphael.

"Where are we?" Karol said.

"We're still in the Bronx but on the other side of town."

She looked up at a skylight covered with grime. "What the hell do you want?"

"Just to talk."

"You could have called. You didn't have to kidnap me."

"You wouldn't have listened."

"Nobody snatches a cop in broad daylight."

"So arrest us." Raphael slid his hands into his pockets. "Nobody's going to hurt you."

Karol snorted. "You got that right."

Elias moved beside Raphael. "Don't overestimate yourself. There are four of us."

Karol sat back into the sofa. "Don't pull this good cop, bad cop routine on me. I've played both roles too many times, and I'm running out of patience."

"We want information," Raphael said. "You're the only person who knows what's really going on with the authorities."

"Why should I tell you anything?"

"Because we're Wolves like you."

"I share that information with Gabriel. If you want to be in the loop, ask him. I'm doing what I do for the good of the pack, and the last time I checked, you tore up your membership card."

"We're all at risk now. We need to know what's happening."

"What's happening is that any of our people who can be tied to you, Gabriel, the Wilsons or the Lourdeses, and everyone who was in that meeting hall last night is heading for the hills because of your impulsive stupidity."

Raphael's voice remained soft. "What's done is done. Some of us plan to remain in the city with the majority of the pack."

"Why, so you can lead it? You're not ready for that, and if you stay, you jeopardize everyone else. You need a reality check, and you need to get away from people who only tell you what you want to hear." She stood. "You'll never be the leader your father was, and you'll never be the leader your brother is. You'll never lead anyone besides this motley outfit of yours."

"Who are you calling motley?" Leon said. "I hear you dogged a human. I call that sleeping with the enemy."

Karol moved closer to Raphael. "Congratulations, you're the cock of the walk. This is some pack you've made for yourself."

Raphael's features tightened. For a moment, Karol thought he intended to Change.

"If you want to leave this room, tell us what you know," he said in an even tone.

"Or what? You'll beat it out of me?"

"Don't doubt it," Elias said.

Raphael raised a hand to silence him, but his gaze stayed on Karol. "You don't have time to waste here, and neither do we. You know it isn't possible for me or Elias to go to Gabriel because we're wanted just like he is."

"How do you know your flunkies weren't seen abducting me? How do you know someone didn't see their license plate or cameras didn't track you? My other people could be heading here right now."

"All the more reason for you to cooperate. We have as much right to know what's coming as the rest of the pack does. It's to our mutual advantage that you tell us what you know."

Karol exhaled. Raphael was right. "The feds and the police are working together here in the city. I'm sure the FBI has its own operation running in addition to the task force I'm serving. The local government may be giving Rice's story the brush-off but only to deflect attention while they try to capture you two, Gabriel, and Gomez. They want you alive, which says it all. We've been compiling a list of names by tracking the friends, families, and associates of the Wolves who have already been killed. A lot of our people are on it. I've been feeding those names to Gabriel. Except for you guys and Gabriel, everyone else in that video has left the country or is doing so now."

She looked at Elias. "The FBI has an informant for the Brotherhood, and his information has allowed them to track your movements and connect a lot of the dots in the laptop we recovered in Newark. Your picture is going up in every airport, train station, and bus depot in the country, so your days are numbered."

"We'll see about that," Elias said. "I've eluded authorities all over Europe. It's my specialty."

Karol turned back to Raphael. "Thanks to Rice, everything is going to spiral exponentially. It's just a matter of time before the FBI, CIA, and Homeland Security take over this whole situation and the task force is shut down. Then I'll be out of the loop."

"Can you get us files?" Elias said. "Copies of files? E-mails and memoranda with the names of high-level officials calling the shots?"

"No way. I won't even do that for Gabriel. The minute

anyone but Mace suspects I'm working both sides, I'm finished."

"There's the female FBI agent too," Elias said.

"So far, they've both got my back."

"We should have killed her along with Mace and his wife when we had the chance," Elias said to Raphael.

"That kind of talk will get you nowhere. If you go after any of them, I'll come after you, and I won't be using chloroform. We're done here." Karol moved around the two men and walked toward the entrance. Then she stopped and turned. "Where's my phone?"

"We broke its memory card and threw it away," Raphael said. "We didn't want it used to track you if we had to keep you here longer."

Karol rolled her eyes. Now Rhonda couldn't reach her. "Whatever you're thinking of doing, forget it. Just get the hell out of here while you can, if it's not already too late." She resumed her walk to the door.

"Man fucker," Leon said as he got out of her way.

Karol opened the door and stepped outside into the bright sunlight.

Waiting for his breakfast to be served, Carl took out his cell phone at the booth in the diner and checked his messages. He sipped his coffee, then called Colleen.

"Where have you been all morning?" Colleen said in a flustered tone.

"A pair of the city's Gestapo agents took me downtown for questioning," Carl said.

"Without a lawyer?"

"Do you know how expensive lawyers are?"

"The station could have provided you with one. Where did they take you?"

"I was sitting in the heart of werewolf central, and it wasn't much. Me and Mace watched the mayor's press conference."

"He didn't do either of us any favors."

"Are you feeling the heat?"

"I'm getting third-degree burns. I need to see your copy and have it approved by the station board members before you go on the air."

"Sure, sure, no problem. But I want to do a remote from that community center."

"Taped, not live."

"Whatever makes it easier for you."

"And that's conditional upon your copy getting a green light."

"Oh, I'm not worried about that."

"What have you got up your sleeve?"

"I've got information on the new star of the FBI's most wanted list."

"Michalakis?"

"Maybe."

"Tell me more."

"Not just yet. But if what I have pans out, it will not only match last night's victory—it will remove your bottom from that hot seat it's on."

"I really hope you're right. If I lose my job over this, I'll never work again."

"I should go on at four thirty, not six. That way all the big boys will have no choice but to cover our coverage at five and six."

"You'd better be right."

The server set his breakfast on the table.

"Ciao." He hung up and smiled at the server. "Thank you."

The young woman stared at him. "Are you that reporter who was all over TV last night?"

"I certainly am."

She lowered her voice. "Oh, my God, can I have your autograph?"

Carl experienced a moment of holiday cheer. No one had ever asked him for his autograph before. "Of course you can."

The server tore a page from her order pad and handed it to him along with her pen. "Could you date it too? I want to show that you did this the day after that broadcast."

"Whatever you like. What's your name?"

"Melanie."

Carl wrote, *For Melanie, the prettiest waitress on the West Side* on the back of the page, then signed and dated it and handed it back with the pen. "Have a nice day."

"Thanks. You too." Melanie walked away.

Carl forked polish sausage into his mouth, then made a second call.

"It took you long enough to get back to me," Kerry

Jones, his editor at Winchester Publishing, said.

"I'm pretty busy these days, sweetheart."

"I can just imagine. You looked great on TV last night. I didn't know you had it in you."

"I'm a late bloomer."

"Can we talk business?"

Carl shoveled more sausage into his mouth. "Always. What do you have in mind?"

"Clearly, a third book is in order, covering the Brotherhood of Torquemada, Rodrigo Gomez's escape, and however you got that story last night."

"Clearly. And there's more to come, so keep watching the skies."

"How soon can you deliver a manuscript?"

"If you're expecting it in six weeks, forget it. And if you're expecting me to sell my soul for a ten-thousand-dollar advance, forget that too."

"You sold your soul a long time ago. What do you want?"

"Six figures, all of it up front, 25 percent royalties, and I want a hardcover deal."

"Sixty thousand, half up front, and we're not in the hardcover business when it comes to our true crime line."

"It's time to get in the Carl Rice business, or I'll shop this story elsewhere. Something tells me I won't have to go far, and I expect my phone to start ringing any minute."

"Don't hold a gun to an old friend's head."

"I haven't forgotten how you treated me over the Manhattan Werewolf book."

"You didn't have an ending."

"Well, I do now. Do we have a deal or not?"

"I'll e-mail you a contract by the end of the day."

"Don't keep me waiting too long. We haven't shaken hands yet." Carl hung up and focused on his breakfast. Everything had turned around for him.

Candice opened the passenger door to Grant's SUV and climbed into the front seat.

"What are you doing?" Grant said. "This wasn't the plan."

"It's cold outside. Besides, Carl's eating in a diner two blocks from his apartment. He's obviously going there when he's finished."

Grant frowned. "You're not very disciplined."

"Discipline is something I do to my kids."

"Maybe you're not cut out for police work."

"Says who? *You?*" She sucked her teeth. "Please. I've been a police since before you went to prep school. I know a lot more about it than you do, and I walk the same way in my street clothes that I do in my PO clothes."

"I'm sure they're one and the same."

"You're lucky I don't ground you."

Grant smiled. "All right." He straightened in his seat. "There's our subject now."

Carl emerged from the diner and lit a cigarette.

"He's a human being, even if he is on the sleazy side."

Carl stopped at a newsstand, and with his cigarette clenched between his teeth, he gathered a stack of newspapers one foot thick.

"I'm surprised he didn't take every copy," Grant said.

After Carl paid for the newspapers, he started to walk away. Then he stopped and turned in the direction of the SUV.

"He made us," Candice said.

Carl leaned forward, as if peering into a cage at a zoo, raised one hand, and waved.

"Damn, damn, damn," Grant said.

Grinning, Carl proceeded toward his apartment building.

"Those are strong words for you," Candice said. "It doesn't matter. Our assignment's still the same, to make sure that sorry son of a bitch stays among the living."

Grant shifted the SUV into gear and merged into traffic. He followed Rice at a distance. Rice tossed his cigarette butt away and entered his building.

"Now what?" Grant said.

"Find a place to park. It doesn't matter if he sees us. He can't send us home."

Carl whistled as he walked through the corridor to his apartment. If he hadn't been lugging the stack of newspapers, he might have danced a jig. It was a glorious day: after years of scrounging around in the muck, he had secured a television gig, a newspaper column, and a book deal all in the span of twenty-four hours. His mother would have been proud of him if she was still alive. His father was alive and wouldn't give a damn.

Holding the newspapers at shoulder level, he used his free hand to take out his keys and unlock his door. Carl stepped on the mat, kicked off his shoes, and entered the dining area. He dropped the newspapers on the table, peeled off his scarf and then his coat, which he draped over a wicker chair.

As he made his way toward his computer, he rubbed his arms. His apartment almost never got so chilly. He moved to a window and opened the blinds, allowing sunlight in.

"Hello, Carl."

Carl jumped so high the floor shook when he landed. "Jesus!"

Pivoting on one heel, he saw a figure detach itself from the shadowy mini-kitchen.

"Where have you been all morning?" the man said.

It took a moment for Carl to recognize Rodrigo Gomez.

TWENTY NINE

Carl froze. "You're naked."

"You noticed," Gomez said. "Very observant. No wonder you're a reporter."

Carl swallowed a lump of fear. "There are two cops downstairs protecting me."

Gomez moved closer and stood toe to toe with him. "They won't do you any good down there."

Carl felt himself shaking. "Please . . ."

"Please what? Please don't kill you?"

With tears forming in his eyes, Carl nodded.

"You must own a voice-activated recorder, right?"

Carl sniffed. "Yes."

"Where is it?"

"In my coat pocket," Carl said, gesturing at the table.

Gomez leaned so close Carl smelled his breath. "Don't

go anywhere."

The Full Moon Killer walked barefoot to the table and searched Carl's coat pockets. He took out the small recorder and switched it on, then set it on the table next to the stack of newspapers. He picked up a copy and caressed it.

"Very impressive," he said. "I read the online edition on your computer. Who knew all that about the Brotherhood of Torquemada? Just Terrence Glenzer, I guess. Anyway, congratulations on your newfound success. You've really made the big time."

"What do you want?" Carl said, stammering.

"I want the same thing you do." Gomez raised his arms like Christ on the cross. "I want to be famous. Or infamous."

"You already are."

Gomez crossed the room and clasped Carl's shoulder. "Thanks to you. You really made my name with your first book."

Sweat dripped into Carl's eyes, stinging them. "I tried to paint an accurate picture—"

"You made me look like a goddamned psycho," Gomez said in a raised voice that caused Carl to squeeze his eyes shut and look away. "That's a term applied to humans, and I'm not human. I'm *super*human."

"I can see that," Carl said.

Gomez grunted. "You see nothing." He paused. "But you will."

"What do you want, money? I don't have any right now, but soon . . ."

"I'm a Wolf, but you're a jackal—a hyena. You pick at the bones of the weak and the dead, and you feast on their carrion. You make me sick with your weakness."

Carl's bladder betrayed him, and hot urine ran down his thighs.

Gomez stared at the stain spreading in the crotch of his prey's pants. "I was in your second book too, wasn't I? Only there was no new material about me. You just regurgitated the same information. Tony Mace captured the Full Moon Killer. Tony Mace gave riveting testimony at Gomez's trial. Tony Mace visited Gomez in Sing Sing at the height of the Manhattan Werewolf's murder spree."

Carl's gaze darted from side to side. Was Gomez jealous that he wasn't featured in *The Wolf Is Loose: The True Story of the Manhattan Werewolf*? "The second book was about the Manhattan Werewolf. Mace was in charge of the investigation."

"I killed three men when I escaped from prison," Gomez snarled. "I killed three more people for the hell of it and an old lady yesterday. What did I get for my trouble? One stinking day of front-page coverage."

"I'm not an editor. I have nothing to do with what goes on the front page."

"You bumped me the next day with that story on Gabriel and Raphael Domini."

"I'm sorry!" Carl swallowed. "I'm sorry. But you're still in the news."

"I'm front-page material."

"I just made a deal today to write a third book. You'll

be prominently featured, I swear. It will tie the other two together and—"

"You didn't even cover my escape. Do you expect me to believe you'll give it the same attention as you will that video you shot of those guys turning into werewolves? A picture is worth a thousand words. A moving picture is worth a fucking book."

"Just tell me what you want me to do, how to make it better."

Gomez's smile stretched so wide that Carl expected the corners of the man's mouth to tear and spill blood. He pointed at the computer in the far corner. "Fetch your camera."

Carl didn't want to go to the computer. He wanted to go closer to the front door in the opposite direction. It seemed to take forever to reach the desk. For the first time in his life he wished he owned a gun. He picked up the camera. Turning, he faced Gomez.

"Turn it on," Gomez said.

Carl switched the camera on and opened its flip screen. The camera focused on Gomez's nude body and shook in Carl's hand. "I'm recording."

"Go up and down my body," Gomez said.

Carl started at Gomez's feet and tilted to his head.

"Now do a close-up."

Carl fumbled for a button, and the camera zoomed in on Gomez's face. He went back down to his feet, doing his best to ignore the man's dangling penis.

"Now, go wide, so you can see as much of my body as possible."

Carl reversed the zoom. "Got it."

"How much of me can you see?"

"From your knees to the top of your head."

Gomez held one hand a foot above his head. "Do I have head room?"

"No."

"I need head room. Give me about a foot."

Swallowing, Carl adjusted the frame to give Gomez the requested space above his head. "Okay, got it."

Gomez held up one finger. "Am I in focus?"

"Yes."

"Okay, now, watch carefully." Gomez drew in a breath and clenched his fists. The irises in his eyes expanded until there was no white in them. His body trembled for an instant, then his feet grew longer, forming leg extensions that made him stand a foot taller; claws burst out of his toes and fingers; a canine muzzle emerged from his face; his ears grew pointy; and a coat of black fur spread over his muscles. The entire process lasted only seconds.

Flinching, Carl dropped the camera. As terrifying as Gomez had looked on the camera's flip screen, he looked even worse standing ten feet away and seven feet tall, a ferocious beast with jutting fangs, a pointed snout, and saliva dripping from his curled lips.

The monster bounded forward, and Carl pivoted on one heel. He was willing to dive through the window and take his chances on the fall rather than face Gomez's wrath. He took but a single step before long claws seized the back of his shirt collar. A moment later he flew through the air and crashed into the table on the other side of the room. The table tipped over, and he slid to the floor with a pained cry.

Then Gomez charged forward on all fours, and Carl released a scream before fangs and claws tore into his flesh and black fur filled his vision.

Norton stood at Mace's desk, showing him a printout of names. "We can't find Minjun Kim, the owner of that Korea deli, anywhere. He's vanished. So have his wife and daughter. Also, we've been unable to locate Mildred Ramirez who worked at the community center."

Mace gave her a solemn look. "I guess you'd better add their names to the list."

"I already have. I've also notified Missing Persons to relay any new cases that come their way."

"Right." He felt more than ready to ditch the charade.

"Tony!" Landry raced into the office, his eyes wide. "Get Channel 2 News on now!"

Mace switched the channel from Manhattan Minute News to Channel 2 and raised the volume.

An ashen-faced newswoman sat at the anchor desk. "We're waiting for confirmation from police regarding the authenticity of this video footage."

"Go to YouTube," Landry said.

Mace keyed the name of the website into his browser. "What the hell's going on?"

"Gomez just killed Rice."

"*What?* Holy hell!"

Norton seized the remote and changed the channel back to Manhattan Minute News, where a weather forecast continued. "If that's true, MMN has been scooped on its own story."

Mace typed in *Carl Rice*, and a page full of news clips appeared. His phone rang.

Landry pointed at a clip. "That one. Rice's own You-Tube channel."

Mace clicked on the link and answered the phone.

"What the hell is going on now?" Jim said.

"I'm trying to find out," Mace said.

On his computer screen, video footage of Gomez standing naked and talking to the camera appeared beneath the words Piggy Squeals.

"There it is," Norton said.

On MMN, Sandra Piazza, one of Cheryl's former colleagues, appeared distraught. "We've just received an unconfirmed report that Manhattan Minute News's own Carl Rice has been killed."

On the computer, Gomez continued to talk.

"Why the hell are we learning this on YouTube?" Jim said.

"This footage just premiered on YouTube and another network," Sandra said. The YouTube footage replaced her, with Gomez's penis blurred.

"I don't even know what we're looking at yet," Mace said to Jim. But he had a bad feeling that his suspicions were correct.

On YouTube, Gomez transformed into a Wolf in one continuous handheld shot, and Rice dropped the camera.

"Radio Candice and Grant," Mace said to Landry.

On the TV, Gomez turned into a werewolf in living color.

"Jesus Christ," Norton said.

On YouTube, the camera lay on the floor, aimed at the leg of a sofa, which went in and out of focus. A crash reverberated over Mace's speakers, followed by screams and wild animal snarls. The screams stopped, and the tearing began.

"Oh, Lord," Mace said.

The camera lost focus as someone picked it up and swung it around the apartment. A wide shot revealed a red wall, red furniture, and a red lump on the floor.

"Is that him?" Norton said.

On the TV, Rice started screaming again.

"I need to know exactly what's going on," Jim said.

"I'll let you know when I know," Mace said and hung up.

Telephones rang all over the squad room, and clerks answered them.

"Let's go," Mace said to Norton. "Do your best, Ken. Try to get ahold of Karol and tell her she's got to call me."

Mace and Norton ran out of the squad room.

THIRTY

Candice and Grant ran into the foyer of Carl's building. Candice tried the inside door while Grant pushed buzzer door buttons. Candice held her Glock by the barrel and used it to smash a pane of glass in the door. She reached through the new space and opened the door. They sprinted inside.

"What floor is it?" Grant said.

"Four."

They ran up the stairs. By the time they reached the fourth floor, Candice felt winded. When they found Carl's door, Candice put on a pair of latex gloves. Then she drew her Glock, and Grant did the same. They looked at each other and nodded.

Candice tried the doorknob, which turned. She threw the door open and entered, holding her gun in both hands.

"Police," she said.

Silence greeted them.

Candice moved along a dingy hallway to the living area. Turning left, she gasped. Blood spatters decorated the walls. Flesh and blood dripped from a table knocked on its side, and a shape lay on the floor beside it. It took a moment for her to realize it was a human body that lacked a head or arms. One arm lay on the sofa, its fingers frozen in a claw.

Watching her step, she made her way toward the bedroom door. Halfway there, she spotted Carl's head, its eyes and mouth open, resting upright on the computer keyboard. So much blood covered the face that it did not look real.

Candice opened the bedroom door and swept the small room with her gun. When she stepped out of the bedroom, she faced the wall. A circle, almost a foot and a half wide, had been painted on it in blood. "Check the bathroom," she said.

Grant kicked the bathroom door open and went inside. A moment later, he reappeared.

"The roof," she said.

They rushed out of the apartment and up the final flight of stairs to the rooftop exit. Candice pushed the panic bar, and the door swung open. Skyscrapers and clouds filled her vision.

A low barrier separated the roof from that of the building next door. She hurried over to it, stepped onto the next roof, and ran across it with Grant at her heels. A chasm three feet wide separated the roof from the next one. She took the jump, and the toe of her right foot caught on a cable. Fearing she would plummet five stories to her death, she pointed her toes and brought her heel to her buttocks, freeing her foot. She landed on the roof, and pain shot through her ankle. She then limped over to the edge and gazed at the next roof, fifteen feet below.

"He got away," Grant said.

Mace sped uptown on Broadway, his siren wailing and lights flashing. His phone rang in its docking bay, and he saw the task force's phone number. "Put it on speaker."

Norton picked up the phone, set it on speaker, and put it back.

"Go ahead, Ken," Mace said.

"Rice is DOA. From Candice's description, it had to have been Gomez."

"We'll be there in ten minutes."

"That video's gone viral. The local stations interrupted Lindberg's televised briefing to show it. This is escalating fast."

A beep came over the speaker.

"I have to go, Ken."

Norton picked up the phone, pressed its screen, and set the phone down again.

"This is Mace."

"It's Colleen. Is it true?"

"I have no comment at this time," he said in a flat voice.

"Please, Tony." Her voice cracked. "I need to know."

"I'm sorry." He nodded to Norton, who hung up.

The phone rang again.

"It's Mint," Norton said.

Mace snatched the phone from its bay. "What is it?"

"When I call, you answer."

"I'm driving to the crime scene at fifty miles an hour. Do you want me to hit a pedestrian because I'm talking to you at the same time? I'll call you when I have something to report." He set the phone down.

Norton's phone rang. "My turn," she said.

When they arrived ten minutes later, two patrol cars had arrived on scene, and a third was double-parking. Mace had to park halfway down the block, and they hurried to the building.

"No press," Mace said to the PO stationed outside. "No one enters who doesn't have a key."

"Yes, sir."

They entered the building and took the stairs two at a time.

"Containment at this point is unrealistic," Norton said. "I wonder how Lindberg's press briefing went."

Mace didn't answer her. On the fourth floor they slowed down and caught their breath as they walked to the apartment guarded by a PO. They put on rubber shoe covers and latex gloves in silence, then entered and followed a long hallway to where Grant shot photos of Carl's head in the far corner and Candice shot photos of the wall to Mace's left.

"Watch your step," Candice said.

Mace stared at the remains of Carl's corpse. All the blood made it hard to tell where the shredded clothing ended and the shredded flesh began. He stood beside Candice and looked at the circle painted in blood on the wall.

"It's like the Manhattan Werewolf all over again," Candice said. "What do you think it means?"

"It's the moon," Mace said. "He's signing his work."

Norton crossed the room. "How long was Rice up here before Landry called you?"

"An hour, tops," Grant said.

Norton stared at Carl's head. She reached down and tapped the mouse next to the keyboard, and the monitor's screen lit up. Norton leaned over the head to get a better look at the screen. "This is the home page for Rice's YouTube channel. The footage was uploaded almost an hour ago. Only his subscribers could see it at first. It's been downloaded sixty-four times, and now it's public." She scrolled down the page. "He previously uploaded the footage from the community center, but that's set to private."

Mace stepped around the bloodshed to join her. A camera lay on the floor, an arm on the sofa. "Carl must have been logged in. All Gomez had to do was insert the memory card, wait for the video to load, and set it to public."

"He went upstairs to the roof and escaped that way," Candice said. "Maybe he got dressed while he waited for the video to load."

"He didn't have to wait long," Norton said. "This is a Mac Pro."

Mace's phone rang. *Jesus, Jim, let me do my job.* "Hello?"

"Oh, my God, is it true?" Cheryl said.

Mace crossed the room to the hallway. "I can't say

anything right now. Everything will be okay."

"I want you home."

"I can't do that, but I'll make sure a second car is sent over to watch you. I don't want you to worry."

"If you don't come home, you'd better kill him. Do you understand? *Kill him.*"

Jim walked through the door.

"I'll talk to you later," Mace said.

"Well?" Jim said.

Mace gestured inside the apartment. "Come see for yourself."

Jim stared at him for a moment, then entered the living area, where Candice, Norton, and Grant stood.

"Jesus H," Jim said in a weak voice. "How could you let this happen?"

Mace grabbed him by the back of his arm and turned him away from the living area. "What do you mean? You've had us working three different major cases with a skeleton crew, on top of the one everyone thinks we're working on. We're undermanned and overworked so you and Hollander can play things close to the vest. We're so busy crisis managing the media we don't have time to be real cops. I had Grant and Candice bring Rice in for questioning at 10:00 AM like you wanted. During that time, no one was available to watch the building because they had to see where he went when he left our squad room."

"You had him in your office three hours before he was killed? This is going to be a nightmare."

"What kind of a nightmare? A public relations

nightmare? Rice is dead. He's out of the picture, right?"

Jim ran a hand over his face. "No one's going to buy any spoon-fed cover stories. This is never going away."

"Maybe it's time we stopped trying to cover this up and acted like cops. Forget about the Dominis. Forget about Michalakis. The only one who matters right now is Gomez, and we have to catch or kill him. Be clear: no one on this task force is going to pay for the bad decisions you and Hollander and whoever else have made so far. If this comes down on anyone, it comes down on you."

Jim turned away. "I have to call Hollander."

Hector and Suzie appeared in the doorway. They allowed Jim to exit, then entered.

Mace called Landry. "I need another car parked outside my house and increased patrols around the block. Make sure uniform in Bay Ridge has his shotgun ready."

"You got it," Landry said. "The phones are ringing off the hook."

"Did you get ahold of Karol?"

"Negative."

Maybe Karol had already made a run for it, Mace reasoned.

"Jesus Christ," Hector said, looking at the gore in the apartment. "It's déjà voodoo all over again."

THIRTY-ONE

In the kitchen of her Canadian cabin, Angela Domini washed dishes by hand and toweled them dry. Gareth and Damien, Gabriel's twins, played with a handheld video game in the open living room. She loved her six-year-old nephews and had enjoyed spending time with them in close quarters despite the circumstances.

Melissa, their mother, joined her at the sink. "Let me do that."

"Don't worry about it," Angela said. "You and the boys are my guests."

"You've already done enough for us. Besides, it will take my mind off things."

Angela doubted that, but she smiled. "All right."

Melissa took over the chore, and Angela was about to check on the boys when the front door opened and Arick entered.

"They're here," Arick said.

Angela grabbed her coat and hurried to the front door.

"They're here!" Damien said to Gareth.

"So?" Gareth said. "Keep playing."

Standing on the front porch in the chilly air, Angela watched a compact car and an SUV growing closer.

"There can't be many of them," Melissa said behind her.

The vehicles parked near the cabin. The door on the driver's side of the SUV opened, and Micah jumped out. Arick ran over to him and gave him a hug. The other doors of both vehicles opened, and passengers climbed out and stretched. Angela recognized Minjun Kim and his wife, and she assumed the young Asian woman with them was their daughter. Angela hadn't seen her in five years, and it surprised her how much she had grown. All of them wore grim expressions. Angela knew it wasn't easy to give up a lifetime of connections and memories and move away.

Cecilia Perez got out of the car. So did her husband and son, who looked two years older than Gareth and Damien. Another Hispanic woman got out too. In her midthirties, she wore glasses and had long curly black hair.

Melissa greeted each of the newcomers. She had a way with people, which made her a perfect wife for Gabriel.

Micah came over to the porch. "Thanks for taking us in, Angie."

"I didn't have much choice, did I? You're welcome. Did you have any trouble at the border?"

"No, we came when Ricardo was on duty, just like Gabriel said. I had his cell number, so we just coasted through using our fake passports."

"How is Gabriel?"

Micah shrugged. "Worried."

"And Raphael?"

"Trouble through and through. Elias Michalakis has his hooks deep into him."

"Raphael isn't weak-minded; he's just impulsive. He would never be anyone's puppet. He and Michalakis must have more in common than you think." Angela raised her voice. "Come inside, everyone. Melissa and I have cooked you a big lunch. Then Arick will take you to your cabins, and you can get settled in."

The refugees filed onto the porch, nodding and smiling at Angela.

"I'm Millie," the Dominican said to Angela, then hugged her. "Thank you."

Not long ago, they had all treated her like a pariah. Angela had been excommunicated from the pack for having sexual relations with John Stalk. "You're welcome," she said.

The refugees went inside, and Micah waited on the porch.

"How many more are coming?" Angela said.

"Fifteen," Micah said.

"That makes twenty-three, plus the five of us already here. There are six cabins. We'll manage for now. When will Gabriel arrive?"

"I don't know. He's got to make sure every loose thread is tied, and that's a tall order with everything that's happening."

Angela knew that Gabriel would not leave the United States without Raphael. At least, she hoped that was the case.

In his Williamsburg, Brooklyn, safe house, Gabriel sat on the sofa watching the news. The doorbell rang, and he cast a suspicious glance in the door's direction. Then he got up and crossed the room and peered through the peephole. Karol Williams stood outside. Wrinkling his brows, he opened the door and let her inside. "What are you doing here?"

"Don't worry. I wasn't followed."

He closed and locked the door. "How do you know?"

"Because I was lost to begin with. Nobody knew where I was except for your brother and his goon squad. They snatched me off the street."

"Are you all right?"

"I'm fine. They didn't hurt me, but they drugged me. I still feel terrible."

"What did they want?"

"They wanted to make me talk. And I did. There didn't seem to be any point in keeping our plans from them."

Gabriel led her into the living room. "Did you see the news about Rice?"

Karol froze in the threshold. "No, Raphael threw my phone away. I'm completely in the dark."

"Gomez killed him in his apartment. He made Rice videotape him transforming, then he uploaded the footage to YouTube. All the stations have played it."

"Shit." Karol took off her shoes and crossed the polished wooden floor in her stocking feet. She sat next to

Gabriel on the sofa.

"It's out there now. Everyone knows about us."

She touched his shoulder. "I'm sorry."

"This is the danger when a berserker is on the prowl. They're like rabid dogs, striking out with no regard for the pack or species."

Karol looked around. "Where is everyone?"

"Gone." Gabriel sat back and crossed his legs. "George and Bennett left for Canada with their families. Micah should be there now. The council members are all on the road. Everyone who was in that meeting has been sent away to start a new life."

"Then why the hell haven't you gone too?"

He looked her in the eye. "Why haven't you?"

"Rhonda's missing. I have to find her."

"The drug dealers killed in the Bronx?"

She nodded.

"Why didn't you tell me?"

"You had enough on your plate already, and I thought it was better for everyone if Gomez took the fall for them. But you've got nothing left to stay here for. Your family's already with your sister. You belong with them."

Gabriel raised one finger. "Not my entire family."

"Forget about Raphael. There's no reasoning with him. He's not worth the trouble."

A faint smile formed on Gabriel's lips. "He's my brother. I have to try. But he's not my primary concern right now." He stood. "Come with me."

Gabriel led her upstairs into an office, where he

crouched and dialed the combination on a safe in one corner. He swung the heavy safe door open, revealing stacks of money.

"How much is that?" Karol said.

"Just under four million dollars," Gabriel said. "Our investments, our retirement money. I've been liquidating it over the last few weeks. I've given each of our people who fled forty thousand dollars. It isn't a fortune, but it's enough to start over, and many of the refugees won't stay in Canada, which is probably a good thing."

"Why show me?"

He handed her a banded stack of cash. "I want you to have your share. Take it. Run now."

"I already told you I can't do that."

He gave her another stack of cash. "Find Rhonda. Give this to her. Then run for your life."

Karol stood looking at one stack of money in each hand.

Gabriel took an envelope from the safe and handed it to her. "Take this as well."

She stuffed the cash into her coat pockets and took the envelope. "What is it?"

"The combination to this safe. I have to try to convince Raphael to leave with me, just as you have to convince Rhonda to leave with you. But I have a larger responsibility, and I'm unloading some of it onto you. Once the council members are out of the country, the rest of the pack should be safe here as long as they avoid one another. Many of them will want to leave anyway, and they should. If anything happens to me, I want you to give that combination to someone you trust so he or she can disburse the rest of these funds. Each Wolf should have the option of a fresh beginning."

Karol slid the envelope into her coat as well. "You can count on me."

"I know I can."

"There's something you need to know. Raphael and Elias were fixated on the records at the task force headquarters. I told them everything I know, but I got the feeling they wanted to see for themselves."

"What time does that office close?"

"One o'clock at the latest but 6:00 PM isn't out of the question, especially with the hours we've been pulling."

Gabriel shut the safe and turned the combination dial. "Isn't there a hotel across the street from that building?"

"A fleabag joint for hookers and dopers. It's on the corner, though, not directly across the street. You're not thinking of checking in there, are you?"

He smiled. "Don't worry about me. I have ways of getting around unnoticed."

Angela and Melissa stood on the porch of the cabin again, this time watching Arick, driving Angela's truck, lead the two vehicles along the driveway to where cabins waited for them.

"I want to go back to the city to help Gabriel," Melissa said.

Angela put her arm around her sister-in-law. "I know you do, but the answer is no. It's too dangerous, and you have young ones here."

"I don't know what I'll do if anything happens to him."

Angela gave her a reassuring smile. "You'll do what you have to do, what we all have to do, whatever it takes to survive. That's the way it's always been for us."

"I never believed we'd reach this point. I took my life for granted. We were fools to think we were safe. None of us knew how fragile, how precarious, our existence was. I wonder if anything will ever be the same again."

"Let's go inside. We've got a mess to clean up after all those Wolves and another meal to prepare."

"I'll come in a minute."

Angela went inside, leaving Melissa to gaze at the wilderness.

THIRTY-TWO

Standing tall, Big Kwamie pumped himself into the woman writhing on her hands and knees on the leather sofa in his office.

"Yes, yes, yes," the woman said, whimpering.

He didn't even know her name. Grabbing her hips, he pulled her toward him while he slammed into her.

"Yes, yes, yes!" she said.

He wished she would just shut the hell up.

Someone knocked on the door.

"Who is it?" he shouted above the woman's cries.

"St. Thomas," a man said.

"Can't you hear I'm busy?"

"Sorry. Bedlam is here."

Fuck. "Give me a minute." He drove himself harder into the woman, then doubled over her and roared. The woman collapsed beneath him, and he grabbed the back of the sofa for balance. He didn't bother to look at her as he bent over, pulled up his underwear and then his trousers, and fastened his gold belt buckle. He took out his roll from one pocket, peeled off a hundred dollar bill, and tossed it onto her sweaty body. "Get dressed. Playtime is over."

The woman dragged herself upright and got dressed.

Kwamie put on his jacket and arranged his dreadlocks, then opened the door.

St. Thomas, his right-hand man, entered with Bedlam, who gave the woman an approving look.

"Let yourself out," Kwamie said to the woman.

She left the office.

Kwamie sat on the sofa with his arms spread wide on its back. "What's the word?"

"Those young punks haven't been seen," Bedlam said.

"'Course they ain't. They scared. With good reason. You know who they are, right?"

"I know their faces," Bedlam said.

"Well, learn their names and smoke 'em out. I don't care if you have to take out their whole families. I want them gone. Every day they're still alive makes me look like a chump. A couple of pigs came in here last night trying to push my buttons. Motherfuckers all but laughed in my face. That kind of disrespect requires an answer. You feel me?"

Bedlam nodded.

"We got a lot of people looking for them," St. Thomas said.

"I want *everyone* looking for them."

"Then that's what you'll get."

"Nobody messes with me," Kwamie said.

Two gunshots rang out upstairs, causing all three men to flinch.

Bedlam drew a nine from his waistband. "What the fuck was that?"

An agonized scream followed.

St. Thomas drew a nine of his own. "That's Big Whitey."

They waited for more screams, but none came.

"You got any product on the premises?" Bedlam said.

"Hell, no," Kwamie said.

"Then we can always call the cops."

Kwamie sneered at his lieutenant. Then he strode over to the corner of the room. He pulled a section of the paneled wall out, revealing a hidden compartment, and removed an AK-47. He popped a clip into the weapon and flipped the safety switch. "Let's take care of business."

St. Thomas opened the door and peered out, then stepped into the hallway and motioned them forward. Bedlam followed, with Kwamie bringing up the rear. They passed the restrooms and janitorial closet, the nightclub above silent.

Kwamie watched his men ascend the wide, carpeted stairs to the club. He tightened his grip on the AK-47. Who the hell would be dumb enough to attack him in his own place? He hadn't reached his position in the drug trade by being political.

They emerged onto the dance floor, deserted except for one body: Big Whitey lay in the center of the floor. With their guns raised, the three men formed a triangle around the three-hundred-pound albino. Big Whitey's throat had been torn out, and his right hand, which still clutched his Glock, had been severed from his wrist.

"What the Jesus goddamned fuck?" St. Thomas said.

A shadow glided across the floor.

Kwamie aimed his AK-47.

"I don't like this," Bedlam said.

Kwamie activated the custom laser sight on his weapon and aimed the red beam in the darkness. Another shadow scampered behind the bar. All three men turned their guns in that direction. A shadow darted behind a table, claws scrabbling. The men turned in circles.

"Come on out," Kwamie said. "We got you covered. There's no way you're getting out of here alive. Just show yourselves, and we'll deal with this like businessmen."

A low growl came from the darkness.

The gun in Kwamie's hands shook. "What the *fuck*?"

A rattling sound came from overhead, and he looked up at the lighting grid suspended from the ceiling. With the lights off, the lamp houses were hard to see against the black ceiling. Something was wrong, though. A few of the lights appeared to be missing . . . or something covered them. He took a step back. Something was up there.

Three dark shapes dropped from the grid at the same time. Kwamie saw wide jaws parting to reveal canine teeth.

St. Thomas jumped back.

Kwamie brought the barrel of the AK-47 up too late, and the lupine creature landed on top of him, digging its claws into his upper body. The impact forced him to his knees, and he triggered the gun, filling the club with a deafening roar. Bedlam and St. Thomas screamed around him, but neither of them got off a shot. Then he found himself on his back, staring into the eyes of a monster that defied reality. He had heard the stories on the news and had made jokes, but now he knew that werewolves existed, and for some reason he could not fathom, they had come for him.

Two more creatures tore into Bedlam and St. Thomas, and one ran onto the dance floor. A second monster joined the first on top of Kwamie, and a flurry of bites and slashes opened him up. He tried to fire his weapon again, more as an angry punctuation to his demise than a futile effort to save himself, but his trigger finger would not respond. A second later, he knew why: the first werewolf held his severed hand between its jaws. He kicked, but his legs found only emptiness, and then both of the beasts buried their muzzles in his flesh and went to work on his organs.

He closed his eyes and prayed for the end to come.

Rhonda sprang upright and changed to human form, Kwamie's blood dripping from her naked body. Daniel continued to gnaw on Kwamie's corpse, and the others feasted on Kwamie's bodyguards.

"That's enough," she said, her breasts rising and falling.

Daniel and the others pried themselves away from their victims and assumed their human shapes. They rose one by one, covered in blood.

"Check their pockets," Rhonda said.

Daniel turned out Kwamie's pockets and held up a roll of cash. The others collected wallets and rolls from the other corpses.

"Get the clothes," Rhonda said.

They rushed into the table area and retrieved the backpacks in which they had stuffed their clothing. First they removed the wet towels they had packed.

"Just your faces, hands, and hair," Rhonda said.

They wiped the blood from their flesh, dressed, and pulled on their socks and sneakers.

"Bolt," Rhonda said.

They sprinted onto the dance floor, giving a wide berth to the pools of blood around the four dead men, and ran straight to the back exit doors. Rhonda threw herself at a panic bar, and one door flew open. They emerged into the fresh air of an alley and stood on the sidewalk.

"How do you guys feel?" Rhonda said to T-Bone and Lincoln.

"Fuckin' A," T-Bone said.

"Like new," Lincoln said.

She turned to the others. "Go home and wash up good. I'll see you at Lincoln's later."

Rhonda had gotten half a block away when she heard the first siren.

THIRTY-THREE

When Mace and Norton entered the squad room after eating a late lunch, Landry came over to them. "Mount Pleasant PD reports the homicide of one Savana Silvestri, age eighty, in Valhalla. She was dismembered in her home. Her granddaughter found her. The O'Hearn family's SUV was parked in the garage, and Silvestri's Lexus is missing."

"So Gomez went to her house the night of his escape and used her car to get into Manhattan," Mace said.

All three of them went into his office.

"I put out an APB for the car. Do you want to send someone out there?"

Mace sat behind his desk. "Who would we send? Half our team is tied up with Rice's murder. Did you ever hear from Karol?"

"No, I'm getting worried."

"Don't be. She'll turn up." He wondered if she had already crossed the border.

A female clerk in khakis knocked on the door. "Excuse me, but Detective Andeli from the Four-Five is on line seven and wants to speak to the captain. He says it's urgent."

"Thank you," Landry said.

She exited and Mace answered the call.

"Captain, we have four DOAs at Kwamie's Spot in the Bronx."

Mace felt a familiar tightening in his stomach. "Is Kwamie one of them?"

"It's hard to tell. There isn't much left of any of them. This is just like the four DOAs the other night in the wrecking yard."

"I'll be there as soon as I can." Mace hung up and stood. "Back on the road," he said to Norton. "Ken, tell Hector and Suzie to get to Kwamie's club in the Bronx, then call Mint and Hollander."

Mace took East Houston Street to FDR Drive north. Twenty minutes later, Mace parked behind several emergency response vehicles outside Kwamie's club. Dozens of people stood behind crime scene tape, and television camera crews were at the ready. He and Norton got out and made their way through the gauntlet.

"Captain Mace!" a female reporter shouted. "Is this the work of Rodrigo Gomez, or are there other werewolves in the Bronx?"

"You're supposed to be investigating the Brotherhood of Torquemada. How do these murders relate to that investigation?" another reporter said.

"Do you have any comment on Carl Rice's murder?" a third asked.

Staring straight ahead with a grim expression, Mace nodded to one of the POs stationed at the front doors and entered the building with Norton at his side.

"The price of fame," Norton said.

At the top of the stairs, Mace opened a door for her, and they entered the club, which seemed larger without any patrons inside. Hector and Suzie were shooting photos while two detectives and two POs watched.

"It's like we never left," Norton said.

The two detectives joined them.

"I'm Andeli," one of them said. "This is my partner, Martin. I hope you're here to take this off our hands."

"I'm afraid that's not the case. We're shorthanded, and you're already here. You're the primaries." Mace moved closer to Hector. "Gomez?" he said in a low voice.

"Only if he's got friends." Hector pointed at bloody paw prints all over the floor. "It's kind of hard to tell how many there were. Did they walk on two legs or four? It looks to me like all four guys went down at the same time, and they weren't exactly harmless. There were three Glocks and one AK-47 between them."

Norton's cell phone rang, and she took it out. "This is Norton . . . Yes, sir." She hung up and turned to Mace.

"That was Hollander. As soon as we're done we need to report to FBI New York."

Mace looked at Hector. "I think we're done."

"Do you ever feel like quitting?" Norton said as Mace drove back to Manhattan.

"All the time. You?"

"No, I'm too career-oriented. I don't know what I'd do with myself if I had a normal life."

"I'd like to get out of the city, go someplace with grass and trees."

"You want to mow the lawn and shovel snow?"

"Something like that."

"It sounds like you're just having a midlife crisis."

"I've been having it for two years, then. I've been in the city all my life, and I'm beginning to wonder if it's natural for us to be living on top of each other like this. I want to raise my daughter someplace where she can experience nature other than on TV. I'd like to walk on a lawn barefoot and feel the grass between my toes."

They drove through the concrete canyons surrounding Foley Square. The Jacob K. Javits Federal Building at 26 Federal Plaza provided a home to several government agencies including the FBI's New York City field office and the Department of Homeland Security. Norton directed Mace where to park, and they walked a quarter of a mile to the tallest federal building in the country. Lawyers and federal employees crossed the sidewalks.

Inside the massive lobby, they showed their IDs and weapons to armed security and walked to the elevators. They took an elevator to the twenty-third floor, where they entered the FBI field office and signed in at the reception counter.

A black woman working behind the counter smiled at Norton. "Hi, Kathy. Hollander's expecting you."

"Thanks, Bonnie. This is Captain Mace from NYPD."

Bonnie held out her hand. "I recognize you from TV."

Mace shook her hand. "Hello."

Bonnie picked up a phone. "Special Agent Norton and Captain Mace are here." She waited. "Yes, sir." She hung up. "Go right in."

Norton led Mace through wide corridors lined with spacious offices and conference rooms. They rounded two corners before she stopped at a door with Hollander's name on it. She knocked and opened the door. Hollander and three other men in suits standing around his desk looked up.

"Wait here," Hollander said to the men. He crossed the carpeted office to Norton and Mace. "Come with me."

Hollander led Norton and Mace down the corridor to a room with a panoramic view of the city. All three of them sat down.

"Here it is," Hollander said. "We've obviously failed to contain this situation. No one blames either of you for that failure."

Big of you, Mace thought.

"As we speak, the powerful brokers in D.C. are forming a joint agency to deal with the Class L menace."

"Excuse me," Mace said, "but if we're operating on the belief that there's a secret society of these creatures, one rogue Class L doesn't constitute a national threat."

Hollander gave him a perfunctory smile that resembled a muscle twitch. "The formation of this joint agency, which doesn't have a name yet, began the minute we took custody of the carcasses of the Class Ls killed by the Brotherhood of Torquemada. The events of the last few days necessitated the process to be expedited. Your team held down the fort while we assembled the foundation for this agency. You did a good job with limited manpower."

"We'd have done better with the detectives promised us," Mace said.

Norton gave his ankle a gentle kick.

"I understand your ire, Captain, but decisions on national threats are made at a higher level than you're used to," Hollander said.

"I maintain there's no evidence that the Class Ls pose any kind of threat," Mace said.

"You can maintain whatever position you like, but be aware that certain statements could be perceived as disloyal to our nation's interests. Are you also maintaining that Gomez killed those drug dealers in the wrecking yard and the four in that nightclub today? Because evidence suggests otherwise." Hollander glanced at his watch. "Your investigation into the Brotherhood of Torquemada is officially closed at midnight. Go back to your offices, file your final reports, and send your people home. Tomorrow Special Agents Norton and Grant will take custody of your files and computers. You and your lieutenant will assist them in that transfer, and then your detectives will be debriefed here and reassigned to regular duty. You'll stay on as a consultant, but your field days are over. Your profile in the media has become far too visible."

"Through no choice of my own," Mace said.

Hollander rose. "Be that as it may, any additional investigations into murders committed by Class Ls will be initiated by NYPD and then handed over to this office."

"What about Jim Mint?" Mace said.

"He's set to announce his resignation. I understand he'll be pursuing a career in the private sector. In any case, you and your people are to be commended for your handling of the Brotherhood of Torquemada. I understand the president plans to honor you all with medals at a ceremony in two weeks. Congratulations."

Hollander exited the office, leaving Mace and Norton alone.

Mace waited until he and Norton had left the building to speak. "Jim dragged me into this, and now he's throwing himself on his sword," he said as they walked back to his SUV.

"Or he was pushed," Norton said. "He was out of his depth. Either way, this is how things are done. Just be glad you can go back to living a normal life. Isn't that what you want? Willy and Shelly are gone, but the rest of your people came out of this with their careers intact. The only one you need to worry about is Williams. If she disappears, it's going to raise serious questions about what you and I know."

"Medals," Mace said. "They won't let me do my job because I've become too famous, so their solution is to make me more famous."

"That's the way of the world."

"It sounds like you'll be staying in New York."

"I can't complain," Norton said.

"Do you ever?"

"I learned a long time ago that you don't get very far in law enforcement by rocking the boat."

"What do you think my responsibilities as a consultant will entail?"

"Oh, they'll probably give you an office here or at One PP, where you'll read reports and make notes on them. You'll work nine to five like most other professionals, and you'll get home in time to have dinner with your wife and daughter."

"It sounds like retirement before retirement," Mace said.

"Don't knock it. When you do retire, you can get that house in the woods, or you can move into the private sector with the bureau's recommendation."

"Just like Jim Mint."

"That's—"

"The way the world works."

Karol saw her SUV had not been touched and moved it to the opposite side of the street. She didn't expect to spend much more time in it, because fleeing the country in a police vehicle seemed like a bad idea.

In the lobby of her building she collected her mail. She would pay her bills before she disappeared. No need to add utilities companies to the list of entities that would be hunting her. She took the elevator upstairs, looked from side to side, and unlocked her door. She didn't own a landline, and without her phone she felt cut off and wondered how alarmed Mace had become.

As soon as she entered the apartment, she saw Rhonda's bedroom door was open. She closed and locked the front door, and Rhonda appeared in the bedroom doorway, a startled look on her face. Karol had never been so happy to see anyone in her life.

"Where the hell have you been?" she said, moving forward.

"You don't need to know that," Rhonda said.

"I know you're one of the Wolves who killed those drug dealers the other night."

"They were hit men. Assassins, just like the Brotherhood of Torquemada, except they didn't know what they were getting themselves into. It was self-defense all the way."

Karol stopped six feet away from Rhonda. "What were you doing out there in the first place? Who were the other Wolves?"

"Friends from my class."

Karol knew she had to control her temper. "I respect that you've been through a lot, but you broke our laws. Even if it was self-defense, you have to take the needs of the pack into consideration. You and your friends should have hidden those bodies, not just left them out like calling cards."

Rhonda grunted. "The Greater Pack is finished. Me and my friends will form our own pack."

"I'm sure their parents will be delighted. As delighted as they'll be when they find out their offspring are berserkers."

"Everyone thinks Gomez killed those guys."

"Not for long. Forensics will prove otherwise."

"You and Mace will keep that from the public."

"I won't be doing anything with Mace. I'm going to Canada, and you're coming with me."

Rhonda laughed. "I'm not going anywhere with you. I'm striking out on my own. I only came home to get my things."

Karol drew her Glock. "You are going to Canada, girl. It's just a matter of time before the brass orders Mace to bring you in, and then you'll disappear for good. You'll wake up in some black prison outside the country where CIA and Homeland Security can do whatever they want to you. Gabriel says—"

"I don't care what Gabriel says. I don't care what you say. No one is making me go anywhere I don't want to go. If you're going to shoot me, then shoot me, because I'll never be anyone's prisoner again."

Karol's jaw tightened. Rhonda had called her bluff. She lowered her weapon, resigned that she could not save the girl. "Where will you go?"

"It's better if you don't know." Rhonda went into the bedroom and came out with her coat on and a large bag slung over one shoulder. "Thanks for letting me crash here and for putting up with my drama. Good luck in Canada."

Karol holstered her gun. "Wait." She reached into her pocket and removed a bundle of cash. "This is from Gabriel. Forty thousand dollars. It's yours."

Rhonda took the money and stared at it.

"I know that seems like a lot, but it isn't, so spend it wisely. Find yourself a nice, illegal basement apartment somewhere, with owners who don't claim their rent as income."

"Thanks for the tip," Rhonda said. "And thank Gabriel for the cash."

Then she left.

THIRTY-FOUR

When Mace and Norton entered the task force base on Mott Street, the desk sat empty. Inside the squad room, two clerks packed their things. Grant sat at his desk keying in a report, and Candice and Landry did the same in their office. Landry saw Mace and Norton and came out, followed by Candice.

"The clerks were told to go home," Landry said.

"They're shutting us down," Mace said. "Everybody, finish up your paperwork and go home."

"What about our case?" Candice said.

"It's not yours anymore."

"Hallelujah." Candice collected pages of a report from a tray in the printer. "I'm finished now."

"Report to FBI tomorrow morning for debriefing," Mace said. "You'll get your new assignment then."

"I hope it's good and boring," Candice said. "I don't want any more werewolf details."

"What about me?" Landry said.

"Show up here at 0800 tomorrow, and help me turn everything over to Norton and Grant. Plan on spending the rest of the week at FBI, and then you'll get your new assignment."

"Karol still hasn't called back. I'm really worried."

"I'm sure she's fine. I told her to take the day off if she needed it."

Candice stapled her paperwork, signed it, and handed it to Landry. "My final report, sir."

"Thank you."

"I'll see you at the ranch tomorrow." She turned to Mace. "I can't say it's been a pleasure, but it's been unforgettable." She extended her hand. "If anything ever comes up in the future, don't even think of requesting my service."

Smiling, Mace shook her hand. "Good luck."

Candice clapped Grant on the shoulder. "See you around."

Mace took the report out of Landry's hands. "I can handle that. Get out of here before they change their minds. You too, Grant."

"I'll just get my things," Landry said.

Mace went into his office and dropped the report on his desk. Then he sat and called Cheryl. "I'll be home in a few hours, and then it's all over. They're shutting us down and reassigning us. I'm told I'm being put out to pasture; I'll be spending my last two years reviewing reports at FBI."

"Thank God," Cheryl said. "What about Gomez?"

"You and Patty will continue to have protection until he's stopped."

Landry entered, carrying a box filled with his belongings.

"Come home soon," Cheryl said.

"I will." He hung up and stood.

"Any idea where they're sending me?" Landry said.

"None, but I'm sure you'll do well." He held out his hand.

Landry shook it. "Thanks, Tony. I'm glad we all get to go home this time." He turned and left.

Mace walked back into the squad room. "Hurry up, Grant."

"I'm just finishing up." Grant shook hands with Mace. "I'll see you tomorrow."

"Right."

"Good night, Kathy."

"Don't do the secret handshake in front of Tony," Norton said.

Grant smiled and left.

"It looks like it's just you and me," Mace said.

"And only four murders to write reports on," Norton said.

Gabriel sat at the window of his hotel room on Mott Street. Despite the thick layer of grime on the glass, he had a clear view of the building where Mace's task force had set up operation. Only their fourth-floor windows glowed in the dusk.

Most of the people exiting the building were Chinese women, and he guessed a factory of some kind occupied the floors below the police base. Then three people who weren't Chinese exited within minutes of each other: a black female, a black male, and a white male. Every one of them looked like the law. Gabriel wondered if anyone else was in there besides Mace and the FBI woman.

The telephone beside the bed rang.

Gabriel froze and stared at the device, which continued to ring.

Someone knocked on the door.

Rising from his chair, Gabriel tiptoed past the ringing phone to the door. He leaned close to the metal door, listening. A peephole would have been convenient. The phone stopped ringing.

"It's Karol."

Exhaling, Gabriel unlocked and opened the door, and Karol entered the room.

Gabriel closed the door and locked it. "What are you doing here? You're supposed to be looking for Rhonda."

Karol crossed the room. "I found her."

Gabriel joined her. "Then you should both be on your way to Canada."

"She's not going, and I can't go."

"Why not?"

Karol pointed at the window. "Because those are my people too. I already lost Willy, and I'm not going to let anything happen to Mace or Norton. They've had my back. I have theirs."

"We don't even know if Raphael's really going to try something."

"I'm a cop, and my cop gut tells me it's a marvelous night for a moon dance." She looked at the bed. "Speaking of which, that's disgusting. I can't even count how many different body odors I smell coming from that mattress."

Gabriel sat in his chair. "I don't intend to sleep on it."

"I'm glad to hear it." Karol pushed the dresser away from the wall, and a rat scurried away. "Ugh."

The rat disappeared under the bed, and she pushed the dresser close to the window and sat on it.

"Here comes the night," she said.

Norton knocked on Mace's door. Darkness had settled outside. "How's it going?" she said.

"One down, one to go."

"I'm about to make you a very happy police captain."

"Oh?"

"Get out of here. I've got one left too, so I'll finish yours."

Mace raised his eyebrows. "Really?"

"It's not like I have anywhere to go. Suzie and Hector are still working. I know you and Cheryl will both feel better if you're home."

"Thanks." Rising, he looked around the office. "I'll pack this stuff tomorrow." He put on his coat, and Norton moved out of his way, and he exited his office. "You're all right."

"You too."

"See you tomorrow." As he crossed the squad room, it occurred to him that Norton reminded him of Patty Lane.

The telephone rang, and Cheryl seized it.

"I'm on my way home," Mace said.

Cheryl exhaled. "Really?"

"That's what I said. It's still rush hour, so don't expect me too soon."

"That's okay. I'm just glad you'll be here."

"I love you," he said.

"I love you too." Cheryl hung up and moved to the high chair where Anna had taken over feeding Patty. "Guess what? Daddy's coming home!"

Patty grinned.

"You can go home early tonight, Anna."

"I don't mind staying."

"Don't be silly. I'm so grateful for all the time you've spent here keeping me company this week. I can't tell you how much it's meant to me."

"I was happy to do it. I'll leave as soon as Captain Mace comes home."

Cheryl put her hand over Anna's. "No, I want you to go now. You've been so helpful, but you need some time to yourself."

"Mrs. Mace—"

"Anna, go home. Study. Get some sleep. I'll see you in the morning."

Anna looked displeased as she stood. "Call me if you need anything, okay?"

"I promise, but I'll be fine."

Anna opened the door and stepped into the hallway, then closed the door.

Cheryl turned the locks, lifted Patty out of the high chair, and twirled her around. "Daddy's coming home!" Patty laughed.

"There goes Mace," Gabriel said.

Karol leaned closer to the window and saw Mace walking away from the building. "That just leaves Norton."

"It's only six thirty. There's no way they're all leaving for the day with everything that's going on."

"I can't believe Tony's leaving early," she said. "I wonder if anything's changed."

"Everything's changed," Gabriel said.

Gomez circled the block wearing baggy clothes, glasses with thick rims, and a Rasta hat. Two police cars idled outside Mace's house on Eighty-fourth Street, just as they had all day. At the corner, another squad car patrolled the congested traffic on Fifth Avenue. He passed a pizzeria, an electronics store, and a hair salon. Rap music blasted from a passing car. Tough-looking teens loitered outside, smoking cigarettes, and weary-looking adults walked home from work. Christmas lights in store windows blinked on and off, and carols played over speakers mounted outside businesses.

At the corner of Eighty-third, he turned left at another pizzeria and cruised down the dark residential street. At the far end of the block, people appeared in droves on Fourth Avenue, discharged from the nearby subway stations. Gomez counted the houses on his left, and when he had passed six of them, he veered into a driveway and followed it to a narrow garage. Behind the garage, he encountered a six-foot fence separating the property from the Maces'.

Setting his hands on top of the fence, he vaulted high into the air and landed on all fours on the other side. Lights glowed on each floor of the house, and bars covered the windows in the rear just as they did in the front. Curtains masked each window, preventing him from seeing inside but also preventing anyone inside from seeing him.

Discarding the colorful Rasta hat, Gomez ran to the house and crouched at the nearest basement window. It had no bars because it was made of glass blocks. Extending the fingers on one hand into claws, he pulled out the narrow hatch in the window with ease and set it on the grass, then started yanking out the glass blocks one by one. Only the cracking of the mortar that held the blocks in place made any noise, and he timed his actions to avoid any rhythm.

It took him only two minutes to create a space large enough to squeeze through, and he slid his feet through the opening and backed into the darkness. Once his hips had cleared the window, he lowered himself to the floor and turned. A washing machine and dryer, a slop sink, and shelves covered with paint cans and accessories crowded the basement. He walked its length to the stairway and stared at the wooden door above.

Norton finished her last report. She saved it, backed it up, and transmitted it. Then she printed a copy and went to the copy machine, where she waited for the full document to unfurl.

She would miss working in the task force with her colleagues, but she knew it was best for all of them, especially Mace, to move on. She had no idea what the future held for her or for the Wolves, but she sensed the world as she knew it changing. She doubted she would be in a position to continue helping the strange creatures without Mace at her side, but she hoped she would always be able to follow her conscience. As the pages of the report slid into the tray, she contemplated if she and Suzie had a future together.

Then every light on the floor went off, including the monitors.

"There go the lights," Gabriel said across the street.

"Norton must be leaving now," Karol said.

They waited.

Pools of illumination from the emergency lights mounted on the walls cast eerie light on the ceiling. Looking around the squad room, Norton noted half the emergency lights didn't work, resulting in a strange imbalance and swaths of darkness. She went to the windows and peered through the dirty glass at Chinatown below. Red and yellow lights splashed glare over the crowded sidewalks.

No blackout, she thought. *Maybe an internal failure?*

She put on her coat and walked into the reception area. The light in the inside alarm key pad had turned dark.

Someone killed the power to breach security.

As she reached for the knob, the metal door shook on its frame from what sounded like the impact of a body. Norton flinched and covered her mouth to prevent herself from crying out. A body crashed against the door again, and she drew her Glock. Another smash and she stepped back. The door bowed inward. Another crash. She ran back into the squad room, lit by lights outside. The door flew open.

Central Alarm would notify Mace and the Fifth Precinct, which would dispatch a car. All she had to do was survive that long.

Norton turned in a circle, looking for a hiding place. She dropped to the floor as silhouettes appeared near the reception area. With all the stealth she could manage, she crawled under the desk that had been Willy's and pulled his chair close to hide her. She heard claws scrabbling over the floor and panting.

A shadow passed on the floor before her and then a furry four-legged body.

THIRTY-FIVE

A second four-legged creature covered with coarse black fur passed the desk, this one on Norton's left-hand side. She took a slow, careful, deep breath. Two more Wolves appeared, crossing paths before her. Four in all.

They moved toward Mace's office, then rose on their hind legs. They seemed to melt, and Norton gaped at the pale legs of four naked human males. She lowered her head closer to the floor to see their faces. The emergency lights cast harsh shadows on their features.

"Mace should have the most data on his hard drive," a man with curly dark hair said, looking at Mace's office door. Norton believed he was Elias Michalakis.

"Grab it," Raphael Domini said to one of the other men. "We'll try to figure out which of the other ones belongs to the FBI."

One of the men entered Mace's office, and the other three fanned out. Norton's back and knees ached. The man in Mace's office disconnected cables running from the monitor on the desk to the computer beneath it. She lost sight of Raphael, Elias, and the remaining man. Desk drawers opened and closed around her, producing hollow echoes.

"Look at this," Raphael said inside the conference room. Norton craned her neck to see Elias joining him at the wall where the task force team had posted several photos, maps, and charts.

"That was taken in Philadelphia," Elias said.

"There are cameras everywhere," Raphael said. "Maybe we should torch the place and set them back a day."

"That wouldn't do any good. Whatever's on these computers is also on computers at One Police Plaza and FBI headquarters. All we'd do is call even more attention to ourselves. They won't publicly admit that we stole these computers."

A pair of hairy male legs stepped before Willy's desk, and Norton held her breath, her eyes bulging. The man opened and closed the drawers, each movement ricocheting around Norton's head like a bullet. He padded away as Raphael and Elias emerged from the conference room.

"Any luck?" Raphael said.

"There's hardly anything in these desks," the man said. "It looks like they're cleaning the place out."

"Then we were just in time," Elias said. "We were right not to wait."

"Let's go," Raphael said to the man in Mace's office.

They filed through the squad room, the fourth man carrying Mace's computer. Norton listened to their retreating footsteps until the sound of her phone's ringtone blocked them out and sent a spasm of fear through her body. Her heart did double time, and her phone rang in her pocket again.

"What the hell's that?" one of the men said.

Norton reached into her pocket and closed her hand around the phone, which she turned off mid-ring.

"We cut the power," Elias said. "No phone should be ringing."

Norton drew her hand from her pocket.

"Someone else is in here," Raphael said.

Norton tightened her grip on her Glock. She sensed, rather than heard, movement around her. Did she hear paws padding toward Willy's desk? Her breathing grew shallow and labored. She wanted to run.

Shadows moved on the floor.

Norton felt a scream rolling around the inside of her throat and mouth, trying to claw itself free.

A reverberating thud behind her meant one Wolf had leapt onto a desktop. A thud to her right told her another one had done the same thing. Then a third banging to her left. The Wolves jumped from desk to desk. One remained on the floor somewhere, she thought.

Something large and heavy landed atop Willy's desk, the thundering impact echoing around Norton, who stifled a cry. With her heart jackhammering, she raised her Glock in one hand, her view obstructed by the office chair. A long, furry arm knocked the chair over, and an upside-down lupine head lowered into view, eyes trained on her and canines bared as the monster growled a sound not unlike laughter. Norton stuck her Glock in the beast's face and pulled the trigger twice, destroying the eye and cheek on the left side of its face. The beast issued a strangled gasp and toppled to the floor in front of her, blood gushing from its face.

Norton scrambled out from under the desk and clambered over the kicking beast's form. She didn't have time to consider its immense size and fled to the cubicles near the conference room. She didn't look for the other monsters, but she glimpsed raging shadows leaping to the floor.

As she reached the end of the cubicles, a second werewolf leapt before her, and she knew it had stayed behind in case she attempted to flee. Her body jolted, and she heard herself cry out. The creature roared at her, and she stopped in her tracks, raised the Glock in both hands, and fired at its chest four times. It howled in pain and fell to the floor. Claws scrabbled on the floor behind her.

Norton bolted into the reception area, stopping only to pull the fire alarm on the wall, and a clanging filled the building. Then she scurried over the fallen door, brushing aside a piece of the frame that dangled before her. The Wolves had left their shoes and clothes near the elevator. She knew the elevator wouldn't be working, so she opened the emergency exit door, stepped into the stairwell, and slammed the metal door behind her. Emergency lights cast a harsh glare everywhere, and the fire alarm rang here as well. She rushed halfway down the first flight of concrete steps, then leapt to the landing, the impact echoing.

The door flew open above her and slammed against the wall. Claws scraped concrete overhead, growing louder.

Norton hurried to the next landing and opened the door, emerging into the third-floor sewing shop. A hundred workstations for seamstresses stood empty, and she zipped between the rows toward the back. A howling merged with the fire alarm. She continued toward the rear of the floor, wondering if she could double back to the front, where the windows offered access to the fire escape. Two werewolves chased her on all fours, and she ran faster.

She stopped at a wooden gate over a freight elevator shaft. A handwritten Out of Order sign had been pinned to the gate. After holstering her Glock, she pulled the rattling gate upward and stared into darkness broken only by the freight elevator cables. Cold air met her face.

The werewolves panted behind her, their claws slipping on the tiles.

Without turning to see their proximity, Norton took off her blazer and held it in both hands. As she dove into space, a claw raked her back. For a moment, she wondered if she would plummet three floors to her death, but she caught the taut cable. Her right leg slammed into the cable, the impact eliciting a pained grunt, and she almost lost her grip.

She glanced over her shoulder at the two werewolves, silhouetted and snarling within the gateway, just eight feet away and four feet above her.

Mace had just left the Fifth Precinct parking lot when his cell phone rang. The words *Central Alarm* appeared on the screen. Frowning, he took the call.

"Captain, this is Central Alarm Station. Can you give me your password?"

"Gypsy One," Mace said.

"We have an alert at your Mott Street location, probably caused by a power failure. Do you wish us to report this issue to the police?"

Mace's heart thumped in his chest. "Yes."

"Shall we contact you with their findings?"

"No, I'm going to the site now." Mace hung up and stomped on the brake, then stepped on the gas pedal. He had to drive all the way around the block to reach Elizabeth Street and drive north toward headquarters. He honked his horn at the vehicles ahead of him and pressed autodial for Landry.

"Is everything okay?" Landry said.

"No. The power's down at base, and I left Norton there alone. Call in the marines."

"Copy, copy."

Mace hung up. Halfway across Canal Street, traffic reached a standstill. He banged on his horn. "Come on, you morons!" He had not felt so helpless since sitting in an undercover van listening to Janus Farel tear Patty Lane apart in a moving vehicle. Horns honked around him, and he saw the lights of the buildings around headquarters three quarters of a block uptown. Twisting his steering wheel, he eased his SUV into a throng of pedestrians crossing the street, scattering them, and drove onto the sidewalk. Civilians jumped out of the way and shouted at him, but he only in-creased his speed on the narrow sidewalk.

When he reached the dark building, he parked the vehi-cle and jumped out. The fire alarm clanged inside. Drawing his gun, he ran inside and unlocked the inside door. The alarm pad was dark, and emergency lights cast an eerie glow over the lobby. He bypassed the elevator and went straight to the emergency stairwell.

"What's that alarm?" Karol said.

Gabriel pointed out the window. "Look!"

A black SUV sped along the sidewalk and screeched to a stop outside the building across the street. Mace jumped out and sprinted inside.

"Let's go," Karol said.

They ran for the door.

Gomez stepped out of his shoes, kicked them aside, and removed his socks. He peeled off his coat and allowed it to bunch at his feet, then pulled off his shirt, unbuckled his trousers, and dropped them. He didn't wear any underwear.

He crept up the carpeted wooden stairs. At the top, he set his hand on the doorknob and gave it a slow turn. The door creaked open, and he stepped into the hallway. Facing the door to the first-floor apartment, he listened for signs of movement on the other side, his nostrils flaring. He left the basement door ajar and moved to the bottom of the stairs leading to the second floor.

Norton turned away from the werewolves and loosened her grip on the cable just enough to slide down it, her jacket protecting her hands. The fire alarm sounded quieter in the shaft, and the wolves howled in anger. Looking below, she saw only blackness. She passed the second-floor gate, visible because emergency light shot through its slats, and gained speed, the wolves' howls echoing around her and the alarm continuing. Glancing up, she saw the silhouettes of the creatures, smaller now.

Just when she wondered how much longer it would take to reach the top of the freight elevator, she passed the first-floor gate, and her feet slammed onto metal. The impact sent a shock wave through her bones that caused her to lose her balance, and she let go of the cable and crashed onto the elevator's top.

Lying on her back and wincing in pain, Norton squinted up at the third-floor gateway. She drew her Glock and aimed it at the patch of dull light, then fired a series of rounds at the wolves, which howled in protest. The sound of the gunfire ricocheted off the walls. She ceased fire and waited for a reaction.

One of the werewolves jumped into space and grabbed the elevator cable, and then she lost sight of it.

Mace took the stairs two at a time. He knew the intruder had waited for him to leave before killing the power in the building to shut down the security alarm. Norton had pulled the fire alarm, which meant she was alive or had been just minutes ago.

Gomez, he thought. *It ends here.*

Gabriel and Karol ran through the narrow lobby of the hotel, which consisted of nothing but a cashier window, a garbage can, the stairway, and ratty furniture by the door.

At the door, Gabriel caught Karol's arm. "You go first. I don't want any security cameras in the neighborhood recording us together."

Karol was about to argue when she saw the wisdom in his decision. Without commenting, she turned and sprinted across the sidewalk to Mott Street.

Keeping her eyes and Glock trained above her, Norton rose on one knee, then stood. She fired the gun several times, glimpsing the descending werewolf through the muzzle flash that dazzled her eyes. The monster had reached the second floor. With a better idea of its location, she opened fire in a continuous burst. The gunfire grew deafening and blinding, and she couldn't tell if she had hit her predator or not.

Then she ran out of ammo.

Mace emerged from the stairwell onto the fourth floor, his breathing heavy. He swept his Glock from one end of the hall to the other, then gazed at the floor, where four piles of clothing lay.

That meant the Wolves were from Gabriel's or Raphael's faction, or they were the rogues who had attacked Kwamie and his soldiers.

Not Gomez.

Sitting at the dining room table, Cheryl spooned mush into Patty's mouth. She'd feel better when Tony got home, but she knew she wouldn't feel safe until learning Gomez had been killed.

"Dada!" Patty said.

"Yes, baby, Dada will be home soon."

A low growl rose from the floor, and she turned her head. Sniper stood near the door, staring at it with an intensity Cheryl had never seen in the animal before. The dog gave a warning yelp. Someone—or some*thing*—lurked on the other side.

Oh no, Cheryl thought, fear spreading through her veins as she stood.

The doorknob turned, and Sniper barked.

Norton ejected the cartridge from her Glock, took another from her pocket, and slapped it into place. The sound of the wolf landing a few feet away in the darkness joined the cacophony of noise disorienting her.

With spots still dancing in her eyes, she opened fire, the muzzle flashes illuminating the wolf like a dancer in a strobe light. Dark splotches appeared in the hyperintense flashes. Once she had found her rhythm, she continued to fire at her assailant, moving closer to her attacker but keeping the elevator cable somewhat between them.

The wolf howled in pain. Norton ran out of ammo again.

Mace entered the reception area with his gun drawn. Four Wolves prowled the premises somewhere. He moved through the short hall leading from the reception area into the squad room, where he conducted a perimeter sweep. The clanging alarm prevented him from hearing even his own footsteps. Sirens wailed in the distance, growing closer.

Mace headed toward his office, his arms outstretched with his Glock clenched in both hands. He had emptied a .38 into Janus Farel at point-blank range, and the bastard had transformed into a Wolf before his eyes and chased him down. Only Farel's blind faith in the Blade of Salvation had saved Mace's life. Mace didn't have a sword now, and these

Wolves didn't believe in the Blades of Salvation anyway.

He stopped in the middle of the floor and conducted another perimeter sweep. The emergency lights and the glare of the buildings across the street cast long shadows across the floor, and the patches of darkness between the pools of light felt palpable.

One shadow charged at him, and as he jerked his head, it snatched his gun by the barrel, almost taking his fingers with it. He jumped back and watched the Wolf merge into the shadows once more. Spinning on one heel, he glimpsed a Wolf stand erect on a desktop a dozen feet away, silhouetted by the light outside. On his left-hand side, a second Wolf rose on another desk. On his right, the Wolf that had snatched his Glock stepped into a pool of light.

Janus Farel times three, he thought.

The Wolves growled, their thick fur bristling. They licked their chops, slathering saliva over their sharp teeth.

Cheryl unclasped the straps that held Patty to the high chair and lifted her out of the seat. Sniper barked a challenge at whoever stood on the other side of the door, and the noise caused Patty to squirm in protest. If Cheryl could just make it to the window in the living room and get the attention of the police outside . . .

Maybe.

The home invader struck the door, and Cheryl heard wood splintering.

Sniper leaned forward, then drew himself back for a launch.

I'll never make it.

Holding Patty in her left arm, Cheryl reached on top of the computer hutch and took Tony's .38 revolver from her purse just as the door exploded off its hinges.

Sniper leapt right, avoiding the door as it fell to the floor. A figure seven feet tall and covered in black fur stood in the doorway, its pointy ears touching the frame. Sniper barked in a frenzy, causing Patty to cry. Opening and closing its claws, the wolf snarled at the barking dog. Cheryl turned her body so Patty couldn't see the monstrous creature that had come to kill them.

Gomez, she thought.

Still barking, Sniper jumped left, then right, distracting the creature.

Cheryl flipped the safety off the revolver and aimed it with one hand, then remembered Tony's instructions to always hold its butt with both hands.

The wolf entered the apartment and hunched forward, roaring. Sniper dove at the wolf and sank his teeth into Gomez's throat. The wolf thrashed around, trying to shake Sniper loose.

Cheryl managed to grasp the gun with both hands, supporting Patty between her arms. She aimed at the wolf, but the flurry of motion kept putting Sniper into her line of fire. She didn't trust herself to hit Gomez in the head. Patty wailed in her ear.

Cheryl fired twice over Gomez's head, hoping to bring the police inside. The gunfire caused Gomez to flinch, and Cheryl pivoted and ran down the hall toward the bedrooms.

An instant later, Sniper let loose a shrill cry and turned silent.

THIRTY-SIX

In the dark elevator shaft, Norton stepped back just as the wolf swiped a claw at her face. She didn't see the move but felt wind on her face. She knew her disadvantage: the wolf could see in the dark, but she could not. She positioned herself behind the cable for protection and reached into her pocket for another ammunition cartridge—her last one.

The alarm stopped ringing, and she heard the wolf step to its right, its claws scratching the top of the elevator. Maybe help had arrived.

Sudden pain flared in her right hand, and she dropped her Glock. She didn't know if the wolf had bitten her hand or slashed it with a claw. The gun clattered on the edge of the elevator and scraped the wall of the shaft before landing on the basement floor beyond her reach. Instead of the clip, she took out her phone and pointed its glow at the darkness, illuminating the wolf, which roared at her. Blood flowed from a dozen or more wounds in the beast's hide, slowing it but not stopping it.

The wolf lunged at her, and she jumped to her right. The beast grabbed the cable, almost losing its balance. Norton removed a small canister from her pocket, and when the beast lunged at her again, she discharged a blast of pepper spray into its eyes, eliciting an anguished howl.

The two Wolves on the desks leapt to the floor. One had a bloody face and only one eye. Norton had not backed down from them. They advanced on Mace, accompanied by the third Wolf, which crept forward on all fours. Mace clenched his fists and felt blood flowing through the fingers on his right hand.

"Raphael!"

The Wolves jerked their heads in unison, and Mace looked over his shoulder as Gabriel and Karol entered the squad room.

Thank God, he thought.

The unscathed Wolf stood straight and roared at Gabriel and Karol. The wounded Wolves dropped to all fours and charged. One Eye leapt onto Mace, who fell backward and kicked the beast over his head before it could inflict any damage. The move had worked against Janus Farel, and now it worked again. But he knew it would not work a second time this night.

The second Wolf knocked Karol to the floor, and as they rolled, Karol transformed into a Wolf with her clothes still on.

"Stop it!" Gabriel said. "We have to work together, not against each other."

Raphael, the unscathed Wolf, tore out of the office.

Gabriel shape-shifted into a Wolf and took off after him.

Karol and the Wolf she fought bared their fangs at each other, and Mace found himself crouching like a football player against One Eye. The beast leapt on him again, and before he knew it he was on his back with the beast on top of him.

Cheryl ran into the bedroom with Patty in one arm and Tony's revolver in her other hand. She slammed the door shut, pushed the button lock on the doorknob, and set her crying daughter on the bed. She tried to push Tony's armoire across the room to block the door, but it wouldn't budge, so she tipped it over instead. The wooden armoire crashed against the door, then fell to the floor with a thundering impact.

The door opened four inches and slammed against the top of the armoire. Cheryl threw herself onto the floor and pushed her back against the wall, bracing her legs against the base of the armoire and forcing it against the door, which closed. Gomez crashed into the other side, and Cheryl clenched her teeth, straining to keep her legs straight. The armoire held the door shut.

A clawed fist burst through a panel in the door.

Cheryl recoiled, but she refused to scream in front of her daughter. "It's okay, baby. Don't cry. Mommy's right here."

Gomez retracted his hand, and then eight elongated fingers reached through the broken wood and pulled it in opposite directions, making the hole larger. The wolf pressed his face against the door, his eyes on fire.

Cheryl raised the .38 in both hands.

The wolf snapped its jaws at Norton and managed to sink its fangs into her left shoulder, driving her onto her back. She heard and felt her collarbone snap, and she dropped her phone but held on to the pepper spray with all her strength. Warm blood flowed over her neck and left breast.

The wolf raised its head, tearing her flesh and muscles, and her blood spattered her face as she screamed. The monster straddled her, and she rammed her right knee where she estimated his scrotum to be. The wolf howled, an agonized sound that echoed up the shaft.

Ignoring the pain that shot through her left arm, Norton forced her hand into her pocket and took out a lighter. She raised the lighter and sparked it to life with her thumb. A tiny yellow flame burned in the darkness, barely illuminating the wolf as it moved in for the kill, its lips peeled back to reveal fangs jutting out at different angles. With tears filling her eyes, she lined up the pepper spray behind the lighter and triggered a long, steady spray that burst into flame. The fire ignited the pepper spray already on the wolf's face, and Norton directed the spray at the creature's torso and sternum.

The wolf howled nonstop, its fur catching fire. It staggered backward and slammed against the cable. Norton stopped spraying and dropped the canister, then rolled over and pushed herself upright against the wall of the elevator shaft. The wolf staggered toward her, the stench of burning fur and flesh turning her stomach, and she moved out of its way. It sank to its knees, then thrashed around, its howls sounding almost human.

Norton grabbed the cable for support and watched the wolf stop moving, the flames consuming its carcass and rising higher.

Gabriel chased Raphael out of the task force headquarters and into the hallway leading to the elevator. Raphael went straight to the stairwell door, threw it open, and charged up the stairs toward the roof. Determined to save his brother, Gabriel scrambled after him.

Karol snapped her jaws at Leon, drawing blood. Leon kicked at her thighs with his hind legs, shredding her slacks. They rolled around on the floor, biting and slashing each other.

Then Leon sprang up, looked in the direction Raphael and Gabriel had run, and tore after them.

Karol whipped around on all fours and was about to give chase when she saw Mace struggling with Elias on the floor. Blood flowed from bullet wounds in Elias's mangled face, and she sensed the Wolf had been blinded. The Wolf lunged at Mace's face, and Mace twisted his head from side to side, dodging the attacks, and attempted to push the Wolf's head away with his hands.

Her first loyalty was to Gabriel, the leader of her pack, but she couldn't leave Mace in such a helpless position. She dove into Elias, knocking him off Mace. They rolled across the floor, and she raked his muzzle with her front claws. Elias roared in anger and took a swipe at her but missed.

Karol ran toward the reception area, then disappeared into the hallway.

Mace grabbed a desk and pulled himself up. He had to find Norton. Bright light filled the windows, accompanied by the steady roar of a chopper outside. Wincing, he glanced at his right hand. The Wolf strike had slashed all four of his fingers, and the gashes revealed bloody bones. He opened and closed his fingers, which felt numb, and wondered if they would ever function again.

He took one step forward and froze: the bloody Wolf that had attacked him padded back into the squad room and stood erect.

The creature moved straight for him, but its movements seemed tentative, and he wondered if it saw him.

Mace crouched behind the desks where Willy and Karol had sat.

The Wolf snarled at him and flung the first desk aside, flipping it over, then did the same with the second.

Mace fled in the direction of his office and heard the Wolf close on his heels. He didn't want to end up facedown on the floor, unable to defend himself, so he turned around just as the Wolf crashed into him, knocking him to his office floor.

The Wolf slammed one claw over Mace's face, breaking his nose, and Mace seized the monster's wrist with both hands and held it in place, hoping to prevent it from tearing off his face. But the Wolf only wanted to pinpoint his head and throat, and it leaned in for the kill.

Mace released the Wolf's wrist with one hand and pressed his palm against the creature's nose, knowing it could bite his hand off at the wrist. Blood from the Wolf's bad eyes trickled into his face, and he drove his thumb into the beast's left orb.

The Wolf's howl was louder than any sound Mace had ever heard a living creature make.

When Karol entered the stairwell, Raphael and Leon had backed Gabriel into the far corner of the landing above. The three Wolves traded barks and snarls, and Gabriel almost seemed to cower.

Karol ran up the stairs and sank her teeth into Leon's Achilles tendon. Leon howled in pain, and Karol ground her teeth, tasting blood as she severed the tendon. Leon kicked at her with his other hind leg, but Karol refused to release him. Instead, she dragged him back down the stairs, allowing Gabriel and Raphael to settle their differences one-on-one.

With the playing field leveled, Raphael turned and bolted up the stairs, and Gabriel followed.

Cheryl was about to squeeze the trigger on the .38 when she heard excited voices in the living room. Gomez heard them too, and the Wolf turned in that direction.

The police, she thought. Her protection had arrived.

Gunshots rang out, and Gomez roared. A barrage of gunshots followed.

Cheryl's eyes welled with tears. *Thank God.*

The gunshots stopped, and the house turned silent except for Patty's wailing.

Norton backed as far away from the burning carcass as possible to avoid breathing smoke. The flames illuminated the elevator shaft, and she scooped up her phone, which reignited the pain from the lacerations on her trembling fingers. Sinking to her knees, she vomited from the stench.

Then she crawled to a hatch in the elevator's ceiling and threw it open. The interior of the freight elevator was dark. She slid her legs through the opening and held on with her uninjured hand. Allowing her legs to dangle, she let go and dropped to the floor below. A shock wave of pain radiated through her left shoulder and broken collarbone, and she cried out.

She called Mace, and when he didn't answer, she tried Landry.

"I'm almost there," Landry said. "Where the hell are you? What's happening?"

"I'm in the freight elevator in the basement," she said, gasping. "I killed one of them. It's right above me on top of the elevator, and it's on fire. Get the fire department in here, but make sure they're protected. There're three more of them up there somewhere."

"Are you all right?"

"I'm bleeding bad," she said.

Then she dropped the phone and closed her eyes.

With her breaths coming in tortured bursts, Cheryl aimed the revolver in both hands. A long moment that felt like forever passed. Then a shadow appeared on the wall visible through the hole in the door. The muscles in her face twitched, and she could not make them stop. The snout and ears of the Wolf appeared, wet with blood, and Gomez turned toward her.

Cheryl looked at Patty. All she wanted to do was hold her crying baby, but she had to protect her. When she looked back at the door, the werewolf's face filled the hole. Cheryl fired two shots into the Wolf's skull, and the black shape fell to the floor. She had saved two bullets, one for Patty and one for herself, in case Gomez made it into the bedroom.

The door opened, pushing the armoire aside, and the bloody werewolf rose to his full height.

The Wolf seized Mace's neck and choked him, a human method of killing. Mace grabbed the beast's wrists and pulled on them, but he couldn't wrest them from his throat. The stranglehold cut off Mace's oxygen supply, and he twisted his hips in a feeble attempt to throw the Wolf off him. He felt tired and old and helpless, and he didn't believe he could defeat this creature as he had Janus Farel.

His cell phone rang in his pocket, and he wondered if Cheryl was calling him. God, how he loved her. He wished he had quit his damned job and stayed home with her and Patty, experiencing life instead of his own death.

Mace's head shook, he felt himself turning beet red, and the muscles in his throat locked.

A thrumming filled his head: the sound of his heart-beat. His vision faded, then blossomed, then faded again.

Then he lost consciousness.

Raphael burst onto the roof of the building with Gabriel right behind him. Both Wolves froze: a helicopter hovered above Mott Street, and it swept a spotlight over them, bathing them in white light, the turbulence from its blades blowing their fur.

Landry pulled his SUV up to a blockade at the Mott Street intersection before the block with the task force headquarters. A fire truck idled at the curb, strobe lights flashing.

He lowered his window and showed his ID to the PO who approached him. "I'm assigned to the task force on the fourth floor of that building. Some of my people are inside, and there's a fire in the elevator shaft in the back of the building. Tell FDNY, and let me the hell in there."

"Okay, but you'll have to walk," the PO said.

Landry shut off his engine and climbed out of the SUV.

"You can't just leave that vehicle here."

"Write me a ticket. Is anyone from the FBI here?"

"Not yet but the SWAT team is."

"I need to speak to whoever's in charge before anyone goes inside."

The PO pointed to a SWAT truck parked in the middle of the street. Three men in SWAT uniforms conferred with each other.

Landry rushed over to them. "There are four Class Ls in there."

"Who are you?" one of the SWAT team members said.

"Landry. I'm with the task force. An FBI agent is trapped in a freight elevator in the rear of the building, and there's a fire in the shaft. FDNY has to get in there, and they need cover. I need to get my colleague out of that elevator."

Karol severed Leon's other Achilles tendon, then climbed on top of him and went for his jugular. She couldn't take the chance that he wouldn't reveal the secrets of the pack when captured, and she was willing to break the laws of the pack to protect it. Leon turned and jerked, and Karol ripped his throat out with her teeth, his blood splashing her blouse. Leon's body quivered and stilled, and Karol felt sick to her stomach.

The sound of the helicopter grew louder, and she forced herself to assume human form.

My shell, she thought.

Every cell in Mace's body seemed to scream with pain, his survival instincts kicking in as the curtain closed. He felt his heart straining and his blood coursing through his veins. Picturing Cheryl and Patty, Mace opened his eyes. They felt ready to explode from their sockets. The air stung his nostrils like smelling salts. A door in his conscious mind swung open, as if his body had refused to expire and had awakened new senses in him.

The Wolf, still choking him, salivated.

Mace thought he had been losing consciousness—that he had been dying—but that wasn't the case. His eyesight was just changing, the color draining from what he saw. At the same time, his olfactory senses exploded, and he took in different smells radiating from the Wolf on top of him. The sound of the helicopter outside became deafening. His heart pounded and pulse quickened, and when he thought he should be dying, he felt stronger than he ever had in his life. The muscles in his body were alive, dancing around his bones. Every nerve in his body tingled, and Mace felt renewed—free. Bones in his body snapped, crackled, and popped, and he unleashed a cathartic cry that became a howl.

The Wolf cocked its head, its nostrils flaring.

Adrenaline rushed through Mace, and he released the Wolf's wrists and seized its throat instead. His fingers elongated into claws, his flesh darkening as coarse fur sprouted out of the backs of his hands and his wrists. And then his face and skull exploded, and his teeth burst from his gums.

This is insane, he thought. *This isn't happening. It can't be.*

But he didn't question the change: he embraced it. Angela Domini had once told him that Wolves who had no idea of their true nature existed in human form and often lived their entire lives in ignorance. Gomez had been suspected of being a sleeper until he had discovered the truth; now it was Mace's turn, and he understood why he had been able to think like Gomez and apprehend him in the first place. The information Angela had provided made him question his own identity and consider the possibility he was more than human. He had never believed that to be the case. Now he set his inner self free, and he felt wild and natural.

Releasing his grip on the Wolf's throat, he lunged forward and fastened his jaws on it instead. One Eye arched his back and howled, and the howl became a gargling sound. Mace tried to climb out from under his foe, but his legs, which now had extensions, proved awkward to control. Tasting the Wolf's hot blood, he closed his jaws tighter, then brought his right leg out from under One Eye and set his rear claw on the floor, bracing himself. Then he twisted his head to one side, tearing the beast's throat out.

The blood tasted good. It felt intoxicating. And as the Wolf who had helped him discover his true nature by bringing him to the point of death went spastic and died, Mace felt alive and aware for the first time in his life.

Cheryl scooped up Patty and ran around the bed to the far window. Using the butt of the .38, she hammered at the glass, shattering it in sheets. She used the gun's barrel to break the jagged edges of broken glass protruding from the frame. There was no way Patty would survive a fall from the second-floor window, but if Cheryl jumped with her, Cheryl could protect her from the impact. The challenge would be to squeeze through the window. She needed to keep one hand free.

Gomez staggered into the room, his fur dripping with

blood. Even hunched over, he stood taller than Cheryl. She remembered covering his trial and interviewing him at Sing Sing. They shared history.

Cheryl raised the .38, took careful aim, and fired twice into the beast's chest, adding to the gore. Gomez stumbled and seized the edge of the footboard to keep from falling. Cheryl dropped the .38 on the floor, then threw one leg out the window. Gomez growled. She held Patty close to the sill and moved her other leg out the window. Gomez lunged toward the bed. Cheryl doubted they would drop before he reached them.

And then Gomez disappeared, jerked into the hallway by some unseen force.

Cheryl blinked in bewilderment. Had he retreated? It made no sense. Frenzied growls reached her, the barks and grunts of other wild animals and the terrible sounds of flesh tearing and blood splashing on the walls, followed by the anguished howl of a vanquished wolf.

Standing on the rooftop, Gabriel could only watch as the blue and white helicopter, emblazoned with NYPD on its side, moved closer. He peered over the edge of the roof. Police cars and a fire truck occupied the street, which had been closed off to the public. Scores of uniformed men carrying guns ran back and forth on the asphalt, and crowds of civilians pressed against the barriers erected at each end of the block. He knew there was no escape.

Inside the helicopter, a SWAT officer fired a rocket-propelled grenade launcher, and a projectile raced toward the roof, trailing white smoke. The Brotherhood of Torquemada had used such a weapon to destroy the home of Rhonda Wilson's parents, killing them along with the plainclothes policemen tasked with protecting them.

A defiant howl filled the night, and he turned to see Raphael facing the helicopter with outstretched arms. Gabriel dove at his brother, knocking him aside, and the missile struck the roof and exploded. Blinding white smoke engulfed the Wolves, and Gabriel realized the missile's purpose: to disperse gas. He rose, coughed, then dropped to his knees. The last thing he saw was Raphael leaping onto the edge of the roof and then diving off it.

THIRTY-SEVEN

"Look out!" Landry cried as Norton opened the front door of the building and stood poised to stagger out.

Drenched in her own blood, Norton froze.

A dark figure plummeted from the rooftop and struck the sidewalk headfirst with a sickening snap. The Wolf lay still in a bloody, broken heap.

Landry ran over to Norton, and she collapsed in his arms. "Medic!" he said.

An army of SWAT officers stormed into the building.

Karol rushed into the squad room, where Mace lay on the floor covered in blood. She snatched her shoes and socks from the floor and moved toward him, her eyes widening and her nostrils flaring. She kneeled at his side and sniffed the air. "Oh, my God."

"I can't move," Mace said. "Every muscle in my body is in agony."

She set one hand on his shoulder. "That happens at first."

He stared at her. "Did you know?"

She shook her head. "You've been a sleeper in human form your entire life. Your scent was human all this time."

"And now?"

"You're one of us." Sitting on the floor, she put on her socks and shoes.

Mace nodded at the carcass on the floor. "Who was it?"

"Elias Michalakis."

He smiled. "Good."

Rising, she went to her desk, opened a drawer, and returned with a water bottle. She unscrewed the cap and poured water over his face. "Drink. I don't think you want anyone to see you with blood all over your mouth."

Mace swished water around in his mouth and swallowed. "What about Gabriel?"

Karol glanced at the ceiling. "I don't know. When I realized Elias hadn't followed me, I had to come back for you."

"Thanks. Who was the other one?"

"Leon, one of Raphael's men."

"We have to find Norton."

Ten SWAT members ran into the squad room with M16As ready to fire.

Karol raised her shield. "This floor's clear."

The lead SWAT member looked at the carcass of the

Wolf, then at Mace. "Is he okay?"

"I'm fine," Mace said. But was he? "We need to locate Special Agent Norton."

"She's down on the street."

"Is she all right?"

"It's hard to say. It looked like one of those things chewed her up pretty badly."

The lights flickered on.

Cheryl remained frozen in the window. Waiting. Listening. Patty bawled. Cheryl set her foot on the floor, then swung her other leg inside. She set Patty on the bed, then walked to her bureau, opened a drawer, and took out the box of ammunition. She picked up the .38, popped its cylinder, loaded six rounds, and snapped the cylinder shut.

Then she picked Patty up and ventured into the hallway, where she gasped.

Gomez was dead, his body dismembered and strewn along the hallway, the carpet soaking with blood and the walls dripping. Cheryl didn't understand. Outside, sirens grew louder. She walked through the hall, finding it impossible to keep her bare feet from squishing blood, flesh, and fur. She emerged into the living room, where she stood holding Patty, the two of them alone.

Mace limped to the elevator, one arm draped over Karol's shoulders. She supported him with one arm around his waist, and he groaned with every step.

"My muscles are on fire," he said. "My bones . . ."

"You should have waited for a stretcher."

"I need fresh air now," he said.

SWAT members swarmed the hallway. The elevator door opened, and Hector and Suzie got off.

"Looking good as always, Captain," Hector said.

"How's Norton?" Mace said.

"She'll be fine," Suzie said. "An ambulance is taking her to Bellevue. You should join her."

"What happened?"

"She killed one of those things in the freight elevator shaft," Hector said. "Badass."

"We need to see that carcass," Mace said to Karol.

They boarded the elevator, and the door closed.

"Gomez wasn't part of this," Karol said. "I don't smell his scent anywhere. The other Wolf must have been Eddie, Raphael's other lieutenant. I saw them together today."

"I have to know," Mace said. "This isn't over until Gomez has been caught."

"You won't be doing anything for at least a week."

His phone rang. "Would you mind getting that?"

Karol slid her hand into Mace's pocket and took out his phone. She showed him Cheryl's name on the screen. He nodded, and she held the phone to his ear.

"Yeah, babe?" he said.

"Where are you?" Cheryl said in a trembling voice.

"Wolves attacked the building, but everyone's alive." It felt good to say that.

Cheryl's voice hardened. "Gomez was here."

"What? What happened?"

"He's dead, but he killed Sniper and two police officers. There are bodies—blood—all over the apartment."

Sniper. Mace had loved the dog. "Are you and Patty okay?"

"He didn't get to hurt us, but he came close."

"I'm on my way."

She hung up.

The elevator came to a stop, and they almost collided with Hollander when the door opened.

"You need to get home," Hollander said. "I have a car waiting to take you."

"Williams will drive me."

"She needs to be checked out by the EMTs, and then she's got a long night of debriefing ahead of her."

Wincing from the pain, Mace raised his left arm and checked his watch. "It isn't midnight yet. I'm still in charge of the task force. She's taking me."

"I look forward to reading your reports." Hollander stared at him, then boarded the elevator.

Mace and Karol went out the front door. SWAT team members crisscrossed the street, and more than one helicopter hovered overhead. On the sidewalk, FBI agents drew a black tarp over the shattered corpse of a Wolf.

"Raphael," Karol whispered into Mace's ear.

"Tony!" Landry raced over to them.

"I know," Mace said. "We're leaving now."

"Are you both okay?"

"Yes." Mace looked at his SUV, which had been cordoned off with crime scene tape. "I guess I need another vehicle."

"I'm parked on the next block," Karol said.

The three of them circled the fire engine, Karol still supporting Mace.

"Do you want me to drive?" Landry said.

Mace tried to smile. "No, you're done. We all are. Let the FBI and SWAT clean up this mess."

Landry raised his eyes. "Look."

Karol had to walk Mace in a half circle so he could follow Landry's gaze. A military helicopter hovered above SWAT team members on the roof, lifting a gurney on a cable into the air. The gurney turned in circles.

Gabriel, Mace thought. At least he was alive.

The gurney disappeared into the belly of the chopper, and a minute later the aircraft departed.

Karol steered her SUV out of Chinatown. Patrol cars, ambulances, and news vans clogged the streets. National Guard troop transports rolled through an intersection.

"Here we go," Karol said.

"It's the dawning of a new era," Mace said. His knees wobbled, and when he set his hands on them they shook too. "Shouldn't you be across the border by now?"

"That isn't going to happen. I have to keep the promise I made to Gabriel. It looks like I'm stuck in the big city."

"They're going to come after Rhonda," he said. The vehicle reeked of gasoline and oil.

"I don't think they'll find her."

"Let's coordinate our stories." *Like how my life changed forever.*

"We were separated and didn't see what happened to each other," she said. "That way we can't trip each other up."

"You're good at this." The muscles in his jaw felt tight, and he found it difficult to speak.

"It's called survival."

"Do I get a membership card?"

"They're worthless now. There's no more pack. It's every Wolf for himself."

Mace opened and closed his fingers. "Gomez taught himself everything he needed to know. Will I be able to do the same?"

"Do yourself a favor: whatever story you tell the FBI, make yourself believe it. Forget what happened. You're still Tony Mace, a middle-aged bureaucrat with thinning hair, a beautiful wife, and a gorgeous daughter. Consider her a miracle, by the way. Few human-Wolf hybrids survive childbirth."

Patty, Mace thought. He had failed to consider the full picture. "We tried to have children for years. Cheryl had four miscarriages, and we'd just about given up. Is Patty . . . ?"

"No. The gene isn't strong enough. Both of your parents must have been Wolves."

Mace narrowed his eyes. And his brother, killed in the war. "And their siblings . . ."

"This may be the worst time in our history to poke at family trees. Leave it alone. And for God's sake, don't ever tell your wife."

Police cars blocked Eighty-fourth Street, and Mace and Karol had to show their IDs to get in. Emergency response vehicles of all types had double-parked along the street, and Karol had to triple-park in front of Mace's house. Mace opened the door to get out and fell face-first onto the pavement.

"Whoa," a PO said.

Karol ran around the SUV and joined the PO in helping Mace stand. "What part of the healing process didn't you understand?"

Mace groaned. "It's getting worse."

"It's bound to get worse before it gets better."

Cheryl sat holding Patty inside the rear of an ambulance, answering the questions of detectives.

Karol helped Mace to the ambulance.

"Excuse me," Cheryl said to the detectives. She climbed out of the ambulance with Patty in her arms, and the detectives parted. Her eyes widened when she saw Mace. "I thought you said you were okay."

"I said we were alive." He kissed Patty's forehead. "Why aren't you in the house? The Sanchezes' apartment isn't hot, is it?"

"I'm never setting foot in that house again."

He took her in his arms and kissed the top of her head.

"I'm sorry I wasn't here."

Cheryl buried her head against his chest, ignoring the bloodstains. Her chest convulsed, and she wept.

"The police didn't kill him." She looked into his eyes. "It was more of *them*. It sounded like an entire pack of dogs fighting."

Mace touched her face. Gabriel had made sure she and Patty were protected.

"Do you want a lift somewhere?" Karol said. "Some luxurious hotel or something? You all deserve it."

"We have Cheryl's car," Mace said.

"Then I'll be on my way. I think I'll go see how Norton's doing."

"Let me know, and give her my best."

"Stay in touch," she said.

"I will." He meant it.

"Good night, Mrs. Mace."

Cheryl wiped tears from her eyes and choked back an embarrassed laugh. "Look at me. Good night . . . Karol."

Karol waved to Patty. "Bye-bye, little one." She returned to her SUV, got in, and drove off.

The front door to the house was open, and a forensics team swarmed the downstairs hallway. In the driveway, the Sanchezes answered questions from two FBI agents.

Eduardo glanced in his direction. Mace made eye contact with him, then gave the man a small nod. He and Cheryl had rented the downstairs apartment to the Sanchezes soon after they bought the house. Gabriel must have sent them here to spy on him in the beginning. He would thank the family for saving Cheryl's and Patty's lives another time.

EPILOGUE

Gabriel opened his eyes, and a sterile white ceiling came into view. He raised his hand and gazed at human fingers that he opened and closed. He didn't remember turning into human form or being transported; he only remembered the sight of Raphael diving off the rooftop of the building on Mott Street.

He touched his throat: a metal collar encircled his neck. His gaze darted around the small room, which had bare white walls, an exposed toilet, a sink, and a shower with no curtain or door. He wore an orange jumpsuit with slippers, and when he sat up he realized the bed was made of wood. The fourth wall was made of Plexiglas or acrylic and looked out at a common area with furniture and gymnastic mats. A camera looked down at him from each corner of the room.

Rising, he touched the walls. They were made of steel.

The clear wall slid open with a quiet hum. Moving to the doorway, he saw no windows in the entire chamber. He walked into the common area and saw that his cell was one of twenty or thirty on the ground floor, with five levels of identical cells above it. All of them were unoccupied.

"Good morning, Mr. Domini," a voice boomed over the wall speakers.

Gabriel faced a large monitor overlooking the common area. A man with a military brush cut filled the screen. He wore a nondescript black uniform.

Gabriel did not answer.

The collar emitted an electric shock that brought him to his knees. He didn't make a sound.

"This is your new home," the man said. "Your permanent home. You will stay here until the day you die, and we will become well acquainted with each other."

Gabriel's chest rose and fell.

"For now, you are alone. We don't expect that to be the case for long. Cooperation will be rewarded, and disobedience will be punished. Do I make myself clear?"

Gabriel said nothing. Another burst of electricity gripped his body.

"If you look around, you will see that there are no televisions. You will not be kept informed of current events, which is a shame because the world has become an interesting place thanks to you. If you wish to know my name, ask. If you wish to eat, ask. If you wish to know the status of your family members, ask."

Gabriel knew Raphael was dead. He prayed that

Melissa, Gareth, Damien, and Angela were safe.

"You will talk, I promise you. And you will not escape."

Drawing in a breath, Gabriel rose. He refused to break and intended to maintain his silence until they killed him.

Rhonda loaded what clothes she had into the back of the Jeep, which she had paid for with cash. She didn't have insurance, and she hoped the vehicle would last until she reached California. Maybe Mexico after that. Her friends stood at the curb of Roosevelt Avenue.

"Don't look so glum, gang," she said.

"I thought we were going to form our own pack," Lincoln said.

"Yeah," T-Bone said.

"The days of the big packs are over," Rhonda said. "From now on, it's all about family. You have families. I don't."

"You don't have to leave," Diane said.

"Yes, I do. They'll be looking for me, if they aren't already. I have to cut off all ties and start over. I don't mind. Sometimes change is good."

Raina raised a fist. "Bitch."

Rhonda bumped her fist. "Skank."

Daniel's eyes reflected sadness. "Take care of yourself."

"You too." She kissed him on the lips, then faced the others. "Keep it real but not *too* real. Stay out of trouble, and lie low."

Rhonda got into the Jeep, keyed the ignition, and revved the engine. She waited until she had pulled into traffic and her friends receded in her rearview mirror to wipe the tears from her eyes.

A fresh start, she thought as she raised the volume on the radio.

Angela and Arick watched a minivan depart the snow-blanketed campground.

"That's the last of them," Arick said.

"Will you be staying?" Angela said.

"That's what Gabriel would want," he said.

"Good." She liked having him around. Although Wolves mated for life and John Stalk had been her man, she found Arick's presence calming.

"I'll go lock the gate after them."

She watched him trudge through the snow to the truck, then went into the cabin, where Melissa read to Damien and Gareth. "It's just us now."

"What about Daddy?" Gareth said.

Angela tried to show no reaction.

"Daddy is helping the pack," Melissa said in a soft voice. "It may be a long time before we see him again."

"I miss him," Damien said.

"So do I."

Angela admired her sister-in-law's strength. They had to rely on each other.

"Aunt Angela says we're our own pack now."

"Yes, we are."

That was the key: smaller packs comprised of family units. Angela intended to be a good alpha female, with Arick and Melissa to help her. And maybe someday they would reunite with Gabriel, hopefully on a small settlement and not in a prison.

One month after the battle on Mott Street, Mace reported for work at 26 Federal Plaza. His new position consisted of reading reports and filing comments on them. He didn't even know who read the comments, if anyone. He passed through security and rode the elevator to the Bureau for Werewolf Affairs on the twenty-fourth floor, where he signed in and followed the maze of narrow corridors to his small office. None of the bureau's professional agents or suits acknowledged him. Despite his fame, he was a dinosaur in this new world, and he liked it that way.

The nameplate on his door said, Captain Anthony Mace, NYPD Consultant. He didn't do much consulting, and he suspected his superiors had assigned him to his current position to keep him out of the limelight. He liked it that way too.

Snow fell outside his window, and he hung his coat and took his seat. A new year had arrived, which felt appropriate. He logged on to the bureau's website and began his morning routine of reading classified e-mails.

Someone knocked on his door.

"Come in."

Norton entered. She wore a padded brace over her collarbone. He had not seen her since the ceremony in Washington, D.C., when the president had presented her, Landry, Candice, Karol, and himself with gold medals for defeating the Brotherhood of Torquemada. The irony wasn't lost on Mace. Willy and Shelly had received posthumous medals, and Mace and Karol had the chance to chat with Willy's mother.

"Welcome back," Norton said. "How was your vacation?"

"Good," Mace said. "We spent it with my in-laws."

"How's Cheryl?"

"She's doing well, taking it one day at a time. We're looking at houses on Long Island, which is where she always wanted to raise Patty."

They had moved out of Bay Ridge. Mace decided to rent the upstairs apartment as soon as Eduardo had cleaned it to help cover expenses since Cheryl had not returned to work. He made Eduardo his superintendent and handyman to justify giving him and his family of *nahuals*

free rent. Cheryl had never voiced her suspicions about the family to Mace.

"I'm still waiting for a photo of that darling daughter of yours."

"Here." He took out his wallet and handed her a photo of Patty.

Norton stared at the photo. "Aw, thanks."

"I hear they offered you a promotion to stay and work

under Hollander. Congratulations."

"I turned it down." She gestured at his office. "This isn't for me. I'm a traveling woman. Besides, I don't want to make any difficult decisions—that's your bag. I'll just go wherever they send me and do whatever needs doing."

He understood. "What about Suzie?"

"I can travel to Manhattan too, right? I hear Karol's accepted a position as an NYPD liaison with the bureau."

"I hadn't heard that." Karol had already told him the news.

"I figured you'd want to know." She winked at him. "Hopefully she'll be in a position to do some good."

He nodded at her hand, where she had received stitches. "How's your injury?"

Norton flexed her fingers. "Better. I have scars all over, though. I'm thinking of getting tattoos to cover them."

"Sexy."

She motioned to his hand. "How about yours?"

He turned his fist so she wouldn't see that the deep gashes in his fingers hadn't even left scars. "Like new."

"Really? I'm glad to hear it. I guess your cuts weren't as bad as mine. Hey, look what I got." She removed an envelope from her blazer pocket. "A subpoena to testify before Senator Prince's subcommittee."

Mace held up an identical envelope. "I got one too."

"Are you going to appear?"

He shrugged. "We'll see what the bosses say. I don't know nothin'."

She returned the envelope to her pocket. "Well, I'd better get going. They're sending me to Seattle."

He knew from some of the reports he had read that a Wolf pack was rumored to exist in Seattle, and vigilantes had taken to torching the homes and businesses of suspects. "Good luck."

"You too."

He watched her leave, then returned to his e-mails. Sooner or later, he expected to come across clues to Gabriel's whereabouts. He never forgot his friends.